D0999783

**"Samantha James writes exactly
the sort of book I love to read."**
Linda Lael Miller

"*You enchant me.
I want to spirit you away.*"

His eyes were glittering. She glimpsed
in them a need that was both thrilling and
frightening.

His voice seemed swathed in silk. Sensation
swamped her. Her skin seemed to burn. This
was it, the opportunity she desired. Claire
had wanted to entice. To lure. But she'd never
expected it would be like this. She sensed a
fervent intensity in him that frightened her.
She glimpsed on his face a passion that was
far beyond her means to handle. *He* was far
beyond her means to—

Mid-thought, his mouth closed over hers.

All her life Claire had wondered what a
kiss would taste like. And heaven above, she'd
wondered what *he* tasted like.

And now she knew. His mouth seemed all-
consuming. It seemed like she tasted him everywhere, resonating through every part of
her. She felt overwhelmed.

She tasted . . . *possession.*

**"James delivers delicious
and exciting romance."**
Publishers Weekly

By Samantha James

Samantha JAMES

The Sins Of Viscount Sutherland

AVON

An Imprint of HarperCollinsPublishers

This is a work of fiction. Names, characters, places, and incidents are products of the author's imagination or are used fictitiously and are not to be construed as real. Any resemblance to actual events, locales, organizations, or persons, living or dead, is entirely coincidental.

AVON BOOKS
An Imprint of HarperCollins*Publishers*
10 East 53rd Street
New York, New York 10022-5299

Copyright © 2011 by Sandra Kleinschmit
Excerpt from *Midnight's Wild Passion* copyright © 2011 by Anna Campbell
ISBN 978-1-61129-616-7

All rights reserved. No part of this book may be used or reproduced in any manner whatsoever without written permission, except in the case of brief quotations embodied in critical articles and reviews. For information address Avon Books, an Imprint of HarperCollins Publishers.

Avon Trademark Reg. U.S. Pat. Off. and in Other Countries, Marca Registrada, Hecho en U.S.A.
HarperCollins® is a registered trademark of HarperCollins Publishers.

Printed in the U.S.A.

The
SINS
Of
VISCOUNT
SUTHERLAND

Prologue

London

The terms were set.

Rutgers Field at dawn.

The young cub chose pistols.

The viscount chose seven paces.

There would be one exchange of fire.

The weather was abysmal. Fog snaked in and out between the trees that surrounded the field, shifting as if it were a living, breathing thing. A driving rain pelted the viscount's cheek as he removed his coat and handed it to his second, the Duke of Braddock.

The duke swore. "By God, man, you were in your cups last night and you're in your cups now. Do you think I don't smell the brandy on your breath? This is the last time I'll take my place as your second, do you hear?"

"As you wish then, Your Grace." The viscount gave a mocking bow.

The duke's expression was grim. "Good as you are, I think you should know—the boy's a crack shot."

All the better.

The viscount shrugged. "I did not provoke this duel. It was he who challenged me. If you hadn't been—how shall I say this—lustily engaged upstairs with your ladybird, you'd have heard him. He accused me of cheating at cards. When I accused him of cheating, he demanded satisfaction. There was no changing the whelp's mind. He made no bones about telling me he preferred a gentleman's way of settling a dispute."

The duke scowled. "The barkeep last night told me that only a fortnight ago he nearly took the arm off a seaman from the docks."

The viscount gave a thin smile. "Well, he can't be much of a crack shot then, can he, if the seaman still lives. Perhaps he should try his hand at boxing instead."

"Do not jest. He has the devil's own temper—much like you, I might add."

The viscount wasn't surprised. The cub was no more than five-and-twenty. Hotheaded, hell-born, and reckless. He, too, he supposed, was hotheaded, hell-born, and reckless. But the cub certainly didn't deserve to die.

The viscount lived each day as if it were his last . . . as if he prayed each day was his last.

Nothing gave him pleasure. Not anymore. He cared for nothing, save his mother. He thought of Brightwood, his family estate. Two years had passed since he left for London. His jaw tightened. He'd vowed to himself that the only way he would ever return was in his coffin.

Perhaps, he decided cynically, it wouldn't be so long now after all.

The viscount handed his hat to the duke. A downpour began.

"Gentleman, take your places." A man named Cavendish cleared his throat. Beside him stood a physician. "Begin the count."

The viscount was already drenched. Rain dripped from the dark hair on his forehead.

One.

The viscount recalled his friend's words. *This is the last time I'll take my place as your second.* With luck, there would be no further need.

Two.

The cub could hardly miss at seven paces.

Three.

Oh, to be free.

Four.

No more guilt. No more pain.

Five.

Please, God. Please.

Six—

A sharp report filled the air. The viscount felt the bullet pierce cloth and flesh.

The impact sent him to his knees.

He gritted his teeth and managed to half turn, still gripping the pistol. Fire scalded his right shoulder. He could barely keep hold of the weapon. One shot, he reminded himself. For himself, he cared nothing about the so-called field of honor. He didn't care that the cub had fired early. But if the cub shot and he didn't . . . All he needed was to get off one round. Why he was concerned with salvaging the cub's honor, he had no idea. But if he didn't, the cub would lose all respect from his peers. He would be shunned.

The viscount gritted his teeth. Blast! He struggled to see through the mist. The fog was so strange, still winding and twisting. At least there was no need to aim.

His hand shaking, he pulled the trigger, firing away from the assemblage that had gathered.

The pistol fell from his hand. He felt himself slipping forward, depleted of all strength.

Footsteps shook the ground. Someone shouted. The viscount couldn't be sure. The buzz in his ears grew steadily louder.

Rain seeped through his clothing. The grass against his cheek was cold. Fire scalded his shoulder.

He knew the wound wasn't mortal.

He wanted to scream in outrage. In blind, tormented fury.

He had prayed this day would see him sent straight to the devil.

Instead he must spend yet more of his days in hell.

Chapter One

*I*t was time to let the night play out.

To one who might look on, Claire Ashcroft was the very essence of aplomb. Of composure. Indeed, one never would have guessed the churning need for vengeance that seared her soul. Knowing her nemesis was near tied her stomach in knots.

He stood near the edge of the ballroom, a figure clad in black—a fitting color for the man. His jacket was stretched taut over wide, muscled shoulders; nary a wrinkle was visible. He stood tall and powerful, like a pillar from ancient Greece. His height was such that he seemed to stretch clear to the ceiling. He embodied power. Confidence.

Her eyes slid over his profile. She couldn't deny he was arrestingly handsome to the eye. His hair was black as coal, cropped short. High cheek-bones slanted above a square jawline. He was clean-shaven, but his jaw was faintly shadowed. It spun through her mind that he must doubtless shave twice each day.

His was a pose most formidable, yet his pose was indolently careless. His expression was impenetrable.

Claire sucked in a breath. The sight of him made her shiver.

His gaze roamed the room, an almost lazy perusal. She sensed boredom. She sensed cynicism. A distance that was almost icy set him apart. And then he turned—

Their eyes locked, for one long, nerve-shattering moment.

So this was Viscount Grayson Sutherland.

The blackguard who had killed her brother. The man who had changed her life forever.

A strange sensation slid up her spine. His examination of her had turned no less than fierce. A hundred feelings went through her in that instant. It was as if everything else in the world stood still.

The sheer physicality of the man was . . . Claire struggled for the proper word. Formidable. Almost frightening. She wasn't prepared for it. It was as if his eyes—were they a pale blue or a silvery gray?—sliced into her. A tremor shook her, a shiver that was almost violent.

A hand touched her elbow. "Claire?"

It was Penelope. Dear, sweet Penelope who had paved the way for her reception into Society. Her dearest friend in all the world, Penelope Grove—her name had changed from Robertson when she wed Theodore Grove.

The two of them had attended finishing school together. Penelope was a year older. They were an odd-looking pair, the two of them. Penelope was as delicate as fine china, her demeanor tiny, her features angelic. Claire was half a head taller than Penelope, her limbs long and spare. To Claire, her proportions always seemed out of kilter.

She and Penelope had become acquainted in a rather unusual way. Claire had always felt odd duck out. She was taller than most girls and, indeed, many boys. Little wonder that she'd start finishing school feeling the outsider. She was aware she was the brunt of amusement for several older girls. She had been a bit awkward, the subject of many a joke. She pretended it didn't hurt, but it did. Outside one day in the schoolyard, she saw an older girl named Ramona deliberately push Penelope into a puddle. The front of Penelope's gown and face was spattered with mud. Claire saw tears in her eyes—and saw red. She helped Penelope to her feet and turned to Ramona.

A moment later Ramona was seated on her

bum in the middle of the puddle. She burst into tears.

Oh, what satisfaction there had been!

Ramona teased neither of them from that day onward.

And, well, Claire hadn't been dismissed, though only because of her parents' intervention.

She and Penelope had become the best of friends. To be sure, it was Penelope who had taught her there was more to being a lady than anything she'd learned in school.

And Claire was no longer graceless. No longer sensitive to her height. She'd grown into a tall, striking woman who earned many an admiring glance. Her carriage was one of pride and grace, her limbs were long and elegant. But on the verge of a come-out, her mother's unexpected illness took the family back to Wildewood, back to the country—all but Oliver. Claire remained at home to nurse her mother through her illness, a lung infection that had been long and difficult. There was neither the time nor the inclination to return to the current of Society. It all seemed so shallow and insipid after those months at her mother's side.

Then came the stunning blow of Oliver's death.

No, she thought. Not his death—

His murder.

"Are you ready?" Penelope's gaze held hers. One hand rested on the small rise of her belly.

Covered by lace and pleats and ribbons, her condition was hardly apparent.

Claire frowned. "Are you all right? The baby—"

"Is merely reminding me of his presence. He moves often now, particularly when I wish to sleep."

Penelope was convinced she carried a boy.

"And as for you, Claire"—Penelope raised her brows—"I would feel better if you told me. Are you ready?"

Claire took a deep breath. She nodded.

"I . . . am ready." Did she sound convincing?

It would seem not. Penelope looked at her closely. "There's still time to change your mind, Claire."

Claire's chin came up. It had taken great care and planning to get to this point. She couldn't have done it without Penelope. Dear, sweet Penelope, whose husband Theo was in the Peninsula fighting that upstart Corsican. It was Penelope's most ardent hope that Theo would be home in time for the birth of their baby.

She suspected that if Theo were here, he might not have approved. But Penelope's help had been immeasurable. Invaluable. Penelope had helped her find lodging, a small, comfortable house—oh, and so many things!

At first Penelope shook her head. "I've seen him at parties, Claire, and he is not a man you should associate with. He is more often foxed than not.

He gambles to excess. And where women are concerned—"

"I'm aware of his reputation," Claire had said quietly. "Indeed, I am counting on it."

"Why? How can you gain satisfaction?"

"You won't approve, Pen."

"I won't help you unless I know."

At times Penelope could be stubborn.

"Very well, then. Given the viscount's predilection for the ladies, it's my hope I can use it to my advantage."

Penelope's apprehension was clear. "How?"

Despite her married state, Penelope could also be decidedly innocent. Claire remained silent, while dawning awareness spread over Penelope's face.

"Claire, no! You cannot—"

"Make him fall in love with me?"

Pen's mouth still formed an "O" of astonishment.

Claire sought to explain. "It's all I can think to do." She was silent for a moment. "Perhaps I am a fool," she said softly. "But I will never rest easy until I make him hurt. I must have some measure of satisfaction. I must at least *try*."

Claire had reached out and squeezed Penelope's hand. "I beg of you, help me, my dearest friend. I've been away from Society for a long time." Penelope was the daughter of a viscount. "You can take me places where I could not otherwise go. Places where he will be present. You can show me to Society once more."

"Claire, the man is the worst kind of scoundrel."

Penelope's expression was pained. She took a long breath, torn, it seemed. Yet she knew there would be no changing Claire's mind. "Very well, then," she conceded. "You are my friend and I will help you."

Claire reached out to hug her. "I know I could count on you, dear. I knew it."

And with Penelope's introduction, the doors to Society had opened. There was Lady Belfield, at whose home Claire had attended tea the other afternoon. And there was Lady Sumpter, whose fete she had attended only last night. And now she was here, at Lady Blakely's ball—her first—in the hope that the viscount would be here.

"No." Claire was adamant. "I won't change my mind, so please do not try to sway me."

"I worry for you," Penelope confided. "I do not want you hurt again."

"He can hurt me no more than he already has." Bitterness seeped through her soul, like slow poison. "He robbed me of my brother. He robbed me of the last of my family." She took a long, steadying breath. "It's time, Pen. Time to make myself known to Grayson Sutherland as your widowed cousin, Claire Westfield, visiting from the country."

Her gaze softened as she beheld Penelope's

worry. "Thank you, Pen. No matter what happens, I thank you."

"I would never abandon my greatest friend in all the world." Penelope squeezed Claire's fingers.

Claire smiled slightly. This was it, she thought. The time had come. Was it a fool's errand she undertook? Panic flared, leaving her breathless for an instant. What if the viscount discovered her intention? Her plan to lure him under her spell— to make him fall in love with her—then cruelly dismiss him as if he were nothing.

As Oliver had been nothing to him, she reminded herself.

No, she thought. *No.* He couldn't possibly. She wouldn't fail. It was just as she'd told Penelope. She wanted this too much. And she and Penelope had been scrupulously careful, painstakingly anticipating every detail.

In those days following Oliver's death, nearly every thought was of Sutherland, and every thought of him consumed her. If she could take a pistol and shoot the blackguard the way he'd shot Oliver, she would. But she was a woman. She hated the helplessness lent her by her sex.

At night she paced, unable to sleep. Thoughts twisted every which way in her mind. There had to be a way to make him pay. There *had* to be.

And perhaps there was. Claire could not say precisely when it occurred to her. Perhaps she was not as powerless as she thought. After all, his reputation was scandalous. It was said no man dared cross him. No woman could resist him. Her own reputation was of no consequence. By God, perhaps she could use the cur's hedonism to her advantage.

So it was that her plan was set in motion. Her intent? To make Viscount Grayson Sutherland pant after her while holding the cur at bay, only to ultimately turn him away. Only a year ago she would have been horrified at herself. Spitefulness was not her way. Malice was not her way. But if she could wound him in some way—strip him of his pride perhaps—it would give her at least some measure of satisfaction. The cost to herself was of no consequence, none at all.

All she had to do was play her part.

Perhaps Penelope sensed her sudden self-doubt. "You're beautiful, Claire. Every man here has eyes for you."

It was only one man Claire was concerned with.

Beside her, Penelope sucked in a breath. "He's here, Claire. Near the dance floor. Next to the man in gray pinstripes, the Duke of Braddock. Sutherland wears black—"

"I see him." An odd sensation seized hold of Claire. Her voice was faint. She sounded so strange as she heard herself speak.

Pen's eyes searched her face. "Are you certain you want to do this?"

Claire's eyes darkened. "I must," she said fervently. "I must." Determination swept away all fear.

"You must be careful," warned Penelope. "Watch yourself. And watch him."

Adamant as she was, in truth Claire was terrified. But she disguised whatever fears she had. This was too important. Indeed, it consumed her entire being.

Her gaze returned to the man who stood across the polished parquet floor. Hatred spilled through her. Lodged in her breast was dark resolve.

This man had robbed Oliver of his life's blood. Robbed him of all that life's journey should have held.

Oh, yes, Viscount Grayson Sutherland would pay, she vowed. He would pay for Oliver Ashcroft's murder.

She would see to it.

It was time to begin in earnest. Time to put her plan in motion.

By heaven, the game was on.

Two men stood next to each other on the fringes of the ballroom. One possessed hair as dark as blackened ink, the other but a shade lighter. When standing, they were evenly matched in height and build. The pair had been friends since attending Eton together. And now here they were, two of the so-called four Lords of Sheffield Square.

They were womanizers, all, but the duke was indeed a particularly coveted prize. Despite his horrid reputation, matchmaking mamas steered their daughters toward Clive Fielding, Duke of Braddock, eager to gain the prize of marrying a rich, handsome duke. It seemed they would overlook his reputation.

Which quite suited Viscount Grayson Sutherland. Many a miss thrilled to a glance from the viscount, but their matchmaking mamas were quite horrified. They shooed their daughters far distant. Gray cared not that his manner was called beastly. It didn't matter to him in the slightest that he was not considered a "suitable" match. Once . . . once he had been a coveted prize indeed—

So much had changed since then, for now with the women he sought out—and the women who sought him out—there existed a mutual understanding. Each sought the carnal pleasures of the flesh, no more, no less.

All sought amusement in the arms of each other.

And now two male gazes had fastened appreciable eyes on the woman who stood near the edge of the dance floor. A beauty he'd never seen before.

Gray couldn't take his eyes from the lovely lady in pale green silk. Her hair was a rich chestnut, gathered in a chignon that set off the slim length of her neck. The sweep of her shoulders rose bare and creamy and silky above her neck-line. He watched as the woman raised a hand to tuck back a stray hair that had escaped from her chignon. He caught the flash of gold. A ring.

On her right hand.

One corner of his mouth curled up. His eyes flickered in satisfaction.

Clive followed the direction of Gray's regard. "The lady has captured your attention, I see."

A smile creased Gray's lips. She had indeed.

"I don't believe I've ever seen her," said Clive.

"Nor have I," Gray murmured. He hadn't yet taken his eyes off the lady. "I believe she warrants closer examination."

"Well, then, if you do not take the first step," Clive said softly, "then I shall."

"I think not, my friend. You have a weakness for blondes. And I should hate to see us quarrel over a woman."

"Ah, never that," Clive said with an arch of one black brow. He paused. "Well, man, what are you waiting for?"

"Indeed."

He advanced. Halfway across the room, he felt a hand on his arm. Glancing down, he saw that it was his mother who waylaid him.

He stopped and gave a low bow. "Mama."

Despite her fragile demeanor, her pale-perfect complexion, Charlotte Sutherland could be an intimidating presence. Still strikingly attractive, her hair was dark as her son's, shot through with only a smattering of gray.

Vivid blue eyes the color of his flashed. "I know your intention, Gray. I saw you and Clive eyeing that young woman." She waved a hand toward where the lady stood.

His mother was nothing if not direct.

She pulled him to an outside wall. "She is young, Gray, too young for you."

"What," he drawled, "have I joined the realm of the ancients at the age of three-and-thirty?"

"I will not countenance your ruination of that woman."

One black brow climbed high. "I but admire a woman who has been blessed with nature's beauty. And you don't seem to have noticed, Mama, but that woman is a widow. She wears her ring on her right hand, but I would wager she's broken many a man's heart before she ever wed."

"Where are the rest of your profligate friends?"

"Ah. I assume you mean the duke?"

"You know very well of whom I speak. Yes, the duke. And of course the earl and the marquess." Her mouth compressed. "Where has the duke gone?"

Her gaze swung wide before coming to rest again on her son. "Is he finding his entertainment for the night? Every young miss in London should be on guard. I'm well aware of his so-called 'extraordinary' prowess in the bedroom.

He is as heartless as he is handsome!" Charlotte's mouth turned down. "And let us not forget the earl and the marquess. I daresay the ball is too tame for their tastes?"

She referred to Bramwell Leighton, Earl of Greystone, and Lucian Tremaine, Marquess of Blackthorne. They were not present this night—

Indeed, they *had* proclaimed tonight's ball . . . insipid.

"Mama, I'm sure I have no idea of their whereabouts tonight. Why do you dislike them so?"

"I'm well aware the duke is known for his so-called performance in the boudoir." Charlotte rapped her fan sharply on his hand. "I do not deny the earl is a man of remarkable good looks, but the knave considers himself quite irresistible, doesn't he? As for the marquess, I'm quite aware of the last affair hosted by the man—an orgy!" She sniffed her disapproval.

"Mama! I am shocked that you know of such a thing. And here I feared your tender ears."

Charlotte's lips were pinched in disapproval. "I am not ignorant of all that goes on in the *ton*. I know of your scandalous reputations, Gray, the four of you. The Lords of Sheffield Square—bah! You are the rogues of Sheffield Square."

"I shall be sure to tell them when next I see them."

"Are you so proud of it, then? Perhaps your efforts would be better put to good use if you sought to save your good name. You haven't been to Brightwood in months. Why, perhaps years!"

"Two," he said coolly. "It's been two years. And I have done my duty with regard to the family estates."

"Have you? There is dignity inherent in our name and your title, Gray. But now, all the world knows of your . . . liaisons."

"Mama, I do not set out to seduce and discard."

"Gray! I know it's in you to love again. Why do you disdain it?"

He stiffened.

"Tell me, Gray. Have you had any kind of lasting relationship since Li—"

"Pray do not speak to me of Lily." His jaw might have been hewn in stone. What his mother said was true. He offered his heart to no one, nor would he. God knew, he had nothing left to give. And what he wouldn't give to forget!

But ever present was the guilt he knew would haunt him forever.

"I do not want a lasting relationship, Mama. I will never marry again. Any woman with whom I am involved expects no more of me than I of her. If you wish me to be blunt, Mama, all we share is a mutual passion—"

"Passion!" Charlotte snapped her fan shut. "Is that what you tell yourself, Gray? Is that how you excuse yourself? You leave her bed and you feel nothing. You sate your lust—"

"Ah, forgive me, Mama. But you are right. I misspoke. 'Lust' is indeed the better word. I merely thought you might find 'passion' more palatable."

"By heaven, if we were alone, I would box your ears!"

"Mama," he drawled, "I assure you, my women, as you call them, are well-satisfied."

"Do not mock me, Grayson Sutherland."

"Do I distress you, Mama? It was you who began this conversation."

Something passed over Charlotte Sutherland's face. "What has happened to you? How can you be so cold? You have changed so much!"

She was right, Gray acknowledged. He had changed. He'd closed off a part of himself tight against the world. Against himself. Once, his life had been so very different. But now he was empty inside. There were too many shadows. Too many memories. Too much heartache.

That life was gone. He could never reclaim it.

How could he have been so blind?

It was that which tormented him. His mouth twisted in self-deprecation. Whom did he fool? Not his mother. Not Clive. Always, the pain remained. It never left him, no matter how he tried to close it away. And he did try to close it off. With drink. With women. But his pain left him in bondage. It put him in bondage to the past. And no matter how hard he tried, it never left. Why couldn't he be numb inside?

In that instant, he resented his mother—resented her fiercely!—for making him feel like this.

"Gray! Oh, dearest! Where is the man you once were? I don't understand—"

"Precisely," he said with lips that barely moved. "You do not understand."

"Then help me. Help me to understand! I want you to be happy. Oh, Gray, I know you lost what was so precious to you—"

Gray's tone was brittle. "I pray you, Mama, cease this lecture."

Charlotte's gaze turned as icy as his. "You use cynicism to mask your pain, Gray. That I do understand, so you do not fool me. I know better." She drew herself up to her full height. "Now, I shall take my leave."

Gray cupped her elbow. "May I have a footman call your coach for you?"

"You may consider me old, but I remain quite capable."

With his mother gone, Gray's gaze returned to the woman who had captured his attention. She was still there, standing by an ivory pillar. He found her intriguingly contrary. She was tall, but there was a delicate air about her. Slender, but he sensed a woman of fire on the inside. He found himself gripped by raw, physical desire. He imagined her naked.

Her legs, he had already noted, would be slim

and long, long enough to wrap around his waist. The thought made his rod swell. And beneath the neckline of her gown, her breasts promised an enticing fullness. He imagined what they looked like, smoother porcelain flesh filling his palm. A dark stab of desire settled in his gut. The prospect of finding her beneath him, his legs parting her wide as he settled over her, made his rod tighten; he relished the idea of finding out for himself. And when he did, he would pleasure her again and then again.

Her profile was exquisite as well, small, perfect nose and long-lashed eyes. She turned his way then, and Gray sucked in a breath. Christ, she was beautiful. His reaction was immediate. Intense. Once again his eyes slid over her.

She did not shirk. She did not flinch from his scrutiny. Indeed, the chit evaluated him with an appraisal just as bold as his.

Precisely the response Claire wanted.

Chapter Two

$\mathscr{H}$ is gaze was so intense she felt scorched by it. Something burned in his eyes, something that nearly stopped the breath in her chest. She fought back a swell of panic, feeling a blush heat her cheeks. She couldn't help it. Her heart pounded a rhythm so fast she feared she might swoon.

All around was the chatter of guests. Lights shimmered overhead. Jewels flashed. But all that faded into nothingness when he stepped up before her with a bow.

"Madame, do I know you?"

Oh, no doubt he considered himself clever. The question gave him segue to engage her in conversation. He did not swagger, but moved with effortless grace.

He wasn't what Claire expected. He was so exceptionally tall that she had to tilt her head back to meet his regard. His nose was long and thin—and arrogant, she decided. His eyes—blue, they were, like pale frost—were a stark contrast to hair and brows as dark as a night with no moon.

She'd not anticipated a man with looks like a god. A man so striking he surely surpassed every other man present. Damn, damn, damn! How she wished he looked a troll. Indeed, she had imagined a troll.

Indeed, she had thought Oliver's killer would look like the monster he was.

"I don't believe so, sir." She felt as if she were shaking inside, yet her voice was composed. She mustered her dignity, marveling that she had so readily summoned the ability to speak. "Why do you think we are acquainted?"

"Yours is a face not to be soon forgotten. On the contrary, in fact."

"You flatter me, sir."

"Indeed I do not. Are you certain we have never met?" He was so damnably self-assured. No doubt he thought to sweep her off her feet with that wicked half smile that grazed his lips.

"Quite certain, sir. I've only recently come to London."

"Then permit me to introduce myself. I am Grayson Sutherland."

"Charmed, I'm sure." She extended her hand. Her fingers itched to slap him cold. "And I am Claire Westfield."

He kissed her knuckles. "How do you do, Mrs. Westfield," he murmured. "I could not help but notice"—he indicated her right hand—"you are a widow?"

"Y-es." Claire was immediately impatient with herself. She mustn't bumble or all might be lost.

"My condolences."

A moment later the musicians had struck up a new song.

The viscount had yet to release her fingers. "Ah," he said. "Will you dance with me, Mrs. Westfield?"

Claire had scarcely taken a breath than she found her hand clasped in his. His other arm slid around her waist.

He whirled her onto the dance floor so quickly she had to clutch at his shoulder. She sought to follow the melody. It had been years since she danced. In that instant, a memory washed over her.

Oliver had taught her to dance.

She had to stop herself from spitting on the viscount.

The thought unveiled, that painful memory still high in her mind, she stumbled a little. The viscount's arm tightened ever so slightly.

They swung past Penelope. She wore a look of surprise, then gave a nod of encouragement.

Claire swallowed. She was disturbingly aware of the chest beneath her fingers, rock-hard and solid. Clearly he didn't spend all his time in the pursuit of women and pleasure.

She was hardly a good dancer. She felt like an elephant. The viscount, startlingly light on his feet, was a far more accomplished partner. She had never been a particularly good dancer, despite Oliver's tutelage.

His fingers curled tightly around hers. All she wanted was for this dance to end. Another whirl and she lost her footing. This time she did clutch at him.

He pulled her to the side.

"Mrs. Westfield? Are you unwell?"

"I'm . . . a bit dizzy." And she was. His nearness truly made her feel strange. Almost light-headed. He guided her through a set of double doors open to the verandah. There was a stone bench just outside. He helped her to sit.

"A breath of air will do you good."

The hostess had appeared; Penelope was directly behind her.

"Shall I summon a physician?" Lady Blakely looked worried.

"No, no," Claire said. "Please return to your guests. I'm sorry to cause such a fuss. Rejoin the party. I should feel terribly guilty if you do not. Penelope, you, too, though no doubt you are weary. I shall take a hack. I shall be right as rain once I'm home."

Her heart was pumping madly.

The viscount's eyes slid over her. "You seem unable to catch your breath. Perhaps your stays are too tight." One lean hand took possession of her waist. "If you will permit me—"

Claire nearly shrieked. "No," she stammered. Why, what gentleman would speak of such an intimate thing! Her hand clamped down over his. She registered heat—and the awareness that his hand was much larger than hers.

For just a heartbeat she could have sworn she saw amusement flare in those pale blue eyes.

Oh, but she should have known . . . Silently she cursed him.

Scoundrel. Scallywag. Devil.

"I'm fine. Or at least I shall be. Please, sir, can you help me to stand?"

The wretch took the hand she extended. Flushing, Claire let him pull her up.

"Pray forgive me." Her laugh was breathless. "I can't imagine what came over me. I've never before been prone to the vapors."

"No need to apologize. Soon I shall have you snug in your bed."

What audacity! She could have cheerfully strangled the man.

Her hair had come down, she noticed. She pushed at it self-consciously.

"Here, allow me to pin it up again."

Which he did quite deftly, sifting his fingers

through it and pinning her tresses into a loose knot on her crown. The feeling of his hands in her hair made her stomach knot.

"There. Not as good as your maid, I vow, but passable."

Claire was too stunned—too furious—to protest.

"I shall take you home," he said smoothly. "Then you shall be off to bed straightaway."

Another innocent choice of words? There was nothing innocent about this man.

She shook her head. "Sir, it is very kind of you—"

"I insist. I would brand myself the worst sort of rogue if I did not see you safely home."

Branded. He was already branded in her eyes, she thought bitterly. He was already the worst sort of rogue. And he was already at the door, speaking to a footman.

"I must let Penelope know—"

"I will see to it she is told," he said smoothly. "Here is your wrap."

A footman had handed it to him, a cloak of midnight velvet. He spoke briefly to the footman, then turned. Strong hands settled it over her shoulders.

Claire felt herself tremble beneath his touch. A part of her longed to run screaming from him, as far away as she could get. But this was precisely what she wanted, wasn't it? She had attracted his notice. Yet all at once she felt dreadfully ill-equipped to handle it.

To handle *him*.

At the rear of the house, he handed her into his carriage. Claire gave him her address.

They spoke only briefly during the ride. Outside, a drizzling rain began to fall as the coach rolled to a stop.

Claire was acutely aware of his hand on her arm as they moved up the cobbled walkway, lending her assistance if she needed it. Which she most vehemently did not, she decided crossly as she fumbled for her keys. Her maid, Rosalie, had not yet appeared when Claire opened the door and stepped across the threshold. She discovered he was smiling as she turned to face him.

"May I see you safely inside?"

"Of course." It appeared she had little choice. Stripping off her gloves, she dropped them on the small table near the door. Rosalie had appeared to close the door, then quietly slipped away. Claire looked up to discover a ghost of a smile on the viscount's lips.

She could not help it; she lowered her head, trying not to tremble.

"Mrs. Westfield? Are you dizzy again?"

"Yes." She heard her own voice faintly.

And she was.

His hands came up to her shoulders. He steadied her. Claire swallowed, raising her head. She stared at the strong column of his neck, the chiseled angle of his jawline, suddenly shatteringly aware of their closeness. There was a scant hand's width between them.

"Are you a woman of delicate constitution?"

"Certainly not!"

"Then is it possible there is another reason?"

Claire frowned. "I beg your pardon?"

A pause. "You said you'd never been prone to the vapors."

"I am not."

His eyes met hers. "There is no delicate way to broach this most delicate of female conditions. But if your husband has recently passed, Mrs. Westfield, is it not possible that you . . . that he—"

He was asking if she was with child.

She was of a mind to slap him for daring to speak of such a thing.

"No. That is impossible." She couldn't quite keep the ice from her tone.

"I've offended you. I humbly beg your forgiveness."

Humbly? There wasn't a humble bone in the man's body. He gripped both of her hands now. It struck her that he doubtless wanted her to ask him in. Her head was spinning. Fate had aided her, for the night was going exactly as she'd hoped. But it was happening so fast.

"No need, my lord. I'm quite recovered." She

took a deep breath. "I insist you come in for tea. Or brandy? My—My husband savored one in particular you might enjoy."

Even as she spoke, hatred spilled inside her. It was Oliver who favored brandy.

"I confess, Mrs. Westfield, brandy sounds just the thing."

Claire stopped herself from looking at him sharply. For some strange reason, she'd neither examined nor pondered why, until now—indeed had told herself no liquor cabinet was complete without it—she'd made certain when she came to London that brandy numbered among the spirits.

Not whiskey, but brandy.

In the drawing room, she moved to a table near the sofa. There, she poured two glasses of brandy. She handed one to him.

"Cheers," he said.

Crystal clinked. Claire took a small sip.

The viscount held it to the light. The brandy was clear and golden. He took another sip.

"Aged in wooden casks," he murmured. "Very fine indeed, Mrs. Westfield."

It raced through Claire's mind that she'd known it would be to the viscount's taste . . . which was ridiculous. She disdained the possibility.

"I commend your husband's taste."

The viscount held the glass so the brew warmed in his palm.

His nearness was discomfiting. There was a scant foot between them. Claire took a sip.

Nay, not just a sip. Her rather generous swallow burned her throat. Her eyes watered. She began to cough.

The viscount took her glass, lest it spill. He patted her on the back. Oh, but he was amused, the wretch!

"No more brandy for you, I think," he said. "Perhaps wine. Do you enjoy wine, Mrs. Westfield?"

She'd recovered the ability to breathe. "I like a glass of wine or two, yes."

"And champagne? Do you enjoy champagne?"

"Actually, I've never had it." Claire was annoyed with herself. She felt like a green young girl.

"That should be remedied, then." He still looked amused, the lout. "I shall see to it."

The viscount studied her for a moment. "You're nervous," he said softly. "Am I the first man you've received since your husband died?"

Claire focused on the knot in his cravat. She hadn't expected such straightforwardness.

"Yes," she said quietly. "You are the first man in my home."

She sought to validate the statement. It wasn't a lie. It was true. Oh, on so many levels!

"Do I embarrass you? Make you uncomfortable?"

She swallowed, rendered immobile by his words. By the very man himself. He had that power over her, she decided vaguely, and she must be wary.

And yet she admitted, "You do." It stunned her to realize her voice was shaking.

He took the glass from her hand. "Thank you for your honesty. I shall be just as frank."

"I beg your pardon?"

"I am not a man of pretense."

Pretense? She was reminded of her charade. What would he say if he knew?

She didn't care. She didn't care in the least what he would say . . . what he would do when he discovered the truth.

"And let us be direct, if you please."

"Certainly." Her pulse began to pick up.

"I confess, Mrs. Westfield, I wonder why I've never seen you before this."

Claire took a breath. "I've not spent much time in London. The year I was to come out, my mother fell ill." That, too, was the truth. "Upon her death, my father fell victim to malaise as well. Then my husband—" She broke off.

There was a pause. "I'm sorry," he said finally. "About your parents. Your husband."

But was he sorry about Oliver?

"You've borne a great deal, haven't you?"

And so she had. She felt the onset of a sudden, scalding rush of tears. She blinked it back, casting an embittered gaze on him beneath her lashes. He did not notice.

He set his snifter aside and rose to his feet. "You should retire, Mrs. Westfield." He took her hands.

Claire didn't want him to touch her. Indeed, she longed to spit on him.

He brought one of her hands to his lips. She longed to snatch her hands away, but the possession of strong male fingers seemed to tighten around hers. Damn the rogue! Yet somehow she was shocked at the strange current that went through her as he brushed his lips over her knuckles. "I wish you pleasant dreams."

Chapter Three

$\mathcal{E}$ arly the next morning, the maid admitted Penelope. Claire sat in the dining room with her breakfast. She usually enjoyed the sun streaming in through the windows, but not today.

Pleasant dreams, he'd said. And for the hundredth time she lost patience with herself.

What a fool she was! So much for her plan to captivate and entice the viscount. Whatever thoughtlessness had possessed her to think she could captivate such a man?

All she had done was play the fool. No doubt Sutherland had guessed her stupid scheme and laughed uproariously at the way she flung herself across his path. How stupid of her to even attempt the role of femme fatale. No doubt he—

When Rosalie announced Penelope, Claire waved her to the chair next to her. "Tea, love? A croissant?"

Penelope declined, patting the swell of her belly. "I'm growing fat as a hen! I dare not." Today she wore a dark navy gown that revealed the bump in her middle.

But Claire chuckled. She loved to tease Penelope about the babe to come. "Oh, pooh. Yes, he grows with each day! But that's good, sweetings. Why, I vow this child will make an appearance this very day."

Penelope was actually nearer her confinement than she looked. A little more than a month was all that remained.

She groaned. "Bite your tongue, Claire. If Theo were home, I should quite agree. I'm sure Felicity is growing as tired as I of fetching the chamber pot three times a night. We shall see if you are laughing when you sit in my place!"

Claire's smile froze. There was a pinch in her heart. A husband—and children—were lost to her now. Society was unforgiving. If she were to accomplish what she set out to do—please, God—her name would be forever connected to the viscount. Forever connected to scandal. No man would have her as his wife.

But it would be worth it. It would be worth it, she decided with all that she possessed. It would be worth anything—everything!—to see that bastard Sutherland humiliated before her.

Newfound resolve gripped her. She bit into her toast almost fiercely.

Across the table, Penelope gave a small sigh. Claire knew she fretted each day that Theo was gone. She'd expected he would be back from the Peninsula by now. Alas, he wasn't. Her friend kept up a good face, though, bless her heart! But Claire knew her too well, and realized that behind her facade there lurked an anxious worry.

She leaned forward. "What's wrong, dear? Are you ill?"

Penelope shook her head. "No, dearest. I'm fine."

Claire took her hands. "Pen," she chided gently. "You know we keep no secrets from each other."

Penelope gave a half sob. "Claire—oh, Claire, I haven't heard from Theo for well over a month. And I so need him! I—I so want him here when the baby comes. We thought he would be home in time for our child's birth."

Claire squeezed her fingers. "He is here in spirit, Pen. With both of you. Every moment. Every second."

Claire reached out and hugged her. Penelope hadn't thought to find strength, but she indeed took strength from Claire.

Penelope sat back, wearing a brave smile. "You realize, Claire, that you've not yet told me if you will stand as godmother."

Claire chuckled. "You are most insistent, aren't you?"

"I am." There was a pause. "Really, it will be a weight off my mind if you agree."

Claire's heart melted. "Of course I will, Pen. Did you think I wouldn't? But you haven't told me yet who will be godfather."

"Only because we haven't decided yet!" Penelope laughed, then sighed. "We planned to let Theo choose—another reason to wish him home."

Theirs had been a whirlwind romance. Penelope and Theo had met the night of Penelope's come-out. Within a scant week she was swept away. Scarcely a fortnight had passed before Theo asked her to marry him. Penelope's parents made them wait some six months, but both of them were prepared to wait forever.

And now they would soon welcome the fruit of that love.

Claire pushed aside her envy. Her wistfulness. She did not delude herself. She hadn't from the start. A husband was the last thing on her mind. The only man in her life was her so-called dead husband.

Penelope's expression grew troubled. "Claire," she said, "if this charade is discovered, you'll never be able to have a family of your own. You'll be disgraced. The best you can hope for is a position as governess or companion."

As always, it was as if Penelope read her mind. And once again a pang shot through her. Claire willed it away. She had known from the start that she could never have what Penelope and Theo had. An abiding love that would never be shaken. A husband who adored her as passionately as she adored him. Children. And children. They, too, were beyond her reach. The course she had begun last night would seal away that possibility forever.

Should she succeed, needled a voice within.

But she would. She *would*.

No, it did not sway her mind.

"We've discussed this." Quietly—but oh, most fervently!—Claire reminded her friend. "I am ready. This is a sacrifice I make gladly."

She poured tea for Penelope, then passed her cup and saucer.

"What happened last night, Claire? I asked after you, but I was told you had gone home."

Claire took a deep breath. "I did."

"And the viscount?"

Raising her teacup, Claire blew on the surface, pretending to cool it. "He escorted me."

"And?"

"And . . . that is all."

"What do you mean—'that is all'?"

"Precisely that. He escorted me home, we enjoyed a bit of brandy, and then he went on his way. His behavior was impeccable." Her tone turned scathingly self-critical. "And this is where you tell me what an idiot I have been to think that one of London's handsomest rakes would fall head over heels with the likes of me."

"You would not be dissuaded," Penelope reminded her. "And this has nothing to do with the way you look, Claire. You're beautiful. That blackguard is not worthy of you. I pray you are well rid of him."

Claire lowered her eyes.

"Tell me, Pen," she said suddenly. "I aroused no speculation when he escorted me home? No whispers of scandal?"

"No. That's one of the advantages of being a widow . . . Oh, Claire, I beseech you. Please! I beg you reconsider. But perhaps you should take this as a sign it can come to no good. I know how close you were to Oliver. But do not let Sutherland ruin your life any more than he already has."

"Perhaps I should see it as a sign I am meant to continue." Claire fell silent, deep in thought. "I wonder," she said finally, "where the good viscount will be found tonight."

Penelope didn't hide her dismay. "I cannot dissuade you?"

Claire shook her head. "Not yet. I've barely begun! It's far too soon for me to give up."

"Very well, then. I will see what I can discover, but I must retire to my lying-in soon."

"I will ask no more of you, Pen. I've been out and about enough that I can ferret out what I need—"

The knocker sounded at the front door. The sound of a male voice reached her ears. Then Rosalie's. Then the sound of the door closing.

Claire sucked in a breath. Her heart was suddenly pounding. She knew that voice. "It's him, Pen." She hurried to the doorway.

In the foyer, Rosalie had already admitted Sutherland. He glanced around as Claire and Penelope appeared.

"Good morning, Mrs. Westfield." He tucked his hat beneath his arm and gave a slight bow. His gaze settled on Penelope. "I believe I did not have the pleasure last night."

Claire hastened to introduce them. "My lord, good morning. This is my dear friend, Mrs. Penelope Grove. Penelope, his lordship, Viscount Sutherland."

The viscount bent low over Penelope's hand. "Charmed, I assure you."

"Penelope was just leaving," Claire said crisply. "Would you care to wait in the drawing room, my lord? I'll have tea sent in."

"Certainly." He bowed. "Good day, Mrs. Grove."

As soon as he disappeared, Rosalie handed Penelope her parasol. Penelope gave a shake of her head. "Claire," she whispered, "you must have a care. His eyes . . . Such an icy shade of blue . . ."

That was the first thing Claire had noted about him too.

". . . He makes me shiver, Claire. He seems— oh, I don't know how to say it! It's as if he's looking right through one."

Claire silently acknowledged that as well. But

she did not shiver, but instead shuddered, she told herself staunchly. She knew she could never destroy him, but she would damn well make a fool of him, no matter the consequence to herself. Relentless purpose filled her heart. She *would* have her revenge.

A quick hug and Penelope was off, then Claire walked into the drawing room. The viscount was standing at the window. Hearing the rustle of skirts, he turned.

"I apologize for the interruption. I shall not keep you long. I came to inquire as to your health this morning. It pleases me to find you well."

"I am indeed well, my lord."

She handed him a cup. Their fingers brushed. Her heart leaped. It spun through her mind that he touched her deliberately, and it was all she could do not to scratch that very handsome face.

"Excellent, then." He stopped. Tipped his head to the side, a slow smile edging across his lips. "Actually, I came for another matter as well. It's a fine day. Will you join me for a stroll in Hyde Park this morning?"

She felt like singing. *Yes, yes, oh, yes!*

"I should love to."

"Fetch your wrap and let us go, then."

Upstairs, Claire changed into a blue muslin gown trimmed with a dainty white lace. Just before she left, she glanced at her reflection. Were her cheeks overly bright? Excitement bounded in her breast. Yes. No. Rats, she didn't want to appear overeager. She brushed a bit of powder over them before joining the viscount downstairs. There, that was better.

Rotten Row was empty except for a carriage far down the track. Later in the day those in the Fashionable Set would parade down the promenade. At this hour, most of the *ton* were still asleep from the activities of the previous night. After he'd left her last night, had such "other" activities kept the viscount from his bed?

The day was already beginning to warm, and Claire needed no more than a shawl around her shoulders.

They walked toward the Serpentine at a leisurely pace. But her heart lurched when he tucked her hand into the crook of his elbow. She was immediately aware of the knotted strength in his forearm and hardness of his bicep.

And did he hold her hand longer than necessary? She wasn't sure, but alarm raced through her. She hadn't been wearing gloves when he kissed her hand last night. Now she recalled the touch of his lips with a shocking vividness that echoed all through her.

She pushed it aside. Taking a breath, she closed her parasol and lifted her face to the sun.

She caught Gray's eye. He raised a brow.

"Oh, come," she said. "It's far too enjoyable a day to hide away beneath a parasol."

"Shall I doff my hat as well?"

He did, spurring a laugh she somehow couldn't quite withhold. "I have no objections, my lord."

They stopped where the waters of the Serpentine glimmered. "You're aware that both of us could be perceived as quite wicked. Quite the rebels. Perhaps we'll both be banished."

"Well," she said lightly, "I suppose I do have an excuse to offer."

"And what might that be?"

"I am a country girl at heart."

"Are you?" He appeared skeptical.

"Yes. Couldn't you tell when you waltzed with me last night?"

"I did not notice," he declared.

Claire bit her lip. He was teasing—teasing her! And heaven above, she had the most absurd notion to laugh!

"It's not often we have occasion to waltz at Wildewood."

"Wildewood?"

"Yes. My home in Essex."

Heaven above—why had she divulged that? Foolish, oh so foolish! If he chose to look further into her background—

Yet why should he? Her plan was progressing even quicker than she had expected. Nonetheless, she must be careful. Because if she wasn't—

All might be lost.

Truths . . . Untruths. She couldn't let them become blurred in her mind.

"I've been called far worse than rebel. Indeed, I need no excuse at all. At times I believe I am received only because of my mother."

Claire suspected he was right.

Now, he looked down at her. "So," he said, "a country girl, eh? I must say, you appear to be finding your legs exceptionally well."

"Except when I'm dancing," she said dryly.

He laughed softy.

"Come with me tonight," he said.

"I beg your pardon?"

The light in his eyes seemed to flame. Claire's cheeks were suddenly burning. He smothered her hand with his—

And she knew it wasn't the sun at all.

He lowered his head. His mouth was so close to her that he brushed her cheek. "Come with me tonight. There is a play at Drury Lane. Join me."

Her composure was shaky, her heart pounding. She wasn't sure if she was elated or afraid! She sensed something dangerous in him. But she wouldn't refuse. There was too much at stake.

She lifted her chin. "I would be delighted, my lord."

Chapter Four

*C*laire could not help it. She was in a tizzy. She lay down for a nap but was far too excited to sleep.

She dressed carefully for the play. She didn't want to appear ostentatious, for that would hardly befit a widow. Instead she chose a dark gold gown with a shimmering pleated skirt that flowed around her legs.

Rosalie clapped her hands together. "I've never seen you look lovelier, my lady!"

Claire was caught between excitement and dismay. "Tell me true, Rosalie! It is not too revealing?" Her hand fluttered up to her neckline. The tops of her breasts thrust up beneath the clinging bodice. "Should I tuck a swatch of lace in it?"

"Oh, no, milady! It is all the rage. Truly, your gown shows far less bosom than most women.

And the color is heavenly. Your eyes look so very green!"

So began her evening out.

For whatever reason, she had not thought to enjoy the play. Instead she found it delightful. She leaned forward, utterly entranced as it unfolded. Yet all throughout, she was singularly conscious of the man beside her every second.

Her gaze inevitably drawn to him, her mouth had grown dry as she watched him cross the lobby. Once again she was struck by the sheer physicality of the man. No one would ever think him a dandy, she decided. And she was certain no man would dare tell him so. He looked every inch the vital aristocrat, his shoulders impressively wide. He embodied raw, primitive strength, from the tip of impeccably shined boots to the crisp white of his cravat. Evening clothes did nothing to disguise the power beneath.

When he had called on her, Claire deliberately kept him waiting for several minutes. Their earlier conversation high in her mind, she decided it best not to appear too eager to see him. His hard mouth was curled up in a half smile as she descended the stairs.

His gaze had wandered over the bareness of her shoulders. The pearls around her throat were Penelope's. Rosalie had threaded a matching strand through her hair, pulled back in soft curls.

And now it was she who waited. She stood

motionless before him while those eyes Penelope had called crystal seemed to devour her in a journey up and down her form that left her breathless. The was no denying the approval on his features.

"You are stunning," he told her.

He settled her cloak over the narrow bridge of her shoulders and they were off.

At the playhouse, she noticed several acquaintances. Sir Brownleigh's wife Rebecca looked startled. She quickly composed herself and nodded a greeting.

Gray's box was in the first balcony. Most of the audience had already taken their places. When she was seated, more than one quizzing glass turned their way. She wished heartily that they had arrived earlier.

Gray was totally unperturbed. "I see you've noticed we're garnering a bit of attention. Does it bother you? Pay no heed. The curtain will rise soon." He laid a hand on her gloved fingertips, clasped together in her lap . . . her lap! Her heart lurched. She felt like leaping out of her seat. She hoped no one had seen *that*.

The curtain was raised high. Then all else was forgotten as she found herself caught up in the play.

After the first act, Gray glanced at her.

"Are you enjoying the play?"

"Oh, yes," she breathed. "It's enchanting."

"I'm glad I asked you to accompany me, then. You've never before been to a play?"

She shook her head.

"Your husband was remiss, then." He cocked a brow. "Shall we go for refreshments?"

She fell quiet when they descended into the lobby.

"Wine?" he asked. "No, there is champagne. Would you like some?"

She nodded.

Gray brought her a glass of frothy champagne. Claire accepted it, her gaze skidding up to his.

She discovered him regarding her with an almost lazy amusement. He leaned forward. "I did promise you champagne," he murmured, "did I not?"

Heads turned. Gray paid no heed. He kept her hand anchored to his sleeve. His own covered it. Touching him like this made her pulse race, the way it had this morning at Hyde Park. Her eyes grazed his; Claire was the first to look away.

Rather nervously, she sipped her champagne. Gray, however, seemed totally at ease. A man near the refreshment table had turned toward them. Lifting a quizzing glass, he stared at them for a moment. If she wasn't mistaken, he had been with Gray last night.

He approached, and Gray greeted him easily. Before he had a chance to introduce him, the man caught hold of her hand and bowed over it. He brought her hand to his lips as he straightened. His manner told her that he was as boldly confident as Gray.

"*Enchanté*, madame," he drawled. "Clive Fielding at your service. And you are . . . ?"

"Mrs. Claire Westfield," supplied Gray.

"Where have you been hiding this gem, Sutherland?"

Fielding had yet to release her hand. She tugged it free.

"I will not share her, my friend," Gray drawled.

Claire bristled. It seemed he was as audacious as Gray! She glanced between the two. Both were tall. Powerfully built. Both possessed a commanding, immediate presence.

And bounders, both of them.

They chatted briefly. It spun through her mind that Penelope would have been quite proud of her. Then once again Fielding kissed her gloved fingertips. "Perhaps we will meet again soon, madame. For now, I shall bid you good evening."

Claire looked after him, her mouth compressed.

Gray noticed. He laughed. "Did he offend you? His Grace has a tendency to live up to his reputation."

"His Grace?"

"Clive. The Duke of Braddock."

Claire gasped. She had very nearly set down a duke! She recovered quickly. "Speaking of which, sir, you neglected to tell me your own title."

"I am honored that you chose to find out."

The lout!

"Does he have as scandalous a reputation as you?"

"I daresay, perhaps equal to mine. But please, you must call me Gray."

Claire could think of a good many things she'd like to call him. "My lord" and "Gray" were not among them.

Just then a tiny woman dressed in black and white satin stopped before them in a swirl of skirts. She offered her hand to Gray. He took it and lightly kissed her fingers.

"Mother," he murmured. "May I present the lovely Mrs. Claire Westfield?"

His mother! The woman looked anything but matronly. She was stunning, her complexion like ivory. What a beauty she must have been when she was young!

Rats! Wasn't it enough that she must guard herself against Gray, lest she give herself away? And now his mother was here!

She sank into a curtsy. "Charmed to meet you, my lady."

"Are you enjoying the play, Mrs. Westfield?"

"Oh, yes, my lady. I find it quite riveting."

"There's no place like London for the arts. Even Paris cannot surpass London."

She wasn't sure what to say to the viscountess. "I've never been to Paris."

"A pity! It's quite divine, or at least it will be when Napoleon is defeated."

Claire thought of Penelope's husband Theo.

The viscountess looked her up and down with her quizzing glass. "I don't believe I've seen you before, dear . . . do you often frequent Town?"

"No, my lady. But I confess, I find it quite charming."

"Charming?" The viscountess laughed. "Perhaps not the word I would use, but life in London is certainly lively." They chatted a few minutes more. Claire discovered she quite liked his mother—and wished she didn't. It was going to make her mission . . . more difficult. She wished fervently that the woman would leave.

Charlotte Sutherland finally tapped her son's forearm with her fan. "Come visit, boy. It seems I see you at these affairs and never at home. Indeed, Gray, I do hope you'll make time to come to your birthday fete next week."

"Mama—"

"Oh, it has just now occurred to me." Her smile was vivacious. "Mrs. Westfield, you must come too! I am hosting a birthday celebration for Gray next week. Please, join us. I vow you'll enjoy it."

For all her fragile appearance, Claire sensed that Charlotte Sutherland could be a woman of icy disdain. She had an impression of ever-abundant energy. It struck her that the countess was also a strong-willed and knew what she wanted. Somehow, she knew that Gray was equally as willful. She wondered if perhaps he and his mother ever butted heads.

Claire shook her head. "My lady, I'm flattered at the invitation, but—"

"I insist, Mrs. Westfield. You simply must come, mustn't she, Gray darling?"

"Mama, it may well be that Mrs. Westfield has a prior engagement."

"Do you, Mrs. Westfield?"

"Well . . ."

"No? It will be a delightful affair, I promise you." She gave Claire no time to respond. "Now then, do enjoy the rest of the play, Mrs. Westfield. And I trust that you'll see that my son behaves."

"Oh, rest assured that I will," Claire said promptly. Too late she realized how that sounded.

Charlotte laughed. "Yes, child, I believe you will."

She bade them good evening.

Claire felt she'd been weighed and measured—and apparently passed muster. Why it mattered, she had no idea. Gray—drat, why did she now think of him as Gray?—kissed his mother's cheek.

Claire's head was still whirling. "I daresay your mother is a bit of a whirlwind."

"At the very least," he said dryly.

"She's very beautiful."

"She is."

"Is your father here tonight?"

Gray shook his head. "My father is dead." There was a pause. "A gentleman asked for my mother's hand last year. She refused. She never said why, but . . . somehow I think she felt that marrying again would be a betrayal to my father's memory," he said softly. "But I think my father would have approved."

All at once Claire wished she had never come. Something inside her twisted. She wished violently that she'd never met his mother. Seeing her . . . it made him too . . . human. Too vulnerable. She didn't want to think of him as a man with a family, a mother who loved him and who he loved in return. He was a cold, heartless killer! Had he cared about Oliver? Had he cared that Oliver had a family who loved him? That he was forever lost to his family?

There was a touch on her arm. "Shall we return to the box?"

"I hated to see it end!"

Claire sighed and settled into the sumptuous cushions of Gray's carriage with genuine regret. It rumbled through the cobbled streets, a carriage lamp casting a golden haze into the velvet interior of Gray's coach, while a warm cocoon surrounded her. The champagne? Probably, she decided. Oddly, she didn't care.

Gray watched her, a lazy smile flitting at one corner of his mouth. "Did you enjoy yourself tonight?"

She tipped her head to the side, hugging the silk of her cloak closer around her shoulders.

"Yes, I quite enjoyed myself, my lord."

He made a *tsking* sound. "Gray."

"Very well, then. I quite enjoyed myself . . . Gray."

"And the company, Claire? Did you enjoy that as well? I must say, I found myself ever more entranced."

He watched her laugh nervously. She had yet to learn when he mocked. "You can be quite the charming gentleman, can't you?"

Gentleman? He was darkly amused. The last thing anyone would call him was a gentleman. Bastard. Scoundrel. But never a gentleman. Not anymore.

He turned toward her. "The evening need not yet end. The hour is still early. Permit me to play the host."

Claire felt her heart begin to clamor. "The host?"

"Yes. I've taken the liberty of having a small supper prepared at my home. Will you join me?"

He was certainly direct. This, too, was uncharted territory, but her very purpose in coming to London. "It sounds just the thing."

"Excellent," he murmured. He leaned forward

and rapped twice on the window. Briefly he spoke to his driver.

It wasn't long before they drew up to a house on Sheffield Square fronted by Georgian brick and a shiny red door.

Gray helped her down. In the foyer, he slipped off her cloak. She was acutely aware of the brush of his fingertips across the bare skin of her shoulders. Her heart began to pound as he led her into the drawing room. The sweet scent from a small vase of pink roses perfumed the air. Soft candlelight flickered across the walls. There was fruit and a small array of cold meats and cheese set on a side table.

Claire steadied her breath. Her mind tripped forward. She had asked herself how she would handle an advance from him, should he make one. *Should he make one?* She chided herself. Ah, but that was the whole point, wasn't it? Despite the fact they'd spent most of the day together, she hadn't expected it quite so soon . . . And he'd created the setting perfectly. Ah, but she must gather herself. She was a widow, she reminded herself staunchly. He had already called her young. She mustn't act the virginal miss to be put to the blush.

Which, of course, she was.

"Come sit," Gray invited. He seated her in a velvety divan before the fire, then filled a small plate for her and poured a generous portion of wine into a crystal glass. Claire ate from the plate and drank deeply of the ruby liquid in the glass.

"How do you find the wine?" he asked.

"It's excellent."

She realized that he'd planned to bring her here all along. She would be fine, she told herself, as long as she kept her head.

But her tongue was loosened by the champagne—and now the wine. She ran a finger around the rim of her glass. She could feel the quick hard pounding of her heart throughout her body.

"Did you bring me here to seduce me?" she heard herself say.

He leaned back. "What do you think?"

Claire raised a brow. The half smile that creased his lips widened ever so slightly.

"I wonder how you would go about it." She marveled at her audacity.

He pretended to consider. "Hmmm. Flowers, I think. Wine. I would flatter you. Whisper endearments in your ear. I would tell you your lips are the same blushing pink of the roses. I would tell you I long to sip the wine from your lips, run my tongue along your lips and taste it."

His tongue? Claire was shocked. She had never imagined such a thing, but she must maintain her charade.

"Is that why you brought me here?"

"My dear Claire, at the risk of sounding boorish, I need not resort to seduction. There is no need."

"Yet you've created the setting."

"Yet you are here."

A rush of heat stung her cheeks. The insufferable wretch.

"You are audacious."

"I am honest."

"That is your intent, then?" she asked. "To seduce me?"

He said nothing. That wicked smile merely widened.

"Are you as roguish as everyone says?" A voice inside was screaming a warning. Grayson Sutherland was far beyond her experience.

He pretended to consider. "There is roguish. And there is . . . charmingly roguish."

"Charming? An insipid term for you, I suspect." A part of her was aghast at her bravado, for that's what it was. Sheer bravado.

He threw back his head and laughed. "I agree. 'Charming' is not a word one usually associates with me. I daresay, my mother would agree. But tell me, what kind of man do you think I am?"

Oh, but he would not want to know . . .

'Ere the thought went through her mind, he shook his head. "Faith, don't answer that."

"I believe we both know the answer to that. From your own lips, you're a rogue. Are you a jaded rogue?"

He was amused. "Is there any other kind?"

Claire caught her breath, trying hard not to tremble. Faith, when he laughed, he was breathtakingly handsome.

"The question has been posed," she said almost primly.

"Good Lord, if you knew my reputation, you would scarcely ask."

"Sometimes we are not always what we seem." Even as she spoke, a little sliver of guilt needled her.

"Perhaps you're a woman of mystery, then."

"And perhaps you are a man of mystery."

Thus they continued to parry.

"Come. Sit with me." He extended a hand and saw her seated on the divan in front of the fireplace. It was hot, so no fire burned on the grate.

But Claire felt as if it did. And her entire body seemed to burn. Shadows flickered on the walls; she hoped Gray couldn't see her face.

But she felt as if he did. He sat so near, their knees were nearly touching.

She watched as he poured another glass of wine for both of them. She sipped it nervously, aware of his eyes on her profile. He did not speak.

Finally he set aside his glass, and hers as well. He caught at her hand.

"Come here, Claire."

She didn't want to. She had to remind herself she had a role to play.

But then . . . oh, but then an arm slid around her back, bringing her into his chest. Her shoulder fit perfectly into the notch between his shoulder. It was as if she was made for him.

His eyes slid over her face. "Do you know what I want, Claire?"

Her hands were trapped between their bodies. "I—"

His mouth covered hers. Her fingers splayed wide on his chest. It was a kiss that gained fervor with every second. A kiss that gave rise to a dozen confusing feelings racing throughout her body. A kiss of almost blinding sweetness, pleasure such as she had never known—and fear of what would come next.

Their lips parted. Warm breath rushed over her cheek. "God," he muttered against the corner of her mouth. "I've been waiting to do that all day."

His mouth returned. It was Gray who controlled the tempo of the kiss. Controlled it—and thus controlled her. The fanciful daydreams she'd envisioned as a young girl hadn't prepared her for this. His hold on her was commanding. Masterful. His kiss was far beyond any imagining she might have had.

She was trembling when he finally raised his head. The moment seemed to stretch out forever.

"What's wrong, Claire?"

Speech was beyond her.

He released her abruptly. "You're shaking! What are you frightened of?"

She leaned back. There was a shimmer of tears in her eyes. She tried to blink them back.

"Tell me what the devil is going on." His voice was very low.

The truth was that she *was* afraid. There was an intensity about him that almost terrified her.

He wasn't a man to trifle with. In that moment, she realized just how true it was. If he'd wanted, he could have laid her back, stripped her clothes from her, and taken her at his will.

And there wasn't a thing she could have done to stop him.

But above all, she couldn't allow that to happen. Her quest for revenge would be lost. She'd come this far. She wouldn't quit now.

"How long were you wed?" he asked.

She opened her mouth, floundering.

"Tell me," he said sharply. "Is it too soon?"

"Too soon?"

He made an impatient gesture. "Too soon after your husband's death."

She seized on it. "Yes," she whispered. "I didn't realize it until now . . ."

She had lowered her eyes. It did no use. His regard seemed to spear inside her.

He caught her chin between thumb and forefinger. "Don't play where you are not willing to go, Claire. You're not a green young girl. You've been married. Not every man would stop. You're undoubtedly aware of that."

What? Did he seek to play the role of gentleman now?

She pushed at her hair, which had come down around her face.

In the entrance hall the clock chimed.

"Come," he said. "The hour is late. Let me take you home."

Chapter Five

*L*ater that night, Gray strode into his oak-paneled study. At his desk, he reached for a bottle and poured a generous splash of whiskey into a glass. He was halfway through it when Dawes, his butler, admitted Clive.

"I saw your light aglow in here." Clive helped himself to a drink and a cigar. "May I ask where your beautiful escort for the night is?"

Gray grimaced, watching the tip glow as Clive lit the cigar. "At home."

"And sleeping in her own bed?"

He took a long draught of smooth Irish whiskey, reminded of the brandy he'd drunk with Claire.

Clive took a pull of the cigar. "Set you down cold, did she?"

His jaw tightened.

"I see," said Clive with a laugh.

Gray thought of the lovely Claire Westfield, the way she'd pulled away from him. The memory had him gritting his teeth. A kiss was the least he wanted from the lady.

He'd wanted to drag her back into his arms. He wanted to crush his mouth against hers. Bury his fingers through the thatch of curls at the valley of her thighs and seek the scalding heat of her flesh. Mount her and drive into the sweet heat of her cleft, feel her melt around his cock. Ride her fast and hard. Yet even as those feelings seized hold of him once more, he wondered about his desire for her. Wondered and hated himself for it. It was too damned keen. Gray was a man with iron-clad restraint. He didn't like what he could not hold sway over.

And he did not like what was happening with the lovely widow. What the blazes had he been thinking?

He hadn't, he decided blackly. At least not with his head.

He didn't take his women to his home . . . No one had slept in his bed beside Lily. Not here. Not at Brightwood. He'd loved only her. And when she died— He cut short the thought. Claire wasn't his woman, he reminded himself. He did not have . . . women. He had lovers. He had bed-sport partners from whom he could disengage once passion was sated, women who wanted no more than he did. Women who graced his bed but not his heart.

Roses. Wine. Christ, had he gone mad? What a fool he'd made of himself!

He wasn't used to being rejected. By heaven, he wasn't through with the beauty just yet. He thought of Claire's mouth, the slight pout of her lower lip, the way he'd run his tongue along the outline of her mouth. When he was with her, he could hardly take his eyes from it. He wasn't satisfied. Not by any means. His pleasure had been cut short. He wanted to taste that delicious little pout that so entranced him. He thought of the grace with which she moved. He recalled the ripe lushness of her breasts against his chest, breasts that rose ripe and full above the neckline of her gown. Oh, yes, he wanted so much more from her. Sensation danced through him as he imagined her on her knees before him, his hands in her hair, holding her as she—

Son of a bitch. He sucked in a breath and gave thanks he was sitting. The thought gave rise to a heavy flood of arousal that was almost painful. Desire stabbed through his middle. He was tempted to go find a whore.

But he'd much rather bed the comely widow— the sooner, the better. Then he could put her from his mind.

Clive gave a shout of laughter. "By God, Sutherland, if we didn't know she'd been wed, she sounds like a veritable virgin. But it seems she's a lady, eh? Not one of your—"

Gray fixed his friend with a glare. It was just as Clive said. If he didn't know better, he just might think the woman was untried. He had no interest in virgins. They were too much trouble. He liked a woman with experience. But then, a sudden darkness came over him.

Lily had been a virgin.

Clive angled a brow. "Do you expect to see her again?"

Gray pulled himself away from the darkness of his dead wife and slanted his companion a look. "I can see what's in your mind," he growled. "And I have not changed my mind. Hands off, my friend."

"I can see why you won't share her. But when you tire of her"—Clive well knew that with Gray it wouldn't be long—"send her my way so she may hearken to my arms for comfort."

Gray gave a shout of laughter. "Since when do you take another man's leavings?"

"I may be willing to make an exception with the lovely Mrs. Westfield. And remember, she isn't *your* Mrs. Westfield yet."

Gray's jaw came shut. He cast his friend an acid glance. He didn't like the idea of Claire in another man's arms. The hell of it was that Clive might indeed be true to his word!

He leaned forward and filled his glass and Clive's. It had been a long time since he was with a woman who didn't tumble into his arms and his bed. He must be honest with himself, though. Claire's denial didn't make him want her any less.

If anything, it only sharpened his desire.

He was a man who had never given chase to any woman. It wasn't arrogance that proclaimed it so. Even Lily . . .

Lily. The thought of her was like a stab in the heart. Lily and—

Raw pain rent his heart. God, would he ever forget her? Would he ever *forgive* her?

"My mother has invited her to the birthday party she's throwing for me next week. For God's sake, I might as well be in small clothes."

Clive's smile ebbed. "She wants you to heal," he said quietly.

Gray's retreat into himself was almost palpable. He hated the reminder, and Clive knew it. His mother knew it. He had nothing left to give. Not anymore.

"I am healed," he bit out, "and say no more if you wish to remain my friend." He thought of his conversation with his mother last night.

Clive let it go. There was a part of Gray that was closed to everyone. He allowed no one to glimpse the blood on his soul. That was something that did not change. It would never change. Guilt would not allow it.

"Your country house party," Gray said suddenly. "When is it?"

"The following weekend. Why?"

He smiled tightly. "Is the beautiful Mrs. West-field on the guest list?"

Clive arched an aristocratic brow. "No. But I'll see that it's remedied."

Gray's eyes glinted his satisfaction. He leaned back.

Long fingers closed around the neck of the bottle. He poured both of them another drink. Their cravats untied, their shirts loosened, they drank nearly a bottle before Clive left.

But even that was not enough to dull the ache inside him. Gray welcomed the numbness that settled in with liquor, but tonight his mind would not rest. Oh, he knew why, and he almost hated Clive for daring to speak of Lily. Now, pushing back the covers, he rose. Naked, he stood at the balcony outside his room, staring out at the roof-tops of London. A midnight breeze ruffled the draperies on the French doors behind it. Dark-ness closed in around him. It was then he heard it, a sound that shredded his very soul.

The sound of an infant crying.

Penelope came for tea the next day. It took but a glance for Claire to glean her friend's mood.

She ushered her into the sitting room. "Pen, what is it? What's wrong?" She searched Penelo-pe's face. "Is it the baby? Is everything all right?"

"It's fine, Claire. He moves so often now. I do

believe there are times when he never sleeps." She tried to smile, a lackluster effort.

Claire's heart sank. It was Theo, then. "Oh, darling, what is it? What's wrong?"

"Claire, I—there still has been no word from Theo." Tears filled her doe-brown eyes. "I've had no letter for weeks now. It—It's never been so long before."

"Don't cry, dove. I'm sure there's an explanation. Perhaps the weather. Perhaps they are in an area where there's no post."

The tears overflowed. "Another commander, Colonel Stokes, he and his men have just returned from the Peninsula."

"Yes?"

"I went to him, Claire. He offered regrets that he had no news on Theo and his company. But he said—"

The tears flowed harder. Claire slipped an arm around her friend's shoulders.

"The colonel . . . he said he had heard the fighting . . . has been fierce. That there had been many casualties." Penelope could barely speak. "Claire, I'm so frightened. What if Theo—"

She tried to choke back a sob. It was no use.

Claire slipped an arm around her shoulder. "Hush, love. Oh, Pen, you cannot allow yourself to think in such a way. Yes, you've had no news, but take heart. All is not lost yet."

She pressed a handkerchief into Penelope's hands.

"Don't cry, Pen. I know it's hard, but it's not good for the baby."

Penelope's tears began to stop. She dabbed at her eyes.

"Dry your eyes now." Claire hugged her. "There, pet. That's better."

Penelope gathered herself. "Claire, oh, Claire! I don't know what I would do without you. From the moment we met at school, you've been my dearest friend . . . well, except for Theo—"

Claire smiled. "That's how it should be, dear. Husband and wife should be the greatest friends of all."

Penelope began to calm. They talked about the viscount, and again Penelope expressed reservations.

"I know how much you loved Oliver, but what good can come of this?"

Claire went silent.

"I would urge you to abandon it, Claire, but I know you are set on this course. I will help you in whatever way I can."

Claire squeezed her fingers. "I've always known I can count on you for anything."

Once again they hugged. Their talk turned to other things. Penelope was preparing to leave when Rosalie rushed in, her eyes huge.

"Miss, the Duke of Braddock is here for you."

"What!"

"It's him, miss, the duke." Her eyes like saucers, Rosalie handed her his card. "What shall I do, miss? Will you receive him?"

Claire wanted to shriek. Instead she shook her head. "Rosalie—you cannot call me 'miss'!"

"What shall I do, mi—ma'am?"

Claire smoothed her skirts. "Show him in. And will you bring tea?"

Penelope's eyes went wide. "Here, I will hurry out the back—"

"Stay, goose."

Penelope patted her tummy. "I doubt a man of Society will want to see me like this."

"Oh, pooh. Babies are in the natural order. Besides, thank heaven for sashes and bows. There's very little to see there!"

Both women curtsied as the duke entered. He took the hand Claire offered. "How lovely to see you again, Your Grace."

"Indeed." The duke had eyes like silver. His frame was lean, but it spun through Claire's mind that he was nearly as handsome as Gray.

"Your Grace, may I present my friend, Mrs. Penelope Grove."

He bowed over Penelope's hand. "Charmed, I'm sure, Mrs. Grove. I believe I'm acquainted with your husband's aunt, the Countess of Tilbury."

"Yes, my husband is indeed the countess's nephew."

He turned to Claire. "Mrs. Westfield, I will take but a moment of your time. The Thursday after next, I am hosting a country house party at my estate in Kent, Waverly Park. It will be relatively informal, just a few friends, but I would be pleased if you would attend."

Claire's mind veered straight to Gray. Would he be present? *Of course,* chided a voice inside.

She wasn't sure if she was excited or anxious. Either way, this was an unexpected opportunity to place herself near Gray. She couldn't refuse.

The duke turned to Penelope. "Mrs. Grove. Of course I would be pleased if you could attend as well."

"Oh, no, Your Grace, I couldn't."

"Oh, Penelope," Claire implored, "it will be good for you to get out of the city."

Penelope started to shake her head. "But wait," she said. "Your Grace, Waverly Park is in Kent?"

"Indeed."

"We have very dear family friends in Kent whom I believe have purchased a summer home in Northrup, Lord and Lady Augusta Trahern. Is that near your estate, Your Grace?"

"It's some five miles to the north."

"Are you acquainted with them?"

"No, but if they have only recently settled, I'm not surprised."

Penelope glanced at Claire. "Claire," she said slowly, "I have an idea. If Lady Augusta should be so inclined to welcome me, this might be an excellent time for me to visit. We could share a carriage."

"Capital idea," the duke approved. "As long as your friends are willing."

"Oh, I should imagine they will welcome me heartily. Before my parents left for the Continent, I recall Mama saying they should love to visit the Traherns upon their return. I will write as soon as I'm home."

The duke wore a faint smile. His gaze shifted to Claire.

"I have a confession to make, Mrs. Westfield. I did not send a formal invitation 'round because I thought it would be harder for you to refuse if I invited you here in the flesh."

"Your Grace, I'm flattered." No doubt that wicked little smile had turned many a lady's head.

In the entrance hall, Rosalie handed him hat and cane. He bowed low and seemed well pleased with himself.

"Ladies, I bid you good day."

Chapter Six

$\mathcal{T}$hat wasn't the only invitation Claire received that day. The invitation to Gray's birthday celebration arrived from Charlotte Sutherland. It was the day after tomorrow. Claire truly hadn't expected to receive one. She quickly penned a response that she would love to attend. She was glad she'd chosen the guise of a widow. It was rather freeing that she needed no escort.

But apprehension filled her at the thought of seeing Gray again. Had he been angry when she left his home the evening of the opera? Silly question, that. Those ice-blue eyes had been sizzling. She could only pray she hadn't alienated him. This was a precarious path that she trod. She was aware that she must watch herself closely, but refused to fall into his arms like a slut. She would not lower herself to that level. But she couldn't risk him losing interest in her either.

Penelope helped Claire dress for the birthday party, a jade green gown that her friend exclaimed brought out the gold in her eyes.

It was nearly eight when Claire set off. She was a trifle nervous, but as soon as she entered, Charlotte Sutherland took her hand and greeted her warmly. It burned inside that this charming, vivacious woman had given birth to such a scoundrel. Claire sensed that despite the difference in age, if not for the circumstances of their acquaintance she and Charlotte might have been friends. Charlotte immediately introduced her to several other guests; she had yet to see Gray.

And then she did.

Halfway across the room, Clive Fielding noticed the sweep of Claire's eyes as she scanned the gathering. Noticed and taken note also of Gray's sudden change of expression when *he* spotted Claire. Clive relished the sudden tightly hewn jaw of his friend. He hadn't seen anger, but at least Gray was *feeling* again.

Gray turned his head, and Claire had a glimpse of his full, sensuous lips, rugged jaw, and penetrating blue eyes. The very sight of him nearly turned her knees to water.

The duke stepped up beside her at that moment. "Wonderful to see you again, Mrs. Westfield."

Claire inclined her head. "And may I say the same, Your Grace?"

"I'm so glad you will attend my house party. I

think you'll enjoy it. My estate is lovely this time of year."

They chatted. In time, her gaze again fastened on Gray. Across the floor, he greeted first one guest and then another. On his arm was a dark-haired woman with sultry eyes. She possessed a ripe, earthy beauty, full lips, voluptuous curves. She laughed up at him and he glanced down at her. She stepped up on tiptoe, so close her lips touched his cheek.

A strange sensation gripped Claire's heart. If she didn't know better, she would have called it jealousy.

Ridiculous, of course.

She remained where she was, just outside the entrance to the dining room. "Ah," said Clive. "I see you've spotted Lady Hastings. She, too, is a widow, like you. Her mother is a dear friend of Lady Charlotte."

"I've yet to make her acquaintance," said Claire. In fact, she didn't want to meet the woman; she disliked her on sight. Her smile was too wide, her jewels too bright.

And her gown too revealing. Oh, yes, far too revealing. Claire suspected that given his height, Gray would have no trouble seeing far more of her breasts than what was exposed. Not only that, she suspected the woman wore not a stitch beneath. The ring of her nipples stood dark and taut.

The gong sounded for dinner, and Clive inclined his head and gave a little bow. "Do me the honor of escorting me in," he said to her.

Claire took his arm. She could see how she might easily find his lazily wicked manner and devil-may-care good looks irresistible. No doubt he was just as she'd thought. A rogue. A bounder.

When everyone was seated, Gray's mother rose to tiny, slippered feet and tapped her fork on a crystal glass. "Hear, hear, everyone!" she called, gathering everyone's attention. "Good evening and welcome to my son's birthday celebration. We will not talk about age—certainly not I!—but I hope you will join me in wishing my son the heartiest of birthday wishes."

Beside Claire, Clive rose and offered another toast. It ended with several more toasts, then everyone joined together in conveying birthday wishes.

The beauty beside Gray framed his face between her hands and kissed him full upon the lips. In the next half breath, their heads were nestled together intimately.

Claire deliberately looked away and reached for her wine glass, praying fervently that the meal would end soon. She didn't notice the disapproving tightness on Charlotte Sutherland's lips.

When the meal was over, she saw the duke engaged in conversation with an acquaintance in the adjoining room, where the furniture had been pushed aside for dancing. Some of the faces were familiar. Claire nodded and smiled. She was growing more comfortable in this world. She didn't particularly care for it, however. She would rather have been home at Wildewood, caring for her garden. Caring for the people on the estate.

But there was nothing left for her there either. Not anymore.

She was gripped by a stark, sudden emptiness. Her heart knotted. Oliver had written home occasionally; he had clearly reveled in this world of parties and balls.

And the darker world that lurked beneath the facade of manners and morals.

Bitterness seeped through her. If only he had been stronger. If only he had reached out to his family. Instead he had succumbed—and lost his life in the bargain.

Claire moved about, restless. In time she made her way outside and into the garden.

She didn't notice that she was followed.

She seated herself on a carved stone bench. Music, laughter, and bits of conversation drifted to her ears. The darkness was oddly soothing. She turned her head, to discover she wasn't alone.

"My word, sir, you gave me a start!"

A man dressed in evening clothes stood before her. Claire guessed he was younger than Gray. It had been another whirlwind of names and faces tonight. She had met so many people since coming to London that they were beginning to blur in her mind. "I'm sorry, sir. Are we acquainted?"

"We are now, aren't we?" He gave a bow. "Gerard Riggs at your service."

Claire extended a hand. "Mrs. Claire Westfield."

He took her hand and kissed it. There was the sour odor of wine about him, quite a lot—and she was sure she wasn't mistaken. A prickle of unease went through her. He had yet to release her fingers.

"I must confess, Mrs. Westfield, I've seen you before. At Lady Blakely's several nights ago."

"An enjoyable affair, wasn't it?"

"Indeed. I hear you're from the country. No doubt you don't know of Braddock and Sutherland. I saw you with Braddock earlier. Braddock is quite the ladies' man, as is Sutherland, so you must be on guard against the pair of them. Of the two, Sutherland is the worst. He's dangerous. No better than a common ruffian."

Claire was annoyed. He still hadn't released her hand. "I am quite capable of taking care of myself, Mr. Riggs. You needn't concern yourself with my safekeeping." She tugged at her hand.

His grip tightened. "I saw you come out here. When you didn't return . . . well, I thought perhaps I had best see to your well-being."

She was already contemplating her next move. "Sir, if you don't unhand me, I am going to—"

She got no further. The man jerked her close. An arm hard about her waist, he dragged her against him.

Wet lips dragged across her cheek. The smell of sour wine nearly made her gag. Fingers thrust hard into her hair and gripped her scalp. "I know what you need. What any widow needs. A man—"

Claire twisted and wrenched back. "By heaven, if I had a gun I would shoot you," she hissed. "If I had a knife I would carve you from ear to ear." An empty threat, but she would do the next best thing. Drawing back her fist, she took aim at his jaw.

There was a satisfactory thud.

He staggered back. "My nose!" he cried. "You've broken it!"

"I believe she has."

A sudden prickle went down her spine. There was no mistaking that smooth, resonant voice behind her.

Gray's tone was one of disgust. "You imbecile, Riggs. You're drunk again, you fool. Go inside."

Gray signaled to a footman, who took the man's arm and disappeared toward the carriage house. He turned back to her.

One of his brows climbed high. "You're a bloodthirsty little creature, aren't you? I vow, had I been Riggs, I'd have been quaking in my boots. And here I was, ready to rescue you."

"I was hardly in need of rescuing," Claire said, her tone rather breathless. Drat! She pushed at her hair, half fallen down her back.

"No? I would have thought a widow would know better than to accompany a man alone outside."

"I beg your pardon?"

"You heard me quite rightly. You're not a silly young girl. Surely you know the workings of a man's mind." He didn't hide his impatience.

Claire's eyes began to blaze, lighting them to honey gold. "I will thank you to be civil when you address me," she said haughtily. "I did not accompany him. He followed me. And I begin to think you are the one who is foxed—and from whom I'm in need of being rescued."

"Everything you've heard about me is probably true, so tell me. Did you come outside, hoping I would follow?"

"The last time I saw you, you were quite engrossed with Lady Hastings."

A black brow arose. "Jealous?"

"You flatter yourself."

"Do I? A possibility occurred to me . . . That night at Lady Blakely's, what if you wanted to put yourself in my path?"

A rush of heat stung her cheeks. The insufferable bastard. Had she been so obvious, then?

She must tread carefully, she told herself, lest he turn away and never come back.

"You have a vivid imagination," she said, dismissing it as lightly as she could.

"Do I? The night of the play, you came to my home."

"Upon your invitation," she reminded him.

"Hmmm. I must say, you were certainly readily agreeable. And you've cast off your widow's weeds. What is a man to think?"

"I suspect you're about to tell me."

"I am a man who knows women, Claire. There are men of whom you should be wary."

"Men like Riggs?"

"Indeed."

"Men like you?"

"Men exactly like me."

It wasn't a boast. No, merely a statement of fact. She hadn't expected such bald-faced candor.

He studied her. Something passed over his face. "I cannot quite put my finger on it, dear Claire . . . You are a widow, yet there is—how shall I put this?—a freshness, almost an innocence about you that is . . . refreshing. And almost a challenge."

Claire's heart climbed to her throat.

"I am not the only man who will find it so. I've no interest in girls—yes, girls—who come to London for their come-out. Those in search of a husband." He shook his head. "Be wary, Claire. Be very wary."

Her cheeks were suddenly burning.

"Surely you can't be as awful as all that."

His laugh was almost harsh. "Ah, darling, you betray your youth, for despite your widowhood, you *are* young, and newly brought into this den of lions. Heed me, lest you become too caught up in it."

A maddening smile now curled his lips. Claire's heart was pounding, fast and hard. She had the uneasy sensation Gray sensed her self-doubt.

"Men like Riggs, Claire"—he shrugged—"they are after no more than a dalliance."

"And you?" she dared. "Are you after no more than a dalliance?"

He gave a sudden, biting laugh. "Oh, Claire, I've hidden nothing about my reputation. I'm the worst of all. Now come here. Your hair has come down."

He left no time for protest. Instead he turned her bodily around. His fingers weaved into her hair. And the silliest thought went through her mind.

He twined it as expertly as did her maid.

When he was done, he spun her around. Claire's pulse was racing. He was so close, no more than the span of a hand separated them.

"No more clandestine meetings in the dark, Claire." That wickedly devilish smile widened. "Unless they're with me."

Chapter Seven

The weekend of the Duke of Braddock's country house party approached. If she could have cried off, she would have. So he would be amenable to a dalliance, would he? Was he so confident in his ability to lure her in?

He was no one's fool. She mustn't allow him to get the best of her. She mentally ticked off the mounting reasons she despised him.

His arrogance.

His mockery.

His presumption.

For he did presume to know her, which infuriated her.

But she could hardly go about the business of making the man fall for her if she stayed in London. Ah, but the question still remained. *Could* she entice him?

By heaven, he would not get the better of her.

She had backbone enough to meet and match him.

Claire shared Penelope's coach. Pen had dashed off a note to the Northrups. They were indeed eager to see her. The trip required a stay at an inn. It was a pleasant journey through the countryside. The sun's rays dappled over the fields. The landscape was rich in color, verdant green, and the sun a bright, vivid blue. The air was clean and fresh; there was no stench of coal and smoke, as in London.

It was lovely . . . and yet a melancholy longing rose up inside her. Rolling through the countryside reminded her of Wildewood. How much she missed it!

At noon of the next day they crossed over a stone bridge and the gently swirling waters of a stream below shortly before turning into the lane that led to the house. At Braddock's estate, both she and Penelope pressed their noses up against the coach window, agog. They sped through soaring iron gates, down a wide lane bordered by trees, past vast green lawns and well-manicured gardens.

"It looks like a fairy princess must surely live here," Penelope breathed.

That same thought occupied Claire's mind.

There were two massive wings on either side of the mansion's front entrance. Several servants were there to help them from the coach and unload Claire's trunk. The duke himself came to welcome her in the foyer, where two wide stair-cases swept toward each wing.

After being shown to her room, Claire took a brief nap, then watched as several more coaches rolled in. She joined the duke and some of the other guests for afternoon tea in the garden. Oh, but Clive did indeed possess a roguish charm. His reputation was almost as bad as Gray's.

There was no sign of Gray.

The opening festivity was a masquerade ball. Claire stood on the side of the dance floor, enjoy-ing some of the costumes. Everyone wore masks, including her. She spied an ancient Roman sol-dier—judging from the rakish tilt of his head, it was Lord Davies. Another chose the costume of a medieval jester.

There was still no sign of Gray.

She had chosen to dress as a Gypsy. Her cos-tume was bright and colorful. Her blouse had puffed sleeves and was off the shoulder, tucked into a long, flowing skirt of bright purple. Tied around her narrow waist was a sash of yellow. She'd left her hair long and loose, caught back by a ribbon, her head covered by a patterned scarf.

Across the room, the musicians began to play, lively, vivacious tunes. Claire caught the mood, clapping and stomping in time to the music. Someone brought her a glass of champagne, then another. A pirate caught her around the waist and swung her around.

She laughed and whirled along with him. Another man claimed her as partner. She pleaded aching feet. "I see you've a liking for champagne," someone said. "Would you like another?"

She gave a reckless laugh. "Please!"

"I obey your every wish, Madame Gypsy." The next moment she was holding a glass. "Drink it and come dance with me."

Feeling reckless, Claire drained it. Her new partner swept her onto the floor. She was still laughing as they spun away.

His hand was warm around her waist. He held her close. Claire registered the plane of hard chest and long, muscled legs. The scent of him drifted to her nose. Caught up in carefree exhilaration, she flung back her head. She loved the way she felt small against his masculine strength.

Her head was spinning. The champagne, she knew. She was used to country dances at neighborhood gatherings and not those of the ballroom. But now she felt as if she'd been caught in some strange Gypsy spell. Her feet left the ground as they whirled around. She tipped back her head, the arch of her throat long and white.

She had yet to identify her partner. She didn't care. Surrounded by the trill of laughter and voices, she liked being able to forget all else.

"Every man here is jealous of me," he whispered.

The thought was exhilarating—and he was

indeed the recipient of other envious glances. He spun her away from the dance floor and out onto the verandah. He didn't stop until they stood beneath an arching trellis of fragrant, climbing vine.

Perhaps there were other couples hiding away in the alcoves of the garden. But it seemed as if it was only the two of them in the world.

Her partner stared down at her. A thousand tiny lights seemed to glitter in those ice-blue eyes. Her heart stood still—

It was Gray.

Her every sense had known it . . . and come alive. He held her around the waist. The span of his palm was almost possessive, fingers splayed wide around her back. It was as if she burned.

"You fascinate me."

Her breath left her lungs in a rush.

"You enchant me. I want to spirit you away."

His eyes were glittering. She glimpsed in them a need that was both thrilling and frightening.

His voice seemed swathed in silk. Sensation swamped her. Her skin felt like it was burning. She realized then that opportunity was upon her. It would begin in earnest. Here. Now. She had wanted to entice. To lure. But she'd never expected it would be like this. She sensed a fervent intensity in him that frightened her. The lights from the house revealed a glittering flame in his eyes, something utterly fierce.

Mid-thought, his mouth closed over hers.

This was nothing like their first kiss. The night at his home was merely a prelude compared to this. His embrace had been tame. This was impassioned. Fierce and urgent. His mouth seemed all-consuming. It seemed she tasted him everywhere, resonating through every part of her. She felt overwhelmed. She tasted . . .

Possession.

There was a dark, sweet pleasure in the way her mouth clung to his. Oh, God. Her heart went wild, even as a voice in her soul cried out in betrayal. How was it she could feel such pleasure with Oliver's killer? Some small sound escaped. He swallowed it. Her lips parted beneath the hunger in his. He roused feelings in her she'd never thought possible. His tongue was searingly blatant. It demanded entrance, with a sweeping claim that shocked her even as desire spilled all through her. She remembered how he'd said the night of the play that he wanted to run his tongue along her lips and taste her wine.

The arm around her back tightened. There was an odd, unfamiliar quiver low in her belly. Her hands came up and clutched at his shoulders. She registered heat. Strength. Hardness.

The world around her spun. The sounds of the night slipped away. His mouth was demanding. Intent. Engulfed in darkness, engulfed in him, she struggled for breath.

Somehow she'd thought it would be wholly in her ability to control him.

What folly.

She knew it the instant his mouth trapped hers.

The fusion of their lips was raw and hungry. Panic surged. What would she do if he did not stop? That wasn't part of the plan. Claire thought she had tasted passion. Need. The other night hadn't prepared her for this. She hadn't expected to feel like this. She hadn't expected *he* would feel like this.

His lips conveyed an urgent, compelling persuasion. The hand at her waist guided her into him. Against him. She was instantly aware of the hard, unmistakable press of male desire between his hips, thrust up against her belly.

"I want to see you again," he said. "Somewhere we won't be interrupted. Somewhere we can be alone." His mouth was on the side of her neck. "Meet me at midnight. Here."

Claire's throat locked. Words were impossible. A stray hand slid her blouse from one shoulder.

Deliberately, he touched her, his hand clamped boldly over the whole of her breast, his eyes delving deep into hers.

With his palm, he circled her nipple. Again. And yet again. It was as if he touched her everywhere.

Claire's mind froze. Her mind was screaming. A hundred emotions swirled through her. Shock.

Panic. The hope and prayer that despite his disreputable character he would remain a gentleman.

And pleasure. Dear God, so much pleasure. In some distant part of her being, she was stunned that she could feel such a thing with this man.

Her hand fluttered up to rest atop his. She tore her mouth away. "Please," she said shakily. "Please don't."

Slowly, he released her. But he stared down at her face, his eyes fever-bright. Claire dragged her blouse back over her bare shoulder. She lowered her gaze, trying to recapture her breath. She felt the weight of those crystal-bright eyes gazing down at her bent head. Her cheeks were flaming. Her scarf had come off; her hair spilled down her back. She was shaken, but she couldn't let him see.

Their eyes locked. A palpable tension hung between them. He picked up her ribbon—it was he who finally broke the silence.

There was a faint and oh-so-maddening smile on his lips.

"A pity, Gypsy lady. I was so looking forward to a midnight assignation." He paused. "Another night, perhaps?"

Claire's jaw snapped shut. He dared to mock her! A fury unlike any she'd ever known seized hold of her.

If it was a battle of wits he wanted, by heaven, she would oblige him.

* * *

Gray hadn't lied. He'd meant it when he said he was fascinated by her.

Most assuredly entranced.

There was something about her, something he couldn't put a name to—a vague restlessness that there was more to Claire than a pretty face. Something wasn't quite right. He just couldn't put his finger on it.

Ah, but who did he fool? he thought with sudden, scathing self-derision.

He wanted the lovely widow in his bed.

And by heaven, he would have her. When Grayson Sutherland wanted something, he usually got it. When he set his mind to it, there was usually no escaping it.

He didn't see Claire until after luncheon the next day.

Some of the other men had walked down to the rolling lawn to engage in various so-called manly games. Some of the women gathered there to watch beneath the shade of a large tent where tea had been set up.

Gray was bored. Affairs such as these usually had that effect on him. It was why he usually avoided them like the plague. Indeed, he wouldn't be here if it hadn't been hosted by someone other than Clive.

It wasn't always so. No, it wasn't always so at all. He'd met Lily at just such an affair. Met her, courted her, and won her.

Indeed, he reflected with a black-hearted smile, who did he fool? He was here because of the lovely Claire Westfield.

So it was that he stood at the top of the hill, searching the rosy-cheeked faces of the women beneath the brim of their bonnets.

She wasn't there. He stayed a few minutes longer, then walked the length of the terrace, stopping where he'd kissed Claire the night before. The scent of hyacinth filled the air. Sunlight played hide-and-seek beneath the clouds.

He turned—and there she was.

"Mrs. Westfield, lovely to see you. Were you looking for me?"

"Do not flatter yourself, my lord."

"You wound me to the depths of my heart."

"Have you a heart?" Her tone was light. "I've heard various accounts to the contrary."

"You mustn't believe everything you hear, Claire. Frankly, you surprised me."

"How so?"

"When Clive sent the invitation, I thought you might not attend."

"What do you mean?"

"The night of the play, I thought I'd frightened you off."

"Because you kissed me?"

"Yes." A cool smile touched the hardness of his lips.

"I'm not so easily frightened, sir."

No, he thought slowly. She wasn't. And he was more certain than ever that the lovely Mrs. Westfield was hiding something.

It only intrigued him all the more. "When I said you wounded me, Claire, it was true."

Piquant dark brows rose aslant.

"I cannot help but remember," he said smoothly, "the other night at my mother's. You didn't give me a birthday kiss."

For a moment she appeared startled. Then, almost primly, she spoke. "Very well, then. Here is your birthday kiss."

Raising herself on tiptoe, she brushed a kiss on his cheek and drew back. "Now you have it." A smile on her lips, she lowered herself to the ground.

"And this"—she slapped him hard across the cheek—"is for kissing me the way you did last night."

In the instant between one breath and the next, Gray was too stunned to say a word. Then his eyes glinted.

"It wasn't the kiss, my lovely Claire. I submit it was when I touched your—"

She would have slapped him again if he hadn't caught her wrist. Gray was flooded with fury. Flooded with pride. So she thought to toy with him, did she? Her slap on his cheek left him bitingly angry. He wanted to crush her mouth beneath his. Ride her and ride her hard. It was time she discovered he was not a man who played games.

"I have offended your sensibilities," he said smoothly. "I can only offer my most sincere apologies. I am truly contrite."

She eyed him warily.

"Allow me to kidnap you for the afternoon, my dear Mrs. Westfield. I believe some of the men are riding off to shoot. The women are off to a day of bird-watching. Accompany me instead. We can take a gig down to the stream. I will be a perfect gentleman."

"You, sir? Aren't you the man who calls himself anything but a gentleman?"

"Indeed."

For an instant he thought she would refuse. Finally, she gazed straight into his eyes. "Very well, then. But I will hold you to it."

Gray inclined his head, still full of angry fierceness. Within a fortnight, he vowed, he'd have her on her back, thighs splayed wide, her legs locked tight around his waist while he plunged hard and deep and fast inside her.

Oh, yes, he wanted more than just a kiss. More than a hand in command of her breast. Much more. And yet there was a part of him that despised himself for his weakness. She aroused feelings he'd thought were long buried. He was coming to realize his fiery craving for the lovely Claire was too intense.

He didn't want to be drawn to her. He felt . . . almost reckless. It threatened his control. And Gray was a man who didn't like to be out of control. He wanted to get her out of his system.

The sooner he bedded her, the better.

Chapter Eight

*A*s it happened, Claire wouldn't have been able to join the other guests on their ride anyway. She hadn't thought to bring a riding habit. She dressed in a gown of mauve that brought out the green in her eyes. At luncheon, Gray explained to Clive that the two of them wouldn't be joining the afternoon riding party. Claire watched as they spoke. There was an easy affability between the viscount and the duke. She couldn't help the direction her mind took. Bitterly she wondered if the duke had known Oliver. Bitterly she wondered if the duke knew his friend had killed Oliver.

Once they were on their way, Claire asked Gray about his friendship with the duke.

"Neither of us having a brother of our own, I daresay we are rather like brothers," said Gray. "Even down to our rivalries. We met at a boxing match at Cambridge. I broke his nose, though if you ask Clive, he'll tell you he broke mine."

Claire's gaze traced his profile, stopping on the slight bump on the bridge of his nose. "Brawling, were you?"

"Quite raucously."

"Who won the match?"

"Well, if you ask Clive," he said again, "he will report that he did. And if you ask me, well, you have only to look at his nose for the truth."

So the viscount could be charming, could he? Impossible, she decreed. But now she wanted to know—

"Have you siblings, my lord?"

"One. My older sister Rosalind lives in Scotland with her husband and three children." He glanced over at her. "And you, Claire? Brothers? Sisters?"

She wanted so very much to lash out at him, to cry out that he had robbed her of her brother. That she had lost everyone she cared for.

Claire looked away. "All my family are gone."

Her mood grew pensive. At least he had family, she thought bitterly. A mother. A sister. But she didn't want to see him in a family role. To her, family meant happiness. Love. Contentment. The knowledge that no matter what, that bond was irrevocable. But now there was an empty void in her breast.

She willed her mind elsewhere, but there was

little else to command her attention. Claire was taller than most women, and many men as well. Yet the man beside her seemed a giant. Occasionally one long leg brushed hers. The same was true of her shoulder. If she raised an arm, it would have fit cozily into the hollow of his arm.

Her gaze shifted. She couldn't help but notice Gray's hands. She watched the play of his fingers on the reins. He hadn't bothered with gloves. His hands were lean, long-fingered, and strong-looking. A dark netting of hair that covered the back of his hands merely added to that unmistakable aura of masculinity.

He guided the horse down a pathway that wove through the trees. Overhead was a leafy bower. The fragrance of May blossoms scented the air. It was lovely. Yet she couldn't distance her awareness of the man beside her.

The gig rolled to a stop beneath a huge tree. Beyond dashed the silver sheen of a stream.

Gray leaped lightly to the ground. Claire stood quickly. She didn't want to touch him. She didn't want him to touch her, but there was no avoiding it.

The thought had no more than spun through her mind than those long, powerful fingers settled on the nip of her waist to swing her down. Something that might have been panic raced through her. He withdrew his hands once she was on the ground, yet it felt as if he touched her still.

"What is it? You're not the sort who will cry if a bit of grass dirties your hem, are you?"

It was almost a dare. "Certainly not, sir. You forget I'm a country girl."

"Ah, yes, I recall you told Riggs that."

Claire wrinkled her nose. "Must we speak of him? That is a subject I would rather not remember."

"My sentiment exactly."

A devilish half smile dallied at his lips. To her horror, Claire knew he was remembering what had come after—his mouth warm and drugging upon hers. The bold way he'd touched her breast.

"We can eat luncheon in the shade beneath that tree," he said. He lifted a basket and blanket from the gig and carried it to the tree. When he returned, another half smile had spread across his lips. This one was different, however. An odd feeling knotted in her chest. When he smiled in the engaging way he did now, he looked younger. And so very handsome she nearly caught her breath.

He had returned to the gig.

Claire watched as he reached inside and took out two long poles. He quirked a lazy dark brow. "Does this country girl know how to fish?"

Ha! She smiled sweetly. "Are you going to show me?"

"Certainly. I will be an excellent tutor." His expression rather smug, he stepped behind her.

The cad. Did he think so much of himself, then?

His hand over hers, he showed her how to bring back the pole and throw it into the stream. He wound the line neatly back. His hand still over hers, he showed her twice more.

"Let me try," she said. "Do you think I can throw it as far as that boulder there?"

"Not with one lesson. It takes quite some time to master casting, but if you want, you may of course try."

His superior condescension made her all the more determined. Claire brought the pole back over her shoulder—and threw the line into the stream.

It landed with a *plop!* next to the boulder. Twice more she reached the very same spot.

Gray's dumbfounded amazement was precious.

"So you're a woman of secrets, eh?"

If he only knew, she thought.

They spent the next hour or so at the stream. When Gray finally stowed the poles back in the gig, Claire had landed four fish.

Gray landed none.

He poured each of them a glass of wine while they ate—a hearty, well . . . country meal. There was cheese and bread slathered with butter, and fresh fruit. Claire drank deeply.

Gray cocked a brow. "You find the wine pleasing? The food?"

"Quite so. Once again I applaud your choice of wine."

"Clive's cook is acquainted with my tastes. It's one I favor."

Her glass was empty. He set it aside.

"Claire . . ." he said quietly.

Her senses were suddenly screaming. He was seated in a pose that was almost indolent, his back against the tree trunk, his wrist upon an upraised knee.

"Yes?"

His gaze moved over the oval of her face. Very softly, he spoke. "Do you know what I want, Claire?"

I want to see you again. Somewhere we won't be interrupted. Somewhere we can be alone.

Dammit, why couldn't she look at him? She despaired her foolishness even as the words he'd spoken last night raced through her. And now they *were* alone. Far distant from anyone.

She saw as he reached out a hand. It curled around the side of her neck, a gesture both provocative and possessive. His thumb beneath her chin, he brought her gaze to his. Claire caught her breath. A fierce light shone in his eyes. The glow of passion. The flame of promise.

And then his lips trapped hers. He claimed her mouth completely. Heat streaked through her. She made a sound low in her throat. The touch of his mouth on hers melted her insides.

"Open your mouth." His voice was strangely thick. "Part your lips beneath mine. Oh, yes, Claire, that's the way."

His tongue slid into her mouth, circling hers, running along the edge of her teeth.

Oh, Lord, what was he doing? Her heart was beating far too fast. With a finger, he nudged her gown from her shoulder, baring her breast. Baring her breast completely. The next thing she knew, his hand completely encompassed soft, rising flesh. And now his mouth was sliding down from her collarbone, that traitorous hand gently pushing warm, swollen flesh toward his mouth.

What!? She gasped. Did he mean to—to kiss the pink tip of her breast, which she was stunned to feel his hand on.

Slowly he raised his head. Claire opened her eyes.

Gray was staring down at her.

"How long since your husband died?"

The question took her aback. "What?"

"How long since poor, dear—" He looked at her. "I don't recall his name."

"Jeffery. His name was Jeffery." She spoke the first name that crossed her mind.

"How long did you say you and Jeffery were wed?"

"I didn't."

His eyes narrowed. "How long, Claire?"

She drew a long, ragged breath. "He's been dead for two years."

His gaze had yet to leave hers. "How long were you wed?"

"That's none of your affair."

He shook his head. "How odd that you are so reluctant to answer such a simple question. Was he the last man you kissed?"

"You were the last man I kissed!"

He gave her a long, considering look. "I think you take my meaning, Claire. And either you are incredibly naive, or your husband was a fool." He shook his head. "Next you'll be telling me your marriage was chaste. Or that he left for the war before you were able to share the marriage bed."

Had she not lowered her regard so quickly, Gray would have caught her stricken expression. "You have no right to ask about what is private between husband and wife." The words came out low and choked. She could hardly breathe.

"Perhaps. But it's puzzling, Claire. Puzzling indeed."

"And why is that?"

"Certainly a widow would know how a man is aroused. You were shocked that I meant to kiss your breast. You were shocked by what you felt between my hips—"

"I wasn't!"

"You were. Shall I show you?" His hold tightened. "I told you I was a man who knew women.

Did you doubt me?" He gave her no time to respond.

Shocked? She was shocked that he dared to contemplate such a thing—that he dared to speak of such things!

"You kiss like a virgin, Claire. I'm not mistaken."

"I thought you were a man who disliked virgins."

"Claire, it's quite obvious when a woman lacks . . . experience."

Her cheeks burned painfully. She wanted to slap him again. "Must you insult me? Must you criticize?"

"I do not insult you, nor do I criticize."

"You do," she charged. She surged to her feet. "What would a man like you know of loyalty? Of love? You, the biggest blackguard in London! If you had any idea of the feelings of a woman for her husband, or a husband for his wife—"

"I am well acquainted with the feelings between husband and wife."

Bitterness choked her. "That's a lie. And you dare to call me naive? I am not so naive as all that to believe that you—"

His lips twisted. "Believe it, Claire. I am many things, but not a liar."

Claire sucked in a breath. No, she thought, that was impossible. Surely he didn't mean that he . . . surely not—

She pushed away from his chest. He didn't release her. The air between them had turned suddenly intense. *He* had turned suddenly intense. He had turned chillingly cold in but a heartbeat. His gaze was unrelenting.

"Does it shock you to learn I was wed? That I, too, have been widowed? Yes, I see that it does. You see the man I am now. You've no idea of the man I once was."

Stunned, Claire could only stare as he spun around and went for the horse.

"Come," he said abruptly. "It's time we went back."

Claire's mind was still reeling when he lifted her into the gig.

He'd been married. Good Lord, he'd been *married*.

Tension rode between them like a huge gray monster.

"Why didn't you tell me?" Her voice was very low.

"There was no reason for you to know."

"And there was no reason for you to be privy to my marriage!"

"I suggest we come to an understanding, then." He was tight-lipped and grim. "The subject of my marriage is closed. The subject of your marriage is closed."

They lapsed into silence. Gray was furious with

himself. A bitter darkness slipped over him. He had lost his temper. He discussed his wife with no one. Those closest to him—his mother, Clive—respected his wishes for the most part. It was rare that Lily's name was mentioned. When such thoughts dared intrude, he had schooled himself to close his mind to her memory.

But Claire had managed to give him a shattering reminder of a chapter in his past that he would rather not remember. A part of him almost hated her for it. God knew he hated himself. There were some who said he had no heart. If only he didn't! He couldn't think of Lily without feeling as if his lungs had caught fire. His hands were like his soul, black and stained with blood. That was something that would never change. Something that could never be erased.

Such was his penance. Such was his pain.

Then there was Claire. Somehow, she had gotten beneath his skin. He had only to be near her to give rise to an erection that was almost painful.

Had he known what effect she would have on him, he never would have pursued her. Every inch of his body was taut, every nerve wound tight. Desire still gripped him. She was tempting as sin. He thought of her undressing him. He wanted to lay her down. He wanted her naked, writhing beneath him while he buried his rod to her very soul.

He wouldn't let her go until he had what he wanted. And he was more certain than ever there was something she was hiding.

It was obvious it had something to do with her marriage.

He didn't understand her reluctance. It made no sense. He'd felt her lips blossom beneath his. She'd returned his kiss, yet he was puzzled by her air of purity . . . her air of almost innocence.

The answer to his questions had only led to more.

At the wide stone steps of the manor house, he stopped. He leaped down and went around to her side to lift her down.

She nearly tumbled in her rush to be away from him.

Gray's jaw knotted.

Inside, she went straight for the stairs.

And she didn't come down to dinner.

The men went to retire with port and cigars. Gray stopped Clive.

"Where is Claire?" he asked.

Clive looked surprised. "She isn't feeling well. She said something must have made her ill this afternoon."

Not some*thing*. Some*one*.

"Didn't you know? I thought the two of you were together."

Gray's expression told the tale all too well.

Clive hiked a brow. "Ah—"

"Don't say it," he growled.

"I see. Then you'll probably not be interested in the fact that she's planning to leave early tomorrow morning."

The little cheat!

Gray didn't plan on joining the other gentlemen. Clive raised a brow as Gray turned away.

"I suspect Lady Hastings would be eager to tend your wounds," his friend said.

Two weeks ago he wouldn't have hesitated. Lady Hastings had a way with her tongue and mouth . . . Now he found the thought of Lady Hastings's full red lips almost distasteful.

"Just remember I've a house full of guests," called his friend. "Unless you want to give them something to gossip about."

If there was a cynical twist to his mouth, Gray couldn't help it. But it wasn't going to deter him.

He climbed the stairs to the guest wing and asked a maid which room was Claire's. Thirty seconds later he stood before the door. He knocked firmly.

"The maid's already collected my tray," she called from within.

He knocked again, more loudly this time.

The door opened. Claire stood there. Apprehension chased across her face. But then her skin paled. The green of her eyes darkened to jade. Her gaze locked on him—

As if he was the devil.

Gray smiled tightly.

"You didn't come down to dinner."

"I've an early morning ahead," she said quickly. "I received an urgent note from Penelope. She cut short her stay at the Northrups. I'll be returning to London with her tomorrow morning."

"How fortuitous for you."

"Are you calling me a liar?"

"Did I say that?"

"That's what you meant! I received a note from Pen when we returned! Ask the duke!"

Gray did not speak. He stepped into the chamber.

Claire retreated a step, her eyes wide with dismay. She wore a dressing gown of white silk that lent her an air of purity, that virginal innocence that puzzled him even as it unnerved him.

"You can't be here, Gray."

"Nonetheless I am."

"You *shouldn't* be here."

"You allowed me in." Deliberately, he closed the door.

"Gray, this isn't proper—"

"Surely you know enough of me to be aware I'm not a man to be concerned with propriety. And I would remind you, nor have you."

He took a step forward. Claire retreated a step. Nervously, she wet her lips.

His regard slid over her from head to toe. He sucked in a breath. Across the room, the moon had begun to shine through the windows. God, she was lovely. Her hair was shot through with amber and gold. Her dressing gown fell in soft folds, barely brushing her bare feet. It hid nothing of the shape of her breasts, her nipples round and pushing against the bodice in enticement.

A primeval surge of desire heated his veins. He didn't welcome it. No, he didn't welcome it at all. But then came the strange awareness—

"Are you afraid?" He laid a hand on her shoulder, curled it around her nape. His thumb dipped into the hollow where her pulse betrayed her. It drummed wildly beneath his touch.

"You are," he said, darkly amused. He gave a shake of his head. "Oh, Claire, you disappoint me. I thought you were braver than this."

"I'm not afraid of you."

"I know women, Claire. I know you."

Darkness stole all through him. Something bitterly ominous had begun to burn inside him. Damn her! he thought. Damn her for making him feel like this! Damn her for making his passion rise to a fever pitch.

"I didn't think you were such a coward."

"I'm not a coward—"

Gray caught her up against him. A hand slid down her back. Almost fiercely he clamped her hips against his, letting her feel the swollen measure of his need. *Making* her feel it. Making her breath thin to a wisp of air as his mouth trapped hers.

His kiss was wild. Ferocious. He captured her lips beneath his, the ragged rush of her breath with his. His mouth was blatantly erotic and bold. He demanded; he took. He kissed her hotly—fiercely—until she sagged against him, supported only by his embrace.

He released her so suddenly she nearly lost her balance.

She stared up at him, her skin white, her mouth wet and red and trembling.

"There," he said harshly. "Now run away, little girl. Run away. I've done my worst. Now you have nothing to fear."

Chapter Nine

S hortly after dawn the next morning, Penelope's carriage arrived.

Claire had just finished breakfast with the
duke. He was the perfect host, to see her off at
dawn while his other guests still slept. And oh,
but what a charmer! With his darkly handsome
good looks, he'd probably made many a silly
young maid swoon. He'd probably left many a
lady with a broken heart.

Claire pressed her lips together. Just like his
friend the viscount, she thought.

The knocker sounded just as they stepped into
the entrance hall. Penelope stepped inside.

Claire took one look at her and rushed forward. "Pen!" she cried. "My word, what's wrong?
What's happened?"

Penelope nearly collapsed against her.

Her voice was shaking. "A message from

London arrived yesterday from one of Theo's lieutenants. There was a battle . . . it went on for days . . . Theo . . . oh, my God, Claire . . . Theo—"

.She dissolved into tears, unable to go on.

Claire slipped an arm about her shoulders. "Dearest, what is it? What's happened?"

"He's dead, Claire. I know it. Theo is dead! They—They couldn't find his body!" She moaned. "My beloved Theo . . . He's gone . . . dead. I know it. I know it! And now my little one will never know his father!"

The duke managed to guide Penelope into the drawing room. A maid brought tea while Claire calmed her. She urged her friend to try to eat a bite before they left, but Penelope was too distraught.

They left within a scant quarter hour.

Throughout the day, the carriage bounced along the rutted roadway. Inside, Claire sat across from Penelope. Exhausted, Penelope had finally began to doze, her head bobbing in time with the wheels.

Run away, little girl.

Claire cringed inside. She didn't want to think of the viscount—but the events of yesterday never left the scope of her mind. The rawness of his kiss rushed back. She couldn't banish the taste of him. She tried to close her mind to what came next. His hand, so warm upon her chest. The blazing path he had taken with his mouth, a trail of fire.

Her nipples had thrust up, as if in anticipation of his kiss. Oh, how he had mocked her! She tried to close her mind against it. *I'm no coward.*

Foolish, foolish words, those! She was angry with herself, angry with her weakness. No doubt Gray had felt her trembling against him.

Who did she fool?

He was right. She was a coward.

She must buck up. She must!

No matter that he had nearly stripped her of her pride. This was too important. She thought of Oliver and her heart twisted. Poor Oliver had died alone. She would not abandon her cause. Not yet! Somehow she must lure Gray back to her. She couldn't leave. The die had been cast. She must see it through, no matter what it took, no matter the cost to her pride.

She must find her way into his breast.

And then she would shatter his heart.

When Penelope's carriage arrived that morning to collect Claire, she hadn't seen Gray. The duke had told her Gray left for a morning ride. Claire was relieved that she didn't have to face him.

A coward, indeed, she thought bitterly.

Once they were on their way, Penelope calmed. She pressed her handkerchief in her lap.

"I'm sorry, Claire. Here I am, going on and on! Tell me of the house party. Was it a success?"

Claire glanced down at her hands. "It was an enjoyable few days."

Penelope peered at her oddly.

She didn't tell Penelope what Gray had divulged—that he'd been married and was now a widower. Why, she couldn't say. She owed Gray no loyalty. No trust. But he was so guarded about it that it somehow seemed a betrayal to tell anyone, though she couldn't say why.

You see the man I am now. You've no idea of the man I once was.

Nor could she allow herself to care. And now rampant in her mind were a hundred questions. Who was his wife? How long had *he* been wed? How had his wife—whoever she was—died. When? Had he changed? Had he loved her?

You see the man I am now. You've no idea of the man I once was.

What the devil did he mean?

The subject of my marriage is closed.

That he had been wounded was something she hadn't considered. Nor could she, reminded a voice inside. It didn't change her cause. It could never change what he'd done.

No, she couldn't abandon her cause. She would have her revenge.

Pen soon tired. Her back ached, so Claire massaged it gently. Claire didn't want to hurry the journey, but Penelope insisted. Not wishing to upset her friend, Claire made the decision to continue traveling.

It was near midnight when Claire glanced out

the carriage window. The moon was full, casting enough light that Claire saw some creature dart across the road in front of the coach.

One minute they were rolling along at an even pace, the next they were going faster and faster, as if racing with the wind. The creature must have spooked the horses. A jarring bump sent Claire tumbling to the floor of the coach; she cracked her head soundly. They zigzagged from one side of the road to the other, Penelope screaming shrilly.

The horses' tack broke free of the main compartment. Claire felt the moment it separated. There was a jarring sound and they tumbled over an embankment and crashed through the trees. There was a thunderous roar—

The world went dark.

She regained consciousness slowly. Her head was spinning. It ached abominably. She struggled to focus. It took a moment for the fuzziness of both mind and body to clear. Down the hill a man's figure lay prone. It was the driver.

But her heart lurched. Pen was moaning.

Claire surged upright. She'd been thrown free of the coach, Penelope was still inside.

Fear lent her strength. She managed to grab hold of one of the doors and yank it free of the hinges so she could crawl inside.

Penelope was curled up on her side. She tried to roll, then winced. She began to cry. "Claire! Oh, Claire!"

Claire crawled up beside her. "Here, now. Let me have a look at you."

Pen began to weep. One hand came to rest on her belly.

Claire stared down at her friend. Awareness closed in. No, she thought in horror. Oh, no . . .

Gray, too, had made the decision to return to London. It was late morning when he bid Clive and his guests good-bye. Restless, he decided to ride his horse back instead of his carriage. Thoughts of Claire kept intruding. He was impatient with himself. He needed to clear his head.

On horseback, he made excellent time. After stopping for a meal, he continued on. Evening shadows streaked the horizon. He slowed his mount to a trot. Pondering thoughts of Claire intruded anew. His lips thinned. The little witch! Did she have any idea what she did to him? She both infuriated and enthralled him.

Not since Lily had a woman so compelled him. Gray steeled himself, as he always did when he thought of Lily. He steeled himself against the stark, sudden shadow that blotted his soul.

Lily. Claire was nothing like her. Lily was softness and light, while Claire was fire and passion. With Claire, it was as if desire ruled both body and soul and there was nothing he could do to stop it.

She was nothing like the women he'd been

with since Lily. She wasn't a worldly sophisticate. She was so young to be a widow . . . too young to be a widow.

And that nagging little thought persisted. Wed for a year, she'd said, her husband dead for two.

His jaw thrust forward. They had not seen the last of each other, he vowed.

All at once he stopped. What was that? A scream? He reined in his horse and turned in the saddle, every fiber in him intent. What the devil . . .

The sound came again. Definitely a scream, but fainter this time.

He urged his horse ahead and down an embankment. There were ruts in the damp earth. Something had come through here. The brush was trampled, he noted, following the tracks. It was then he spied it, a carriage overturned, resting against the trunk of a tree. And a figure calling and waving at him.

It was Claire. His heart pounding, he reached her.

She collapsed in his arms.

"You're hurt." He smoothed her hair, touched a cut, bruised lump on her forehead. "Here, let me—"

"No, I'm fine. But Pen—" She gave a half sob, pointing inside the carriage.

A quick assessment. Penelope was laying on her side. She gave a low moan.

"I'll make a fire, then go for help, Claire. You'll be fine—"

"No, Gray, don't leave!" Frantic, she clutched his arm. "Pen's having her baby."

In that moment, in Gray's sudden presence, Claire saw the broadest shoulders in the land. The arms that closed around her were strong and powerful, the touch of lean fingertips almost tender. She longed to cling to him. The near desperate fear she had glimpsed on his face made her heart catch.

Her trunk had landed a short distance away. Gray went over and confirmed that the driver was dead.

Claire had rummaged through the trunk and found her cloak. She spread it over Penelope. Wadding up a gown, she placed it beneath her friend's head.

Gray's eyes found Claire's. "Do you know anything about birthing?"

She hesitated. "A little."

Gray's expression had turned grim. "Well, we'll have to sort our way through it, eh?"

Penelope's face was streaked with tears. She tried to summon a smile. "You forget, I'm here, too. Of course we'll muddle through it."

Whatever the reason, Gray's presence lent Claire courage. "She hasn't felt well all day," she told him. "Her back began to ache shortly after we left."

"I didn't think it could possibly be the baby. It's too early." Penelope gave another half sob. "It's too early, Claire."

Claire shook her head. "Oh, he's a brave one, Pen," she tried to joke. "A fighter just like his mother and father."

There wasn't room for two of them inside the carriage. Penelope lay on the back cushion. Claire slid in and knelt at her side.

Penelope took Claire's hand and laid it on her belly. "There. It's drawing again." Claire felt the womb tighten beneath her fingers. "Every few minutes now." She squeezed her eyes shut.

Claire shook her head. "You're so brave, Pen. You're doing wonderfully."

Penelope's smile turned into a grimace.

Gray was busy starting a fire and rummaging through the trunks to find something to use as cloths.

The hours passed slowly.

And Penelope's labor intensified. Her breath came in half pants . . . oh, it seemed like hours!

Claire's gaze slid helplessly to Gray's. She was afraid to reveal her worry in fear of alarming her friend further.

By then she and Gray had switched places. She was at Penelope's feet, while Gray had squeezed in next to her. Penelope's gown was lifted over upraised knees, concealing her modesty from

Gray, and she was crying. Claire didn't know how to help her.

With a handkerchief, Gray blotted the dampness from Penelope's brow. She was struggling to be brave but her strength was flagging. Her spirit as well. She strained, holding her breath against the pain.

"No, you must breathe!" Claire urged her. "Breathe, Pen!"

Weakly, Penelope pushed herself up on one elbow. Another contraction and she fell back weakly, as if all the strength had drained from her.

"I can't," she said with a sob. She was losing heart. "I can't go on."

Claire despaired as well. Perhaps she shouldn't have insisted that Gray stay. He might have been back with help by now.

All at once Claire cried out. "Oh, Pen, I can see him! I can see him! He has red hair like Theo!"

Penelope tried to surge up. She couldn't make it. She fell back, her face dripping wet. "Help me," she begged. "Help me."

Gray clasped her hand; it rested on her belly. He slipped his other arm behind Penelope's back to bring her nearly upright. Her nails dug into his hand. She screamed and heaved mightily.

Claire gave a joyous sob. "You have a daughter, Pen! A beautiful little girl who looks exactly like Theo!"

She thrust the little one at Gray. "Here. Tend to her while I tend to Pen!"

The cord was cut, the afterbirth expelled. Hauling in a breath, Gray wiped the slick wee body with a chemise. The baby let out a wavering cry, paper-thin eyelids screwed shut. Wrapping her tiny form in his coat, he looked down at the babe he held, snug in his jacket, still warm from his body.

Memory revived, memory of the last time he'd held an infant—

Memory that tore his heart asunder.

Chapter Ten

*I*t was dawn when another coach approached. Gray waved it down. They were all exhausted, but by mid-afternoon Penelope held her new daughter in her arms as their rescuer's coach stopped in front of her town house. The babe was very tiny, but very perfect. She slept in her mother's arms until they reached London.

At the Grove town house, Gray gently picked up Penelope and the baby and lifted them from the carriage. Just as they reached the top step, the front door was flung wide.

It appeared the arrival of mother and daughter would not be the only excitement.

Penelope cried out. "Theo! Oh, Theo!"

Theodore Grove rushed to clasp his wife and daughter into his embrace.

"My darling! I was just about to set out to the Northrups to fetch you."

Penelope clung to his neck. "How can this be?" she said over and over. "I thought you were dead. Your lieutenant said they couldn't find your— your body."

Theo shook his head. He walked with a cane, but it appeared he'd suffered no other injuries.

"A mistake," he said. "A farmer took me into his home, where I stayed until I was able to travel."

Tears stood out in his eyes. Both mother and baby were clasped tight in his arms. "Oh, you're here, my love. You're here." He gave a husky laugh. "I can't believe I have you in my arms once again."

Penelope wore a beatific smile. "My love, meet your daughter."

Theo pressed his lips to his wife's lips, then the babe's fuzzy red cap. He was too choked up to speak.

"She's beautiful," he said at last. "As beautiful as her mother."

Watching the tender scene, Claire felt a hot ache fill her throat. A pang of envy bit deep. She couldn't withhold it. It merely brought home the truth—

And her heart cried out in bitter loss.

She would never experience such love as existed between Penelope and Theo—and their little one. Never in this world.

Somehow they were all swept inside, husband, wife, and child. And she and Gray were swept along, too.

Theo spoke to the servants, who hurried to do his bidding. While a bath was prepared for mother and child, they were safely ensconced on a chaise downstairs. Theo turned and wrapped Claire in a giant embrace.

"Claire, my wife's greatest friend. If anyone would protect my heart's desire, it would be you. I thank you from the depths of my heart."

The viscount had held back, but Theo turned to him and extended a hand.

"Theo," Claire hastened to say, "this is Viscount Sutherland. If he had not happened upon our coach, I don't know what we would have done."

"My lord, I have no words to thank you." Theo's grip was firm as they shook hands.

If Gray looked a bit uncomfortable, Claire was too tired to notice. When Penelope and the baby were ushered upstairs, it was Gray who escorted her home. Gray, on whose arm she leaned as they climbed the stairs to her town house. She sighed once they were inside. She hadn't planned to be home until several days later, so Rosalie was gone. Her maid had asked permission to visit her sister in Kent. The girl wouldn't be back for several days yet.

Claire draped her shawl over a chair, fatigued almost beyond measure.

Gray's eyes fixed on her face. "Would you like tea?" he asked.

"Yes, that sounds wonderful. Here, let me—"

He caught her elbow and tugged her around.

"Sit," he commanded. "I'll fetch it for you."

"You, sir?"

A devilish smile crept along his lips. "My domestic abilities might amaze you, Mrs. Westfield."

Claire rolled her eyes heavenward.

Gray was surprised to find his lips curved up in a smile.

It wasn't long before he returned from the kitchen. He carried a tray with two daintily flowered cups and matching teapot. He slid it onto a mahogany side table near the divan and straightened.

Claire was leaning back against the cushions—

Fast asleep.

Gray stood for a moment. In but a half breath, a dozen emotions chased through him.

Slowly his gaze traced the ivory column of her throat, slender and delicate and exposed. Her cheek gleamed in the lamplight, smooth and silken. Her hair was half up, half down, which made his mouth turn up on one corner. One long silken rope of dark hair trailed over her shoulder.

His stomach clenched. He sucked in a jagged breath. Temptation spiraled within him; he felt his rod swell thickly, marble hard.

What would the lovely lady do if he dipped his tongue into that delicate hollow there at the base of her throat? he asked himself. Laved that tender hollow and felt the beat of her lifeblood pulsing strong and steady beneath his mouth.

His stomach tightened. He sucked in a jagged breath and fought a searing battle for control. He should leave. Now. Before he succumbed to the heated rush that burned through his veins.

Clenching his teeth, he bent to pick her up, bearing her upward as if she were weightless. She was not frail, not weak, yet felt slight in his embrace. Up the stairs to the landing and down the hallway he bore her, glancing into several bedrooms until he saw one with double doors that was undoubtedly hers.

Crossing the room, he lowered her to the bed, then fumbled with the oil lamp. When it was lit, he reached for her. Unfaltering, his fingers at her back, he undid the buttons of her gown and tugged it free of her form.

Her chemise might well have been sheer. The outline of her nipples was round and dark. He watched them rise against the night air as he tugged her gown free. In the lamplight her skin was like honey. Her cheeks were flushed the soft pink of sunset. Long lashes curled thick and dark against the curve of her cheeks.

Claire stirred but didn't wake. His brazen gaze took an unhurried path down her body. How long he stared at her, his jaw clenched hard, he couldn't have said. His blood pooled hot and thick inside him. Unbridled hunger surged hotly, pounding through his blood. His shaft surged, pulsing with the tempo.

The night closed in. Some dark, still emotion slipped over him. Slowly, as if he could not help himself—as indeed he could not—he pulled the pins free from her hair and tugged them out. For the space of a heartbeat, he threaded his fingers through her hair, letting it sift through his fingers, feeling its warmth, its life, its softness.

One slender hand lay beside her on the pillow, palm up. There was something in the pose, a vulnerability that caught at his heart. Her lips were parted and dewed with the moist warmth of her breath.

His insides twisted. Desire sharpened. Everything inside was screaming. How close he was to settling himself over her, parting her thighs with his knees and plunging his shaft between, she would never know. Gray did not deny his want. His need.

Yet he did not succumb.

No, he would not take her, not now. He wanted her hips thrusting hard against his, crying out, seeking a passion only he could give her. But he wanted at least a taste of her.

His hand closed about her nape, bringing her face up to his. No sweet, tender caress was this. He cursed himself for wanting her. He cursed her for making him want her. He kissed her the way he wanted, hot and devouring. For one shattering instant she lay quiet—then her lips parted beneath the greedy demand of his.

His body was shaking when he broke away. But Gray did not leave her. Instead he stripped—

And slid into bed beside her.

Claire woke the next morning, her limbs heavy, her mind clouded. Little by little the previous day came back. The accident with the carriage. Penelope's fear—the baby, and then such joy at her reunion with Theo.

Beyond that, her mind blurred. In all her days, she couldn't recall such exhaustion. Even Gray—

Her mind teetered. Her eyes flew open. Only then was she aware of something hard at her waist.

She froze.

Gray.

He was here.

Gray.

In her bed.

In her *bed*.

She made a faint, choked sound.

The fingers on his hand resting at her waist moved. In some distant part of her it registered that the span of his fingers bridged the width of her hips.

Claire tried to speak. To tell him . . . what? She didn't know. Words failed her. Her breath caught on a ragged sound.

"Hush." Gray's whisper was low, vibrating past her ear. "Don't say anything. Don't . . . say . . . anything."

She was tempting as sin. Primeval urges rushed through him. Gray felt—he saw—the instant that awareness swept over her. Every muscle in her body tensed.

Blood flooded his erection. He was rigid as stone.

And Claire's heart was suddenly pounding in her ears.

He'd slept with her, she realized. The night through.

And he'd kissed her. Again.

It didn't seem real. But now their mouths were so close. Her eyes locked helplessly on his. Her heart was in her throat. Eyes like blue fire moved slowly over her features.

The air was suddenly leaping with currents. Tension radiated out like a spider's web.

And then his mouth covered hers. His arms engulfed her. Her body jolted as his tongue plied hers. She let him explore the depths of her mouth as he wanted. She couldn't stop him. It was as if someone else had seized hold of her.

"Claire." His words were a low mutter against her mouth. "Don't hold back. I want you, Claire. Let me touch you."

It was more plea than demand. She was never quite aware of him pulling her chemise from her.

The next thing she knew, there was no barrier—none at all—between them.

Something teased her nipples. A strange inner trembling seized her. Claire allowed her mind to roam, and in so doing allowed her gaze to roam.

Gray was already naked. He'd slept with her naked—the knowledge raced through her veins. A part of her was aghast. A part of her shied away. The sight of him made it difficult to breathe. Her muscles grew weak. Yet she couldn't stop herself, and her throat locked as she summoned the courage to look at him—at all of him.

His shoulders were awesome, all sleek and burnished in the morning light. His chest seemed almost impossibly wide as well, covered by a dark mat of curly hairs. She tracked it the length of his chest, across the ridged muscles of his abdomen, clear to where an irrefutable male sex thrust from the bush grew darker and thicker. Her breath left her lungs in a scalding rush.

She knew her face must be flaming. But somehow her hands now lodged on his chest. She loved the feel of the rough, masculine hairs beneath her fingertips. Buried within were the round disks of his nipples. Touching one, she felt him inhale sharply.

And now it was his turn. There was no hesitation as he filled his hands with the fullness of her breasts. Her nipples burned like fire, springing taut against his palms. With a thumb, he traced the outline of one deep roseate center. Pure sensation shot through her. He teased her, toyed with her flesh in a maddening circle that stole her breath. Just when she thought she could stand no more, his mouth replaced his hands. His tongue touched one swollen tip. A jolt went through her. It seemed to thrust into his mouth. He began to suck.

Harder. Stronger.

What little control she had splintered. She'd never imagined such a thing.

Nor could she have imagined what further pleasure awaited.

One dark, lean hand traced a shattering pattern across the soft plane of her belly. Claire's mouth went dry as those daring fingertips threaded into the triangle of fleece at the top of her thighs. She inhaled a ragged breath of shock, then went utterly still, but only for an instant. One bold fingertip ventured deep within damp wet curls. He touched her at will, claiming velvet folds, his touch ever more brash. She jerked as he buried his fingers deep within the soft, weeping flesh that guarded the treasure deep within her furrowed channel.

His breath was ragged. "Claire," he said. "I've been wanting to do this since the night we met."

Her heart tumbled to a standstill. It was as if he ruled her senses. It wasn't enough to kiss him. It wasn't enough to touch him. Her hips began to move with the rhythm of his hand. His thumb circled a tiny kernel of flesh, a burning caress that turned her inside out. Every nerve inside her was screaming. Her breath came shallow and panting.

With the pressure of his chest, Gray stretched out over her, above her. It was time. He made a sound deep in his chest. He could hold back no longer. With the pressure of his knees, he parted her wide. Her hands still curled around his shoulders. She lay open, wide and vulnerable before him. His thighs tensed. The turgid head of his organ probed damp, silken flesh.

She couldn't help it. Startled, unsure, her thighs tensed instinctively. A flutter of panic ran through her.

"Let me in, Claire." Gray's whisper was low and ragged. "Please, sweet, let me in." Over and over he kissed her, until her body melted into his once more, every sweet inch of her.

With a single, burning thrust he plunged inside her. For one split second in time he marveled at the tightness of hot, feminine flesh clinging to his rod. He wanted to shout in pure, male triumph.

But only for an instant. Time splintered. In some rational corner of his mind, Gray was shocked at what he felt.

No, he thought, stunned by the frail resistance of her body. It could not be. Yet in that telltale instant when Claire twisted beneath him—when her nails bit into his naked shoulders and her dark, warm channel stretched to accept his burning rod, and when her jagged half cry echoed in his mouth . . .

Truth lay revealed. Truth did not lie.

It could only mean one thing.

He could not stop. His need was overwhelming. It eclipsed all else. She felt so good. He felt her tremor; it only made him even more aware of the way he was buried inside the hot prison of her flesh. He tried to hold back, but his blood was scalding, there where dark, rough curls lay mingled with hers. The sight drove him half mad.

He couldn't look away. It was too wildly erotic. Too raw and elemental.

His mind urged him to be still. He tried to. He tried, but there was no fighting the scalding urges that commanded his body. Need clamored in his veins. His hips had already began to pump. He tried to keep his plunge slow and shallow. But then—he could fight it no more. He felt his body lunge. Again. Almost frantically. Desperately. Deep into the silken chasm of her flesh. Ever deeper. He could do nothing but yield. He wished—prayed—for climax to claim him. He could feel it sizzling along his spine. But a part of him wanted it to never end. Claire was squirming beneath him, around him, sending him even more deeply into a frenzy of desire and need.

Release claimed him. He cursed her. He cursed

himself, even as an explosion of release sent him collapsing above her.

Claire's body was still burning, the world still spinning as Gray rolled from the bed and stood. A single glance downward confirmed the truth. His rod was stained with her blood and his seed.

His movements taut and jerky, he pulled on his trousers, then turned to face her.

Claire had rescued the sheet and her night-gown from the foot of her bed. She latched onto the sheet and held it tight against her breast like a shield, her head bowed low. She needed that moment to grasp the enormity of what had just occurred.

Gray was swearing, blistering words that made her face burn with embarrassment.

"No wonder you kissed like a virgin. You were," he stated flatly. It was less a declaration than an accusation. "God, I should have listened to my . . . How? How can that be"—his lip curled—"*Mrs.* Westfield?"

He seized her hand. His jaw clenched as he stared at the ring she wore. Claire tried to tug her hand free. His grip merely tightened.

"Oh, do forgive me. Is it *Miss* Westfield, then? Enlighten me, if you would." His voice was dangerously low.

Claire's mouth opened, then closed. She stared into his eyes with dread.

"What? Nothing to say?"

His mockery cut deep. His expression was awful, as blistering as his tone.

Oh, what had she been thinking, to yield, and to *this* man. Her brother's killer. She chided herself bitterly. She must have been mad, to yield her body the way she had. What had she done? Lord, what had she done?

"What did you intend? To blackmail me? Claim I stole your virtue? I won't succumb to such chicanery. I won't be used. Not by you. Not by anyone."

"What?" she cried. She finally managed to drag her hand free of his, then leaped from the bed. Everything inside her was still whirling. It wasn't supposed to happen like this, she thought vaguely. When she'd dreamed of the moment she would confront him—this reckoning of accounts, as it were—she had been the one in control. Not him. Never him.

His gaze pinned hers accusingly. "Dammit, what the blazes is going on? Why this"—he gestured furiously—"this masquerade? This charade? You are not a widow—"

"An astute observation, my lord. May I commend you?"

The air was leaping with currents. Claire didn't care that she stood before him clad only in her nightgown. Their eyes collided, hers flashing with golden fire, his alight with a silver flame.

He reached for her. She knocked his hand away.

He looked at her with narrowed eyes. "Your name is not Westfield, is it?"

"No," she said evenly. "I am Claire Ashcroft." She watched him intently. At his silence, outrage began to smolder in her breast. "The name Ashcroft means nothing to you?"

"No. Why the devil should it?"

Claire stared at him. It couldn't be—

"Oliver Ashcroft? The name means nothing to you?"

"Did you not hear? No. I don't know the man."

She was shaking with outrage. "Oliver Ashcroft was my brother. My *brother*."

"Lovely for both of you. I'm afraid, however, that has nothing to do with me."

Claire did not consider. She delivered a stinging slap hard across his cheek. She would have done it again, but iron-hard fingers curled around her wrist.

"It has everything to do with you!" Raw pain wrenched at her breast. She let loose the storm in her heart. "You killed him, you bastard. You killed my brother! Have you killed so many that you remember none of them?"

Gray released her hand. "Your brother," he repeated. "And when did this alleged event take place?"

"Rutgers Field. A duel. How ironic that it's precisely nine months to the day! A gambling debt, we were told. Why did you have to kill him? Why?" she cried. "He was so young! And it was just a pittance to a man like you!"

There was a moment of complete and utter silence. Something flickered across Gray's features. Claire was too incensed to notice. His hands were tainted with blood—Oliver's blood.

The taste of tears was bitter upon her tongue. "Leave," she said. The word came out low and choked. "Leave."

He reached for her. Lean hands closed about her upper arms.

"Claire. For pity's sake, Claire—"

She tore herself away. "Get out!" she cried. "Get out before I summon the constable!"

His jaw clenched. With a furious curse, he snatched up his clothing and left.

He didn't look back.

With a half sob, Claire sank to the floor in a flood of tears and fury. She had sought revenge.

But all she had gained was shame.

Home in his chamber, Gray went straight to the liquor cabinet. He poured himself a generous portion of whiskey. It burned its way down.

He downed it, then another.

His body was still on fire.

At the washstand, he stripped naked, then glanced down.

Traces of blood still smeared his member.

He splashed his face with water, then wiped his member. The towel was left there on the rug.

Bracing his hands on the washstand, he stared at his reflection in the shaving mirror. Christ, what had he done?

Claire was right. He was a bastard.

Darkness took hold inside him. Turmoil raged in his breast. Cad that he was, he thought, he couldn't help it—a part of him felt betrayed by her lies.

On the dresser lay the ribbon she'd worn the night of the masquerade, the ribbon he'd rescued from the ground.

He picked it up—then crushed it in his fist. Fresh memory of the mind-splitting instant he plunged inside her swept over him, the way her passage clamped around his flesh, hot and sweet and velvet. And tight. Ah, damn, so tight.

Shock had held him motionless, but only for a breath. Dammit, why hadn't Claire stopped him?

But there was the rub. Could he have stopped?

A fresh wave of self-loathing flooded him. Once again he remembered her hands on his shoulders. Had he hurt her? The thought cut through him like a knife. He remembered her body trembling in his arms. Her flesh giving way to the power of his. Lord, it had felt too good. She had felt so good. He could almost feel her again, lunging into her almost wildly.

The truth battered him. He should have stopped the moment he discovered that frail membrane of flesh that signaled her maidenhead. An inner voice sneered at him. A noble man would have. But he didn't have a noble bone in his body. Not anymore.

No, he couldn't have stopped.

And he had just found a new contempt for himself.

His recall was fuzzy, but he remembered the young cub, her brother. Not his name but the deed. His mouth twisted. There had been rain. He remembered the way the cub shot early. His fingers unwittingly went to the scar on his shoulder. Yet what point was there in telling Claire? He'd hurt her enough already, and he wouldn't tarnish her memory of her brother.

Crossing the room, he lay facedown on the bed. No, he wouldn't tell her.

The best thing he could do for her was forget they'd ever met.

Chapter Eleven

*T*here was no more to be said. No more to be done. She had failed. Failed Oliver. Her mother. Her father. Failed in her search to avenge Oliver's death.

With nothing to keep her in London, she fled home to Wildewood.

Yet reminders of her visit to London were impossible to forget. *He* was impossible to forget. Gray. All she wanted was to be rid of him forever. At night when she closed her eyes, she relived afresh the sweet pressure of his mouth on hers. The feel of his hand claiming her breast, branding her as if she were his.

The taste of bitterness was vile on her tongue. She wouldn't hide from the truth. She had let him into her bed.

She had surrendered.

Now all she wanted was to forget they had ever met.

Despite everything that had passed, it was good to be home again. She refused to allow herself to wallow in self-pity. She busied herself with resuming management of the small estate left her by her father.

It was time to begin a new life. A new course in life.

The fall had been a profitable one. Her estate manager had taken good care of the house and property. Winter was settling in, though. The days were chill. There was even snowfall in mid-November.

At the market one day she wandered through the booths, shopping for a warm, woolen scarf.

"Excuse me, miss."

Claire turned to find a man behind her. He looked pleasant enough. Her gaze was even with his.

She hated the way her mind immediately swung to Gray. Gray was far taller than this man—

She bit off the thought, wrenching herself away from the memory.

She didn't recognize the man before her.

"Yes, sir?"

He offered a smile. "I'm afraid I may have missed a turn. I'm hoping you can help me find my way."

"I will certainly try."

"Excellent. I'm looking for Walnut Lane."

"Certainly. Walnut Lane is there behind the church. It ends several miles from here. There's nothing there but a small estate, though. I believe the house is empty."

"Not anymore. Rather, not for long. I purchased the property some time ago, and now I find I don't remember the way."

"Indeed. It appears we are neighbors, then. I live at Wildewood, on the southern boundary of your property."

"I'm very pleased to meet you. My name is Lawrence Townsend." He took off his glove and extended a hand.

Claire shook it briefly. "Claire Ashcroft."

"Perhaps we'll see each other again."

"Perhaps." Claire smiled slightly.

"Good day, Miss Ashcroft. Ah, forgive me. Is it Miss or Mrs.?"

"It's Miss." She inclined her head. "Good day to you, Mr. Townsend."

At next week's market day Claire saw him again.

He hailed her. "Miss Ashcroft!"

"Mr. Townsend. Have you settled into your new home?"

"I have indeed."

She saw him again at the market a week later. Again he hailed her. "Miss Ashcroft!"

"Mr. Townsend. How are you, sir?"

"I'm just the thing. I have a confession to make, though."

"Oh?" She wasn't sure what to think of that.

"My name is Lawrence. I would be pleased if you called me by my given name."

"Very well, then. And you may call me Claire."

"It's good to see you again, Claire."

"Likewise."

"I hope you won't consider me too forward, Claire, but I have another confession."

"Yes?" If she was rather wary, she couldn't help it.

"I came to the market hoping to see you again."

She adopted a faint smile. "And why is that?"

"I would like it if you would join me for tea this afternoon."

Claire hesitated. "Sir—"

"Lawrence. Please call me Lawrence." He must have sensed her reluctance. "If you prefer," he said, "we could have tea now."

Somehow it didn't seem so intimate at the inn rather than at one of their homes. "Very well, then."

At the inn, he seated her at a chair near the window. The owner's wife served them tea and scones.

Claire blew on the surface of her tea. "So how are you acclimating to your new home, sir?"

"I am quite enjoying it. I'm in the process of hiring staff."

"What brought you here, Lawrence?"

"I've lived all my life in the Midlands. I am a widower, you see. I lost my wife several years ago."

Widow. Widower. Claire tensed. Her mind sped straight to Gray.

"I have two sons who are grown and have started their own families. As much as I adore them, they are occupied with their lives, and I think it's time I moved on."

Move on. It sounded so simple. But she was discovering it was not.

With his thinning hair and ready smile, Claire found him pleasant to look upon. They began to meet for tea several times a week. Each provided companionship to the other. Sometimes he made her laugh, when she had never thought to laugh again. She told him of Penelope, but did not speak of her brother Oliver.

Or Gray.

In December a letter arrived from Penelope. Claire lowered it to her lap.

A christening date for little Merriweather had been set. Penelope gaily wrote that of course little Merriweather was anxious to meet her soon-to-be godmother.

Claire did not wish to return to London—heaven save her, there were too many hurtful memories!—but she was anxious to see her friends and little Merriweather.

Beyond that, she refused to think.

Lawrence saw her off from Wildewood several days later. He took both of her hands as she prepared to enter the carriage.

"Hasten home, my dear Claire."

"I will," she said.

He continued to hold her hands. Leaning forward, he kissed her on the lips.

It was a sweet, gentle kiss. One that was more than a kiss of friendship. And Claire loathed herself for the single thought raised high above all else . . .

That Lawrence's kiss was nothing like Gray's.

United at last, the Grove family could not have been happier. Theo was an excellent father, Penelope a doting mother. Only one thing marred Penelope's contentment. Well, actually there were two . . .

Both had to do with Claire.

Claire had closed up the house she had rented in London and returned to Wildewood. Of course, they exchanged letters. But Penelope had known Claire too long not to realize that beneath the surface, there was a spark missing.

Theo was not happy that Penelope had helped with Claire's plan. Both of them had risked their good name. Indeed, Theo thought both had risked the wrath of a viscount. So it was that he was surprised the viscount sent an inquiry asking after the family's health—mother, child, and daughter—and a gift for little Merriweather, a music box.

Oh, yes, surprised and pleased.

Pen and Theo had decided long ago that they wanted Claire as godmother.

As Penelope told Theo, "It often happens that the mother chooses godmother for the little one."

What with Theo's service in the Peninsula, however, they had never decided on a godfather for Merriweather. And so both were in agreement that the choice would be his.

Almost from the moment he had wife and daughter back in his arms, it was very clear in Theo's mind whom he would ask. To that end, he invited Lord Sutherland to dinner one night. Penelope didn't think the viscount would accept.

She was wrong.

It was a pleasant enough dinner. The viscount's manner was polite and courteous, perhaps a bit reserved, Penelope decided.

She had written to Claire to ask if her friend had any contact with the viscount. Claire's reply was short. "I have heard nothing," she said, "nor do I wish to."

Did the viscount feel the same way? If she

were honest with herself, Penelope had to admit that she hadn't expected the viscount to have any further contact with Claire.

Over port, Theo put forth the question.

"My lord," he said, "I would consider it a great honor if you would serve as godfather to our Merriweather."

The viscount was clearly taken aback.

"If not for you," Theo said quietly, "my daughter and my wife might not be here today. That is a debt I can never repay." He glanced at Penelope. "We would consider it an honor if you would accept."

The viscount's gaze turned to Penelope. "And you, Mrs. Grove? Is it your wish as well?"

Penelope chose her words carefully. "It is."

Theo reached for Penelope's hand. "Do you accept, then?"

"I accept." There was a pause. "May I ask who will stand as godmother?"

"Claire Ashcroft," she said.

A fractional pause. "And does Miss Ashcroft know whom you've asked to stand as godfather?"

Penelope's gaze was fixed on his face. His expression was difficult to read.

"Not yet," she told him, her head held high.

The viscount said nothing.

"We would like the christening to take place the following Sunday after next. "Does that suit, my lord?"

* * *

It was late afternoon when Claire arrived at the Grove home. Her plan was to stay only a few days. Penelope was disappointed her visit would be so short, but she understood Claire's feelings.

Claire did not tell Penelope that she'd made love with Gray—odd words, those. Passion. Desire. But in truth no love had passed between them.

Penelope ordered tea for the two of them in the salon. Only a few minutes passed before Merriweather's nurse brought her to the room. Penelope took the child in her arms and cooed.

"Oh, Claire, isn't she the most darling thing you've ever seen?" Penelope reverently touched the blankets wrapped around her baby.

"My word, Pen, she is the very image of Theo!"

Penelope gave a breathless laugh and shaped the babe's head in her hand. The child wore a lace-trimmed cap that covered her head, except for where a bit of fuzzy red hair peeped out.

"It's the exact color of Theo's!"

"It is, isn't it? But I think she has my nose," Penelope announced. "And my chin," she added, almost as an afterthought.

Claire chuckled. "Oh, most certainly."

"We've decided to call her Merry. Merriweather is a tad long."

"Well, little Merry," Claire said gravely, "I am very pleased to see you again." Almost as if she knew what Claire was saying, the child waved a fist and opened one eye.

"There! She likes you. And now she's smiling!"

Claire laughed and gave the wee hand the veriest shake.

That little hand curled around Claire's finger and didn't let go.

"See how strong she is already." Penelope laughed delightedly. "And only two months old!"

"Indeed, she is!" Claire glanced up at Penelope. "She is thriving?"

"Oh, yes. The physician continues to marvel. She is truly a miracle." Penelope gave a blinding smile. "Here, Claire, you must hold her."

"Oh, oh! But she is still so tiny. So tiny I'm afraid to hold her!"

"Oh, pooh. Don't be silly." Penelope passed the baby to her.

Little Merry settled into her elbow. God save her, Claire thought, the weight of a child nestled in her arms felt so—so right! For one fleeting instant she imagined gazing down at her own little one, whispering lovingly into one tiny ear, inhaling the sweet baby scent.

All that was lost to her.

She did not deceive herself. There was no point in it. Marriage was beyond her. There would be no husband. No children.

No man would marry a woman who'd already lost her virginity.

Never would she hold her child, Raw pain wrenched her heart at the thought. She sought to banish it, for to yearn for it so would be but foolish, foolish nonsense.

The nurse came in for baby Merry. Claire finished her tea, but ate only half of a pastry on the tea tray. It didn't set right with her digestion.

"Penelope, I hope you will forgive me, but I think I should like to rest for a bit."

"You do look rather tired, love. Would you like a dinner tray in your room?"

"That would be lovely." Claire smiled her thanks. "It has been a long day. Isn't it amazing how tired one can get from simply doing nothing?"

"It is indeed," Penelope laughed.

The following morning the Grove household was in a bit of an uproar. The christening was set for early afternoon, with a reception following at the Grove home.

In the carriage, Penelope blew a stray hair from her forehead. Theo hadn't stopped grinning all day. Merry looked charming. A tiny little cap covered her head. Her christening gown was of elaborate lace and satin. Dressed all in white, the little one looked like an angel. Upon entering the church, she waved a fist and yawned, oblivious of the commotion about her.

Claire followed behind Penelope and Theo. Heavens, what with all the commotion this morning, she hadn't found time to ask after Merry's other godparent. All she knew was that he would be waiting at the church.

Inside, the robed figure of the reverend stood at the baptismal font. He raised his hand in welcome when he saw them. A tall figure was already there as well, his back to them.

The figure turned his head ever so slightly. A strange sensation swept over Claire. Desperation clutched at her.

No, she thought in mounting horror. No—

It was Gray.

Chapter Twelve

$\mathscr{H}$ow she made it to the baptismal font, Claire was never quite certain. Upheaval raged inside her. Penelope and Theo had stepped to the font, Merry in Pen's arms. Penelope didn't lift her eyes to her. Oh, but she knew why! If Pen had told her they asked Gray to godparent Merry, what would she have done? Refused? She would have wanted to, oh, most assuredly! But Penelope was her dearest friend. She could never have refused her.

Either way, it didn't matter. The moment was upon her. She must make the best of it.

But she couldn't stop her knees from knocking. For one perilous moment her legs threatened to betray her. Sheer will kept her upright. Sheer will—and Gray's fingers cutting into the flesh of her waist.

When it was time for her and Gray to confirm

their role as godmother and godfather to Merry, she managed to speak them, if not loudly, then at least evenly.

A final blessing—and it was over. Hugs were exchanged all around.

Except for the two new godparents.

The reception was due to begin immediately after the ceremony. Once Claire was in the carriage with the parents, Penelope passed Merry to Theo. Leaning forward, she took Claire's hands in both her own.

"Claire," she said, "it was terrible of me, I know. If you had asked after our choice for godfather, I should have told you. But you didn't and . . . and I could not take the chance you would refuse if you knew we had asked Gray. We love you. Merry will love you. I always knew I would have you as godmother to our first child. We have much to be thankful for, and thankful to him as well."

"Merry might not be here if it weren't for the two of you," said Theo. "You and the viscount. Penelope and I knew, almost from the start, that we would ask him to stand as Merry's godfather. We wanted to recognize his part in saving Pen and Merry's life. And, well, here we all are."

Claire squeezed Penelope's hands. "I'm not angry, Pen. You know I would never refuse you anything."

The reception afterward was a joyous, happy

affair attended by friends and family. Claire saw several startled glances slide to Gray. Undoubtedly his appearance was unexpected. One did not equate Viscount Sutherland with virtues like faith and family. Out of love for her friend, Claire had decided to accept his role. Out of love for her friend, she would be civil.

She stepped out to the garden and seated herself on a small stone bench under a tree. With her handkerchief, she blotted the moisture from her forehead and the back of her neck. All at once she felt overly warm, and a trifle light-headed.

She didn't know that piercing blue eyes had seen her slip outside. Gray, watching her, debated himself for an instant, then followed her.

Claire feigned an expression of great surprise. "What! You are still here, sir?"

Gray's jaw grew tight. "I'm sure I have no idea what you mean," he said almost curtly.

"Come now," she said crisply. "You have put in the requisite appearance. Now that you have, I would have thought you'd have taken your leave already."

Gray folded his arms across his chest.

"My leave to do what?"

She gave a trilling laugh. "Why, whatever endeavor a gentleman like you would pursue."

"A gentleman like me," he repeated. "And what might that be?" His tone was silky.

Claire's chin came up. "Oh, I'm sure I wouldn't know."

The little witch, he thought.

"Speculate."

She stood. "I think not!"

One side of his mouth went up. God, she was beautiful. His pulse began to clamor. The mere sight of her did that to him. Her haughtiness— her spirit—kindled his own. And all of a sudden he felt . . . alive, as he hadn't for weeks.

"Ah, Claire," he said with a shake of his head. "After the intimacies we have shared, we can surely be honest with each other. What activities do you imagine I might be about at this hour of the day?"

He was enjoying baiting her.

Her chin came up. "Very well, then," she snapped. "You would doubtless be pursuing whatever dissolute afternoon pursuits you pursue with your equally dissolute friends."

"Are they the same as one's morning pursuits?"

"I wouldn't know—"

His eruption of laughter cut her off. "I beg to differ. Must I recount—"

She turned her head. Gray was but a hair-breadth away. "No," she said, her voice low and choked. "There is no need. And now I would like to rejoin the others."

Satisfaction glittered in his eyes.

Claire started to step past him. All at once she stopped. Something flickered across her face. A slender hand groped for his sleeve.

"Oh, my."

Gray bit off an impatient exclamation. "For pity's sake, Claire, let us both cry off! We've done this before, as you recall. So please, cease your histrionics."

She did not answer.

Almost in slow motion, her knees began to buckle.

"Claire . . . Claire! What the devil—"

He caught her halfway to the ground.

The next thing Claire was aware of were strong, capable hands sliding beneath her and lifting her high.

"Can you hear me?"

It was Gray, his tone insistently prodding. She guided him upstairs to the guest chamber she occupied.

Claire's senses were swimming. Her belly protested the luncheon she'd eaten. When Gray laid her down on the chaise near the window, she very nearly lost it.

"Claire!"

Gray was leaning over her.

"What's wrong with you?" He was scowling fiercely. "I don't know what you're about, Claire, but if this is a ploy to invoke my sympathy—"

Claire gasped. "What!" she cried.

"I'm not a fool. This may have worked once, but it won't a second time."

She knocked his hand away, so furious she was shaking.

"I don't want to see you again, Grayson Sutherland. I don't want you near me. Not ever again."

Gray's entire frame had gone rigid. He got to his feet, his mouth curling. "I see we understand each other then, don't we?"

"Go to hell!" she cried.

His mouth twisted. Dear God, he thought, he was already there.

Claire's illness was brief. By the time she arrived home at Wildewood, it was as if she'd never been ill.

Yet before the week was out, she sickened yet again.

Like the other time, it was short-lived. She was on her feet the next morning. And then it happened again.

Lawrence brought bread his cook had made, still warm from the oven. He brought fresh vegetables from the garden, fish from the stream.

And heaven help it—the sight of several fish still on the line reminded her of the day at the duke's estate when she and Gray had gone fishing. She recalled how cocky Gray was about his ability to teach her his skill—

Something pierced her breast. How she had laughed at him!

She saw Lawrence daily now. He made no demands of her—he had yet to kiss her again, but she knew what he was doing.

Courting her.

She couldn't help it. One day a part of her cried out . . . What if it was Gray instead of Lawrence who was courting her? She recalled the night of the play, how Gray had taken her back to his town house, the way he'd filled his drawing room with flowers. They drank wine . . . and they talked about seduction. What was it he'd said?

God, he'd muttered against the corner of her mouth. *I've been waiting to do that all day.*

He hadn't disguised his intent. And somehow she couldn't imagine Lawrence employing such seductive ways. Somehow she couldn't imagine Lawrence embracing her in that hot, masterful way Gray had. Gray's kiss had gone on and on and on—

No. She couldn't allow herself to think of Gray.

Yet she knew the time would come when she had no choice.

Lawrence escorted her home one day after church services. "Claire"—they had grown comfortable enough to freely call each other by their given names—"my cook makes the best Yorkshire puddings in the county. I do believe it's true. Come join me for Sunday dinner today. I hate taking meals alone."

Claire, too, was aware how lonely meals could be.

She protested one day when he insisted on her riding on his gig back to Wildewood. "Lawrence," she told him as he lifted her from the gig, "I'm not an invalid."

"I want to take care of you, Claire. I want you to lean on me." His hands remained on her waist. "You know that, don't you?"

She sucked in a breath.

"I know we have not known each other so very long, but I grow impatient. I feel in my heart that this is right." He took her hand in his. "Will you marry me, Claire?"

There was a huge lump in her throat. She knew she must be honest with him.

"Lawrence, you are a dear, dear man, and I enjoy your company. Indeed, I have come to treasure it. But I must be truthful . . . Lawrence," she said gently, "I am not in love with you."

"Perhaps love will come later," he said. "I will give you time after we wed. I will demand nothing from you."

Claire bit her lip. "There is more," she said, her tone very low.

"I doubt you will change my mind, Claire."

"Perhaps. Perhaps not. Lawrence, I am expecting a child."

When she had slept with Gray, there was no

thought as to the possibility. At first she didn't want to believe it. But when her belly began to swell, she could deny it no longer.

She was surprised, in fact, that Lawrence had not guessed. If one looked closely, the mound of her belly was small—but it grew more with each day.

For the first time, she made the admission.

She was carrying Gray's child.

"Ah," said Lawrence. "I sensed that something in your past had hurt you. I accept you as you are, Claire. I think we can provide each other friendship and camaraderie through the years to come. I will raise your child as if it were my own."

Perhaps it was better this way, she thought later that night. At least her child would have a father.

She gave him her answer the next day. "You are a dear man, Lawrence. And . . . I will marry you."

Lawrence leaned forward and kissed her. It was a sweet, gentle kiss, longer than their first. Claire kept her eyes closed, waiting—praying— for something akin to longing.

There was nothing. Neither pleasure nor displeasure. Perhaps it was better this way.

So began her plans to be wed.

Chapter
Thirteen

$\mathcal{P}$enelope and Theo were having breakfast in the morning room when Penelope opened her latest letter from Claire. They corresponded often.

> *My dearest Penelope,*
>
> *I hope this letter will find you, Theo, and little Merry in the best of health. The weather here is bright with sunlight, but soon all the leaves will come down. Already it begins to grow ever so cold . . .*

Penelope smiled, then read on:

> *I have news you may find rather startling . . . but you needn't worry so about me, dearest Penelope.*

Penelope's eyes went huge. No, she breathed. Oh, it cannot be.

The letter finished:

> *The ceremony will take place at two o'clock on Friday, here at Wildewood. There is a need for haste, you see. Of course I do not expect you to journey to Wildewood on such short notice, and certainly not with little Merry. But I know you will be with me in spirit.*
>
> > *Your friend always,*
> > *Claire*

The paper fluttered to the table.

Theo took one look at his wife's pale face and leaped up. "Pen, good heavens. Whatever is the matter?"

"Order the carriage!" she cried. "Hurry, Theo! Every moment counts!"

"Pen, what the deuce is going on?"

Penelope shook her head as if to clear it. Her mind raced. "Claire is getting married. We must find the viscount. Oh, Theo, we must hurry!" There was a good chance that Claire would be furious with her . . . there was no certainty the viscount would even care.

At his wife's request, Theo went to see if he could locate the viscount at his home in Sheffield Square. He was not. Despite the early hour, Theo found him at White's, just leaving the gaming table for a table in the corner with the Duke of Braddock.

"Come!" he greeted Theo upon seeing him. "Come join us and I'll buy you a brandy, man!"

Theo discerned that both Sutherland and Braddock had indulged in a number of brandies already. He shook his head. "No, Sutherland, do not sit down! I must implore you to come with me at my wife's behest."

"Your wife! Why should she should wish to see me?"

Theo didn't tell him Penelope had received a letter from Claire. Doubtless, the news of Claire's marriage was behind Penelope's urgent summons.

"I have been instructed to bring you with me no matter what the means," said Theo. He eyed the viscount.

"Well, at the very least, you've piqued my interest." The slash of Gray's eyebrows climbed high.

Half an hour later the two men climbed the stairs to Theo's town house. Penelope was in the drawing room with Merry in her arms. She passed the child to her nurse when they entered.

"Please be seated, my lord." Penelope waved the viscount to a chair. Theo moved to stand near the fireplace. "I hope you will forgive my hasty summons, but I have had word from Claire that I think you may wish to hear."

"Mrs. Grove," he said stiffly, "you are mistaken. There is nothing that concerns Claire that can be of interest to me."

"You are wrong, my lord." Penelope's voice rang with conviction. She folded her hands in her lap. Despite his always impeccable dress, he looked horrible. Good! she thought.

Gray's tone was cool. "My dear Mrs. Grove, aside from sharing roles as godparents to little Merry, Claire and I have no further dealings beyond that, nor will we."

"You may change your mind," she said levelly.

"I think not. You are no doubt aware that our last meeting did not end particularly amicable." His tone was faultlessly polite.

"And you are surely aware that I know everything about the two of you—Oliver's death . . . your part in it . . . Claire's plan for vengeance. I am not proud of it, but I aided her."

"Indeed."

He had assumed a rather bored expression.

"I don't think you heard me, my lord. I know everything about the two of you."

He inclined his head. "Yes, I heard you."

"Everything," Penelope stressed.

She'd given him pause. There!

"You should go to her."

Gray gave a biting laugh. "If you know 'everything,' then you know that I am the last man in the world she will want to see again."

"I would not interfere—"

"Pray, do not."

"—only I think perhaps Claire may not be acting . . . in her best interests." Or yours, Penelope thought. She had the feeling Claire would be furious with her.

"That is not my affair."

Penelope felt like hurtling something at him. "You try to hide it, but you're a good man. If I didn't believe that, I would never have asked you to be a part of my child's life. And . . . oh, it is not my place to tell you what to do! but I will say it again . . . you should go to her."

The viscount got to his feet.

Penelope took a huge breath.

"She's getting married," said Penelope. "At two o'clock. On Friday."

"I wish her well."

"You stupid fool," she said fiercely. "If you don't go now, you'll regret it for the rest of your life. Do you hear me? Do you understand? The rest of your life!"

His eyes flickered. "I have obligations here," he said stiffly. "Perhaps at some point—"

"No," she said. "Now."

Gray looked at her sharply.

"If you don't, it'll be too late."

Gray was exhausted. He'd ridden all night in order to arrive here at the village of Wildewood by two o'clock. A farmer several miles back had given him directions to the Ashcroft home. As he passed the town square, he wondered again why Penelope had been so adamant. He shouldn't have cared. He didn't care.

So why was he on his way to Claire's home?

It passed through his mind to turn around. To head back to London. *Face it, you fool*, chided a voice inside. *Claire won't want you here.*

Something dark stole through him. It was none of his affair whom Claire chose to wed. He felt suddenly ugly inside. *Who did he fool?* chided the voice. He admitted it—the thought of Claire with another man made fiery jealousy scald his insides. The thought of her lying naked in someone else's arms, offering body and mouth in sweet surrender, made the edges of his world seem to blacken. He shut her away the best he was able. Now the pain was intense. Immense.

Penelope was wrong. He wasn't a man of honor. Once, but no more. If he cared anything at all about Claire, he would turn around now, head back to London and to his own self-destruction.

But that was the coward's way out, he told himself.

And he deserved to hurt. He deserved to be punished.

The church was small, set back from the road, constructed of stone, one wall covered with ivy. He saw a coach and several buggies outside. Gray guided his horse there and dismounted.

He was travel-stained and weary, hardly fit to attend a wedding. But would he stay until the vows were spoken?

He must. He must.

The church bell rang. Two o'clock.

Quietly, Gray stepped into the church and sat in the last pew. There were only a few people in attendance, seated at the front. Steeling himself, he raised his head and looked toward the altar.

It was true. She was getting married.

A man stood beside Claire, his hair shot through with silver. Claire was dressed in mauve. In her hands was a small bouquet of flowers.

The reverend spoke a blessing. The service commenced. Gray couldn't take his eyes from the bride. She was smiling as she turned more fully toward the groom.

Gray's eyes fastened on her. His gaze slid hungrily down her body.

Shock rippled through him. He was on his feet in a heartbeat.

A vivid curse exploded from his lips.

At the altar, the reverend looked up. "Young man, we are in God's house! This man and woman are here to be joined in holy matrimony—"

"No," he said.

The man beside Claire spoke up. "Sir! Now see here. We are about to take our vows—"

"No."

"Why the devil not?"

"She's marrying me," Gray said fiercely. "She's marrying me."

Claire was shaken. Stunned. A jolt of shock went through her and she reeled. Gray was here at Wildewood.

She's marrying me.

No. It wasn't possible. She couldn't possibly have heard right.

Her blood roared in her ears. Voices buzzed. Male voices. Words, fading in and out.

Father.

Marriage.

Child.

Wife.

Awareness receded. Claire sank down on a pew, guided by a pair of hands. The air seemed charged with a hundred different emotions.

Shaken, stunned, a dam seemed to break inside her. It was too much. She began to sob. "I want to go home. I want to go home!"

They gathered in the reverend's home adjacent to the altar. Gray was tight-lipped and silent. Lawrence was seated next to Claire, both of her hands clasped in his. The reverend had stepped outside.

Gray stood across the room near the window, powerful arms crossed over his chest. His posture, his countenance . . .

Clearly he did not plan to leave.

Claire swallowed. "I am fine, Lawrence. Please leave us. This—" She swallowed hard. "—this is between Gray and I."

Lawrence squeezed her fingers. "Are you certain?"

She nodded. "I will be fine."

"Very well, then. If you need anything, you know where I will be." Before he left, he cast a fulminating glance at Gray.

They were left alone.

Her eyes cleaved to Gray's. His jaw locked, sending a cascade of uncertainty through her. It was Claire who spoke first.

"Why are you here?"

His eyes seemed to blaze like fiery blue torches. It was as if the fires of hell had leaped high.

She cringed inside. "Pen told you, didn't she?"

"She told me about the marriage. She did not tell me about this."

He pulled her to her feet. The roundness of her belly was slight, but her form was so slender it wouldn't be long before she would not be able to hide it.

But Gray saw it.

He splayed his fingers wide across her belly.

"How far gone are you?"

A shudder racked her body. Her voice was low and choked. "I did not realize it was so obvious."

"How far, Claire?"

His tone jabbed at her, rapier sharp. "Four months," she said at last.

"And this is what you want, Claire? Another man raising my child?"

"What! You expect me to believe that you welcome this babe?" The question was fairly hurled at him. "That you will take care of him as a father should? You, a husband? What is this newfound morality? These newfound principles? You are the last man I would expect to do the honorable thing."

"You doubt my morals? You question my intent?"

"Morals! You have none. You proved that when you murdered my brother! And if you think I will marry the man who killed him, you're mad."

Tears scalded her throat. The piercing score of his gaze was like a knife thrust deep in her breast.

"This child is mine," Gray said fiercely. "Can you deny it?"

"You know I cannot." Her tone was bitter.

"This changes everything. There is a child at stake."

"It changes nothing. My child will grow, knowing he is wanted. Lawrence will be a far better father than you!"

"Do not fight me, Claire. You are going to marry me if I have to kidnap you."

"You would not dare!"

There was a flat, stifling silence. "Do not test me."

He meant it. Heaven help her, he meant it!

She hated his cold finality.

"I will see if the reverend is still here." He started to leave the room.

Claire was stunned. "What?" she said faintly. "You mean to do it . . . now?"

He turned on her with fire in his eyes. "You planned on being wed today. And so you shall be."

Hers met his in fiery rebellion. "Such an eager bridegroom, then! Should I be flattered, Gray?"

His jaw clenched. He said nothing, but cast her a thin-lipped glare.

She lifted her chin. "I must speak to Lawrence."

He was going to argue. But by God, she would remain uncontested.

Finally he gave a terse nod. "I will send him in."

Claire sent a pointed glance at Gray when Lawrence entered. He didn't retreat to the foyer but remained in the doorway. There was naught but haughty pride in Claire's expression when she looked at Gray.

"Will you close the door please?"

Gray complied. Reluctantly, it was clear.

When they were alone, Claire turned to Lawrence. "I never meant for this to happen. I am so, so sorry."

"He is the father of your child, isn't he?"

She had never divulged the identity of the father, and Lawrence—kind, giving soul that he was—had not pressed her.

She nodded. "Yes. Do not blame him, Lawrence. Perhaps—perhaps I should have told him."

In all truthfulness, she had not thought that Gray would care. She truly hadn't.

"Lawrence, you are a good man. A good man and a friend. I hope in time you can forgive me."

He smiled slightly. "Already done, Claire. I would have you make me a promise, though."

"Of course."

He clasped both his hands in hers. "If you are ever in need of anything, Claire, promise me you will come to me. And I promise you that I will always be here for you. Always."

"You are too generous, Lawrence. But I promise." She squeezed his fingers.

A scant quarter hour later Claire returned to the chapel.

It was hardly the wedding of her dreams. *But,* argued a little voice inside her, *neither would it have been so with Lawrence either.*

Upheaval raged inside her. She was pale and quiet during the ceremony, her legs shaky. Beside her, Gray's face was like a mask. She could discern nothing from his expression, not anger, not pleasure or *dis*pleasure. When he took her hands and spoke his vows, her hands were icy cold in his. She dreaded the moment he would kiss her.

It did not come. It might have been a dream, so preposterous was it.

The thought unveiled before she could stop it. She began this day expecting to end it as Lawrence's bride.

Instead she was Gray's.

Chapter Fourteen

They didn't leave Wildewood until the third day of their marriage. Gray had decided he might as well see to changes of the estate management as long as he was there. A part of Claire resented him fiercely. This was her home, not his. She couldn't stop the thought burning through her: it should have been Oliver taking over as lord of the manor.

Not his killer.

When night fell on the day of their wedding, Claire's nerves were wound taut. She wondered almost frantically if Gray expected them to sleep together as husband and wife. She did not broach the subject when she announced her intention to retire. She left him in the study. She spent much of the night straining to hear footsteps coming down the hall. It was near dawn before she fell into a restless sleep.

Gray spent the night in a guest room.

Claire was on tenterhooks the next night as well. But again Gray did not join her. Perhaps, she decided cautiously, in light of her pregnancy, he wouldn't.

The third day after their wedding, they left Wildewood. Gray told her they were going to Brightwood, his home in Dorset. The journey there would take about three days. Claire queried him about his home there, but his manner was stiff. If the oaf could not be civil, she decided, so be it. The less discourse between them, the better.

The morning of the second day of their journey, she woke miserable and tired; it was as if a boiling sea resided in her innards. By noonday she discovered that being jostled in a carriage did not set particularly well. Her stomach heaved. She had to ask the driver to stop.

Gray opened the door and pulled down the step. Claire barreled past him. Nausea welled up in her throat and she fell to her knees.

Her breakfast was lost in the bushes. To her utter mortification, it was Gray who held her and wiped her face. Claire leaned back against his shoulder, welcoming the enveloping strength of his arms around her. He slid a cloth down the slender grace of her throat. She was totally oblivious to the hunger in his expression as she turned her cheek into his neck.

"You should have told me you were a bad traveler," he said gruffly. "I'd have set a less strenuous pace." Gray was also upset with himself for not realizing it sooner.

"But that's the thing! I've never in my life been a bad traveler."

"You've never been with child before either."

Claire sucked in a breath. There was something odd in his tone.

No. She was mistaken.

He helped her upright. "We'll stop at the next town."

"There's no need for that, you silly man."

A slow-growing smile etched across his face.

"What is it?" she asked.

He hiked a brow. "I have been called many things, Claire, but I don't believe anyone has ever called me a silly man."

By the time they arrived at Brightwood, her strength was sapped. She was drained, both physically and emotionally. Gray took in her weariness.

"Would you prefer dinner in your room?"

"Yes, please." She was grateful.

The housekeeper, Mrs. Henderson, showed her to her room. It was huge, more than three times her room at Wildewood. There was a small sitting area in front of the fireplace. Claire sat with her head leaning back. She wondered vaguely if his room was next to hers. But no, there was a door beside the armoire. She tore her attention away from it.

A maid named Paulette brought her a tray, then helped her into her nightclothes. Rosalie was to follow later with the rest of her wardrobe. She climbed into bed, exhausted.

Claire felt much recovered when she woke. The room was done up in yellow and white, a little too bright for her tastes.

She was aware of the maid's puzzled look when she rose from her bath. There was no disguising the thickening of her waist and belly anymore. Her gowns were tight about her bosom as well. She sighed.

"I'll settle the question right now. Yes, I'm carrying a baby."

There would be gossip in the servants' quarters that day, she decided.

Paulette flushed bright red. Quickly, she said, "I can let the seams out of your gowns if you like."

Claire flashed a smile. She liked the girl. "Thank you. My maid Rosalie will be arriving soon with the rest of my clothing. She's started with some others, but it would be much appreciated if you could sew the ones I've brought."

Sitting at the dressing table, Claire let Paulette brush her hair. "Your hair is lovely, my lady," Paulette said. "So thick and shining. Would you like me to braid it and twist it up on your crown?"

Claire smiled. "Certainly." She liked the girl's forthright manner. Paulette caught her hair up in her hand and separated it into three long ropes. While she worked, she told Claire the names of some of the servants.

"Mrs. Henderson has been the housekeeper back when"—was it a pause? Or did she stop short?— "for quite some time now." Quickly she went on. "Edgar is her husband, and the estate manager for his lordship." A host of other names followed. Claire decided she would have to meet everyone before she could remember who they were.

"We were surprised when we learned that the master was coming home." Paulette braided her hair with quick efficiency. "We scurried to work to have all in readiness when he arrived."

Claire was puzzled. "Why?"

"Oh, mum, he hasn't been here for—oh, my word—why, it's surely been three years now. Shortly after the accident." She shook her head. "Oh, look at me, now. Mrs. Henderson would be most displeased if she learns I'm prattling on."

Three years! He'd been gone for three years? How odd. What man would leave his estate for three long years? And what accident? Claire was puzzled—and curious, too. She sensed Paulette had been about to say more but caught herself before she did. She wanted to query her further, but another maid came in and announced that breakfast was served.

Gray was sitting in the dining room when she entered. He stood politely.

"Good morning, Claire."

"Good morning to you, sir."

"I trust you slept well?"

"Thank you. I did."

Claire moved to the sideboard, where an ample breakfast had been laid out. She helped herself to eggs, plump sausages, and toast. The eggs were perfectly cooked, the sausage as well. But her stomach began to pitch.

"Are the sausages not to your liking?"

"They're wonderful," she said quickly. A flush crept into her cheeks. "I . . . um . . . I fear that . . ."

There was an awkward pause. "It will pass."

Claire was annoyed. Who was he to think he had the knowledge of a physician?

"You must be curious about your new home," he said.

"I am."

"Then let me show you."

They spent the next few hours strolling through the house and grounds. To Claire, the house was immense, much larger than Wildewood.

They walked through the grounds, well tended but brown and bare with the coming winter. When spring came, no doubt there would be a riotous explosion of color.

Spring. Spring would bring the birth of her child.

They ended up in the corridor outside her room. Claire opened the door but didn't enter. Instead she turned to Gray, feigning an air of nonchalance. "Where is your room?"

She could clearly make out the suddenly tense line of his jaw. "The next room to the right," he stated coolly.

"I see." Claire's heart had picked up its pace. She stepped across the threshold and pointed to the door next to the armoire. "There is a door locked in my room."

Gray said nothing.

"Does that lead to your room?"

Was he offended by her bluntness? She could have sworn she heard his jaw lock. "Yes."

His forbidding expression kept her tongue in check. But she couldn't withhold the thought that sprang high in her mind. Was it to keep him out? Or to keep *her* out?

A ridiculous thought.

Claire linked her fingers together before her, marveling at her boldness. "I am unsure of my role here."

"You are mistress here." He was curt. She could still clearly make out the tense line of his jaw. "You will tend to all the duties that entails."

Her chin rose. *"All* duties?"

His mouth was tight.

"I expect to be treated as a wife. More to the point—" She swallowed. "—I would like to make clear whether you will expect me to . . . to—"

"Share my bed?"

He seemed to take great pleasure in the words. Claire swallowed. "I will if you wish it."

Not that he would want to, she expected, given her condition.

"Gray?"

He looked at her with murder in his eyes. "Let us be quite clear, then." His tone was clipped and abrupt. "There will be no need to come to my bed."

His expression was glacial. Claire very nearly fell back. She found it difficult to believe this man capable of love.

"There is one more matter," she said, forcing herself to go on. "This room. Was it your wife's?"

"You are my wife, Claire." His tone was edged with ice.

Her eyes flashed. "I believe you know what I mean."

"Yes."

"Is it possible I might know her name?"

Time spun out to a screaming silence. "Lily," he said at last. "Her name was Lily."

"Thank you." Her chin lifted a notch. "May I have your permission to redecorate?"

"Redecorate anything you want. Have the bills sent to me in London. Now, if you have finished, I would like to be on my way."

Claire blinked. "On your way?" she repeated.

"I'm returning to London."

"What . . . now?"

"Yes." He turned and walked away.

She was too shocked to say a word. Fury began to mount. Why, the bastard! Good riddance to the man, then!

One month later, Gray sat in the Duke of Braddock's study. On the corner of the desk was a half-empty, finely etched crystal decanter.

Two lazy curls of smoke drifted to the ceiling. Gray had long ago tugged off his cravat. Both had just had several glasses of Irish whiskey.

Clive guided the rim of the decanter into both glasses. Leather creaked as he leaned back.

"Well, Gray, I do not envy you your predicament."

Gray flicked the ash from his cigar. "An annulment is not an alternative."

"No," agreed his friend. "There's no question about it." Clive shook his head. "I still can't believe this has happened."

Gray's mouth twisted. "I thought she was— how shall I say this?—quite experienced, given her marital status." Well, that wasn't quite true. A voice in his head intruded. *You recall thinking she'd not been wed for long.* The other voice argued, *Who would have expected a widow to be a virgin?*

"She deceived me, Clive. All that time she deceived me."

"You killed her brother," Clive pointed out.

"That wasn't meant to happen. You were there, for pity's sake."

"Nonetheless, it did." Clive studied him. "Have you told her that her brother was the first to fire?"

Self-loathing swelled. Claire had called him a murderer. And he was. He was all that and more. His hands were stained with blood.

Gray gave a tired shake of his head. "For what reason? Would that make it any easier for her? He's dead. That doesn't change what happened."

"And it doesn't change that she's expecting your child, Gray. Man, whatever came over you?"

He grimaced. What, indeed. If he'd known she was a virgin, he wouldn't have . . . He let loose a self-deprecating curse. Controlled himself? It was a lie. Even if he'd known, he wouldn't have been able to stop. No power on earth could have stopped him.

His mouth tightened. He was a man of utmost discipline. Even in bed. He didn't like being out of control.

He clenched his teeth. Out of control . . . That was how he'd felt with Claire in his arms. He'd been driven by the blood rushing hot and thick in his veins, desire scalding every part of him. Burned in his memory was the feel of her body beneath him—memories afresh—her belly rubbing against his as he plied her legs wider. He relived the mind-shattering instant he seated himself inside her—as far as he could go—the way her breath dammed in her throat. Christ, he could still feel her!

Clive leaned back in his chair. "You surprised me, Gray, when you said you took her to Brightwood instead of returning to London."

"I won't subject her to ridicule. For me, it doesn't matter."

"How long has it been since you had been at Brightwood?"

Pale blue eyes glinted. He didn't appreciate the reminder. "Three years," he said tersely. Three years since he'd vowed never to return—except in his coffin. "What can I say, except . . . things change."

Clive watched him closely. "Yes. You can hide her away at Brightwood and resume your life here in London."

A self-derisive scorn filled his chest. Claire had called him a murderer. And he was. He was all that and more.

That was exactly what he had planned. He would return to his life in London. Yet in this past month, scarcely a moment had passed that Claire hadn't been on his mind. Lady Hastings had let him know she wasn't averse to sharing a bed with him again. She, too, was a widow. But her curves and smiles left him cold. He hadn't lain with a woman since Claire.

And most unexpectedly, his conscience prodded him. He'd thought he lost it long ago.

"What about the babe, my friend? Is there any question the child isn't yours?"

"No," he said tersely.

Clive studied him. "I can only imagine how difficult it must have been to return home after so long. After Lily and—well, I don't think I need say it."

A dark shadow blotted Gray's soul . . . He'd missed Brightwood. He hadn't realized how much until he walked through the doors. The past closed in, memories he could not lock away. Damn Clive! He was reminding him of everything he sought to forget! It had taken every ounce of willpower he possessed to walk into his home. Every breath was like fire in his lungs. Even Clive didn't know the truth—

"It was inevitable, Gray, that you return. I know your pride in everything your family has built—"

"You are right," Gray bit out. "You can't know."

And Gray couldn't know that Clive hoped he would finally confront his demons.

"Go home, Gray. Go home and tend to the business of your life. Little one on the way or no, many a man would envy your position. She's a damned beautiful woman, my friend."

Gray's mouth tightened. He raised his glass high with false heartiness. "Well, then, to wedded bliss. Wedded bliss with the woman who despises her husband above all else."

He drained his glass.

Chapter Fifteen

*C*laire threw herself into her new life and home with resolve. In all but the main rooms, furniture had been covered with sheets. It was as if all had been held suspended—left in a state of limbo. Her days were busily spent instructing the staff and taking charge of the household.

It was also the holiday season. The Yule log was cut and carried in, lit on the twelfth day before Christmas. Brightwood was abrim with something the Sutherland household had not seen for many a month.

Laughter.

There had been too much pain this last year, so little to lift her spirits. But now it was enchanting, she decided, the house decorated with ribbons and wreaths and greenery. Fir boughs filled the air with the scent of Christmas. It lifted Claire's spirits.

With the presence of a husband or not, she was determined to celebrate the holidays and welcome the new year with gusto.

And the wonder of new life.

For with the advent of the new year would come the birth of her child. Next year she'd be cradling her babe in her arms. She placed her hand over the growing mound of her belly.

"I'm waiting for you, little one. I'm waiting."

A letter arrived from Lawrence, an inquiry as to her health. Claire wrote back, a very brief note to say she had happily settled into her role as wife and prospective mother.

She didn't know when her husband would return to his country estate—or even if he would. Truth be told, she reiterated stoutly, she didn't care if he ever did.

Hah!

There was a surprise visit one day from a physician, Dr. Kennedy, a bewhiskered man who walked with a cane.

It grated a bit, for Gray had surely sent him. If he wanted to know how she was, then he could come see for himself!

"Has all been well with you, my lady?" The doctor's eyes and manner were kind.

Claire nodded.

He looked her up and down.

"You appear well, m'dear. Have you felt the child move yet?"

Claire blinked. She couldn't imagine a life moving inside her.

"I confess I wouldn't know even if he did."

The doctor laughed. "Just so you are aware, many women say it feels like the flutter of a butterfly."

Claire looked doubtful.

"It will doubtless be soon," he said. "If this little one is like his father, he'll be a fine, strapping lad. His mother was convinced he would be a giant—and from the look of her, it looked to be true!"

Claire was aghast at his frankness.

"Now then. I fully expect your well-being, madam, but I will return in a month or so. Summon me if you feel that all is not well."

Later in the day, she was just coming down the grand staircase when Mrs. Henderson opened the doors. There was a sudden rush of air.

Claire's heart lurched. For an instant she thought her eyes deceived her.

It was Gray. Considering that he said nothing about returning, she was surprised to see him.

And, heaven above, seeing him made her heart catch oddly.

He removed his hat, gloves, and overcoat and handed them to Mrs. Henderson.

He looked up. "Claire! There you are, my love."

My love? She almost rolled her eyes.

He was dressed in vest, jacket, trousers, and boots. Her breath caught as she took in his appearance. Of a sudden, the air seemed filled with his presence, vitality, and power.

His gaze had yet to leave her face. Claire was starkly aware of it. She stood near a table of flowers to the left of the stairway. Gray stood halfway across the entrance hall.

"It occurs to me I've been remiss. We've yet to share our first kiss as husband and wife, haven't we?"

Claire's chin came up. "Do not mock me."

"I do not mock you. Now come. Kiss your husband."

Her lips pressed into a straight line. She remained where she was.

"I'll count to ten, Claire."

Her stomach clenched. Doubt crowded her mind. What was this devil about?

Gray crossed to where she stood. "Time's up," he said softly.

Her lashes closed. Their lips touched. Did she lean forward? Or did he?

His mouth was warm. Not demanding, but persuasive. Oh, so persuasive!

She pulled back. Her breath came in soft pants.

His gaze settled on her lips. "You've also not yet welcomed me home, Claire."

"Oh, stop!"

His hands had settled on her waist. Claire flushed. Her waist had thickened since they'd last seen each other.

His mouth closed over hers anew. This kiss was longer. It deepened until his tongue traced her lips. Her senses hummed.

Once again she was the one who pulled back.

His gaze had yet to leave her face. "Another," he said softly.

Her lips parted. "What? Again?"

He gestured toward the ceiling. Claire looked up.

They stood beneath a sprig of mistletoe. It flitted through her mind that she must have it removed.

And then every thought fled as sparks showered through her. It felt so good, this kiss . . . *his* kiss.

She was acutely aware of the quickening rise and fall of her breast. His mouth still claimed hers. This was the longest, the best, the sweetest kiss of all. There was a spinning sensation; Claire instinctively clutched at his jacket.

"Careful." His voice was husky in her ear.

Her throat was bone dry.

"Why are you here, Gray?"

"This is my home."

"Oh, bother!" she said. "You gave me no indication when you would be back, if ever."

"I apologize." Those intensely blue eyes seemed to scour her features. "No more episodes?"

"Episodes?"

"Have you been well?"

"Yes." She paused. "And what if I had not?" Stupid woman, why had she said that?

"I would have come straightaway."

Liar. Her gaze slid to his. He lifted a brow, as if in remonstrance. Beyond that, his expression gave nothing away. How could he be so composed?

"I confess, Claire, I thought you would have let me know how you fared."

"And I thought you would let me know if you ever intended to return."

"Touché. It seems I've not married a quiet little sparrow, have I?"

She trembled, still flooded with the taste of him, the woodsy smell of him. Oh, but it made no sense! All at once he made her feel safe and protected, in a way that had never happened before. She wasn't in need of protection, dammit!

She mustn't allow herself to be thus swayed. Only a fool would do so.

"The servants said you hadn't been home in several years. I understand that's when your wife died. I know such things can be difficult."

Gray's jaw went tight. He wasn't ready to discuss Lily yet. And how dare she pretend to know what was inside him. How dare she pretend to know what he'd endured.

Claire had noticed his withdrawal. She sensed him closing her out.

"Today is Christmas Eve, Gray. I arranged for the servants to leave early, so they can spend it with their families."

"That's generous of you."

"It was a tradition we upheld at ho—" She caught herself. "My family upheld every year."

"You needn't be defensive." He smiled slightly. "We've always done much the same."

She needn't be defensive, he said. But she couldn't help it. One month they had been wed. And she knew no more of him than she had the day they married.

Not surprising, considering the circumstances of their marriage. Claire ignored the nagging little voice in her mind.

His gaze scanned her features. Claire felt herself flush.

"You look tired," he said softly. "Why don't you rest for a while?"

"Oh, no," she protested, "I couldn't. That would be rude."

He had already taken her arm and turned toward the staircase. "You forget, I'm not a guest. You hardly need entertain the master in his house. In fact, if you don't go, Claire, I vow I'll put you to bed myself. Yes. Why, perhaps I should carry you—"

Put her to bed!? Claire's eyes widened. She stepped out of reach. "There's no need," she said quickly. "I am on my way."

His gaze followed her all the way to the landing. Claire stopped there, unable to resist glancing back.

He was staring up at her with penetrating eyes. No sign of a smile broke his lips; it was somehow disturbing, that expression. She fled down the hall to her room.

She lay down on the chaise lounge near the window. She hadn't thought to sleep at all, but drifted off almost as soon as she closed her eyes.

She woke much later to the sound of her name. "Wake up, Claire, or it will soon be morning."

It was Gray. Her thoughts still murky with sleep, it gave her a start to find him sitting on the edge of the chaise.

There was a light coverlet over her.

Who had put it there? Gray? Rosalie? No. It was Gray. She wasn't sure how she knew, but she did.

The thought of him watching her sleep was disconcerting.

She sat up quickly. Wisps of hair had slipped from her chignon. She tried to tuck them back with her fingers. No success. They escaped once more.

Gray reached out. He pulled out several pins and inserted them again, taming the unruly strands with brisk efficiency.

"Thank you," she said breathlessly.

One corner of his mouth turned up. "Perhaps I should hire on as your maid."

Claire felt herself color, unsure of what to say.

Taking her hand, he pulled her to her feet. Memory flooded her, a scorching revival of the way Gray had touched her that night—and where he had touched her. There had been so much promise. But then came that rending invasion. She wondered if she would ever be able to face him without remembering.

Nor was she the only one who thought of that night with scorching intensity. Gray was all at once reminded how tight and small she was in that instant he planted himself deep inside her.

"Supper is awaiting us in the dining room." He offered his arm.

A light supper was laid out on the sideboard. When both were finished, the dishes were removed. Gray summoned the servants, then dismissed them. They left, all but Mrs. Henderson, who had been granted the next few days off instead.

They moved to the drawing room. Claire poured tea for herself, while Gray had port. After stirring the fire, he set aside the poker and his glass, then moved to the sofa where she sat. He pulled a small, beribboned box from his breast pocket.

"Happy Christmas," he said.

Claire blinked.

"Open it."

She didn't want to. Something bitter washed

over her; she couldn't help it. A gift? Was this his way of making up for Oliver's death? Theirs was certainly no ordinary marriage.

With a fingertip, she opened the catch.

Nestled on a bed of red velvet was a diamond necklace. It was breathtaking, flashing and gleaming as it caught the lamplight in myriad colors.

"Do you like it?"

She touched the dazzling stones. Beautiful as they were, they felt . . . cold. Just as her smile felt . . . cold.

She couldn't explain why—or perhaps she could. Throughout the day, she'd been keenly aware that this was her first holiday without her father and Oliver, now more so than ever.

"I have no gift for you," she said.

"I expected none." His eyes came up to catch hers. "Do you like it?"

"Oh, yes. Yes, of course. It's quite the most striking piece of jewelry I've ever seen."

"Let me put it on." He reached for it.

Her hand touched her throat. "Oh, no, no. I fear I'm not dressed for it."

For the life of her, she didn't know why she said that. All at once her eyes were so dry they almost hurt. No doubt Gray would probably mistake her reluctance for disdain.

Claire touched it. "I . . . Thank you. I did not expect such a beautiful gift." The mood had turned awkward. But all at once there was a commotion at the front doorway. She rose and followed Gray to the entrance hall.

A small, petite woman whisked through the door. "There you are, my darling!" she sang out. "Happy Christmas!"

"Mother." Gray took her hand and kissed it. "I wasn't expecting you."

"Where else would I be? It's Christmas. And I've yet to greet my new daughter-in-law." She reached for Claire and kissed her on her cheek. "I do hope you'll forgive me, child. I'd have been here much sooner, except I picked up the most wretched illness when I arrived back in London. But now I am here, and . . . welcome to the family, my dear!"

Claire thought Gray's mother—who insisted that she call her Mother Charlotte—as beautiful as she was vivacious. There was a marked resemblance between mother and son. Her dark hair was the same color as Gray's, streaked with only a small bit of silver.

"Just think, children, next year we'll have a little one to light up our lives."

So. Charlotte knew that she was with child.

A lump lodged in her throat. She didn't dare look at Gray. At least someone in the family was glad of the baby.

"Come, children. I've gifts for both of you."

There was a pair of ear bobs for Claire, a new chain for Gray's watch—and a dozen tiny little caps and gowns for the baby.

Claire was about to express her regrets, for she had no gift for his mother either. But then Gray left and came back with a beribboned box for his mother. He presented it to her with a flourish.

"From Claire and I," he said.

Charlotte opened the lid and exclaimed. "Oh, children, you shouldn't have!" She lifted a mink hat from the box.

Gray directed his gaze to Claire. "You'll find my mother likes to receive gifts as much as she likes to give them."

"And that's as it should be."

"You'll also find my mother is quite taken with hats."

"A woman can never have too many gowns or jewelry or hats," Charlotte announced. "When you are past your confinement, Claire, nothing would give me more pleasure than to take you shopping in London. I've just discovered a new milliner. You won't mind, will you, darling?"

"So long as you do not garb my wife in peacock feathers," Gray said dryly. "They look quite ridiculous."

My wife. How strange that sounded.

"You see?" Charlotte laughed. "You don't fool me, Gray. You are just like your father. He was ever so generous when it came to opening his pocketbook for his wife's pleasure."

She clasped her hands together. "Oh, but I cannot wait until next year. Lavish I shall be, the doting grandmama indeed, and shower the little one with gifts. No, don't think to stop me. Your sister has learned that I will do as I will and see that the little ones are sure to have every little plaything they desire."

It was Mrs. Henderson who told Claire that Gray's sister Jane lived in Scotland with her husband and three children.

"Dear me," Charlotte said crisply. "I'm prattling on. And look at the hour. I'll have a bit of supper . . . oh, no, dear, you needn't tend me. You scoot off to bed now. You must be sure to take your rest."

Chapter Sixteen

A s Claire discovered, Charlotte Sutherland was a woman of whimsy. She was constantly moving, flitting here and there.

Claire couldn't hold back a laugh. "I cannot believe your energy!" she said one day. "You make me feel like one of the ancients."

"That's to be expected. A woman in your condition tires easily. That is why you must rest."

Claire made a face. "Well, this woman is growing tired of being indoors. At this rate I'll be fat as a sow when the baby comes."

The weather had been dismal the last few days, dismal and cold.

Charlotte stood at the window. She pushed aside a fold of the draperies and peered out. "Oh, look! I see a bit of blue . . . oh, and now the sun!"

She turned to Claire. "Come. You are right. I wager the day will be a lovely one. I vow, too lovely to stay inside." She swung around in a swish of skirts. "What do you say the two of us go for a ride?"

"Ride?"

A peal of laughter rang out when she spied Claire's dubious expression.

"We will take a cart," she announced. "You'll certainly not be riding while you're expecting my grandchild."

"I'm not a very good rider in any case," Claire confided.

"No? When you are able, Gray will have to teach you. He's an excellent horseman. Born to the saddle, his father always said."

Of course, Claire thought wryly. She suspected her husband would settle for no less than excellence in whatever endeavor he took on.

"Well," added Charlotte, "except for the time he fell off his pony and broke two of his fingers. Of course he was too proud to admit defeat. He was back on the pony that very day. I suspect stubbornness played a part there."

Claire bit her lip, holding back a laugh. No doubt, she thought.

Snugly bundled in cloaks and furs, a blanket tucked over their laps, they set out.

Charlotte handled the roan with small but capable hands.

As Charlotte predicted, the sun came out, dazzling the frozen countryside. They trotted along, their cheeks rosy from the brisk wind.

After a while they rolled to a stop along the road. Charlotte climbed down while Claire watched, open-mouthed.

"Oh, I've no need for assistance, my dear. I am hardly as dainty as I look. Of course, I'd never climb down unassisted if we weren't alone."

She extended a hand to Claire, who shook her head. "I'm per—"

"Absolutely not! Here, my girl, let me help you."

Once on the ground, Charlotte looped her arm through Claire's while they walked along the path.

After a while Charlotte stopped.

"Look there. You see the stone fence climbing over the hill? The boundary of Sutherland land extends along that fence there." She smiled. "Gray used to come here quite often, all through his childhood." A smile creased her lips. "He's always had such pride for the Sutherland name."

Claire stared out at the hillside. Barren though the trees were, there was a kind of grandeur in the land. No wonder he was prideful.

Charlotte frowned. "What is it?"

Claire took a deep breath. "I understand he has been away for three years—until now. Was it because his wife died?"

Charlotte's smile faded.

"When I asked him, he . . . all he said was that

things change." Claire paused. "He must miss her dreadfully for it to affect him so."

"He is like many men, I think. They tend to—to close things off, I think."

They turned back to return home then. Claire napped a while, then joined Charlotte and Gray in the dining room.

When they finished the meal, Charlotte sighed. "I find I'm not yet ready to retire," she said. "Claire, are you fond of playing chess?"

Claire made a face. "Not well," she pronounced. "My—" She broke off. She had been about to say that Oliver taught her.

She kept her silence, though, not wanting to dampen the mood.

"Perhaps you and Gray will play," she finished lamely.

"Yes, come, Gray. Claire, come watch. I shall show you how it's done."

Something in Claire's breast seemed to tighten when she saw him smother a smile.

The game ended with Charlotte the winner.

She sat back with a laugh. "There, Claire, you see!"

Gray arched a brow.

"Mother?"

"Yes, dear?"

"What would you say if I told you I let you win because you're not a particularly good loser."

"Poppycock! I beat your father at many a game, too!"

This time Gray didn't bother hiding his smile. "Mother?"

"Yes?"

"Were you aware I learned from Father?"

"Indeed. That's why I came out the winner here. You played like your father."

"My point, precisely."

"Oh, bother. Next you'll be telling me that he—" Charlotte stopped short, then: "He let me win?"

"Yes."

"Oh. Oh! And all these years I thought I truly was the better player!" she said with a chuckle. "And what of your sister, Gray? The two of you played many a game. As I recall, your father taught her, too. Did you let her win as well?"

A pained expression flitted across his face.

Charlotte let out a peal of laughter. "Now you have your comeuppance, boy!"

Not long after, Charlotte rose and announced her intention to retire for the night.

"I think I shall, too," said Claire.

"Let me escort you ladies."

They descended the stairs on Gray's arms, one on each side. Claire wanted to sink beneath the carpet when they bypassed the double doors that led to the master bedroom before stopping at the door to Claire's bedroom.

Charlotte bid her good-night, and Gray opened the door and turned to her. "Sleep well." He bent and brushed her cheek with his lips.

It was the first time he'd done that. Claire stepped into the chamber and slowly shut the door. A pang went through her. Her tremulous smile faded.

Had Charlotte seen it? Had she known that they did not sleep together?

Well, now she knew.

Claire hated that the brush of his lips on her cheek was solely for his mother's benefit.

Her heart squeezed.

She shouldn't care. It shouldn't have mattered.

Yet somehow it did.

Over the next few days, Gray spent the daylight hours tending to estate affairs. Charlotte and Claire repeated their afternoon ride and walk. The three of them met for dinner, then retired.

One afternoon a light rain began to fall.

At the drawing room window. Charlotte fussed. "Oh, pooh. We shall have to spend the day indoors." She let the curtain fall back. "Wait! Claire, have you visited the garret?"

"Not yet."

"Let us go exploring," Charlotte declared.

There were many stairs to climb up to the garret. They had both begun to tire when they finally spied a door.

Reaching it first, Charlotte swept it open.

"Oh, good heavens!" She traced a finger across the arm of a chair and held it up. It came away covered with dust. She picked up a broom and swiped at the cobwebs.

The garret was a hodgepodge of furniture and trunks.

"Oh, I could see little girls exploring here," said Claire, "perhaps dressing up and playing lady of the manor."

"Oh, yes, as I recall, the children spent many a rainy afternoon here—just like the two of us!"

They explored further. "Oh, look," exclaimed Charlotte. "Here is the cradle Jane and Gray slept in."

"It's beautifully carved, isn't it? All it needs is a bit of paint." Claire admired it. "I should love to have it for the baby."

"Excellent idea, m'dear."

Claire couldn't hold back a smile. "I have a difficult time envisioning Gray as a baby."

"Do you? I believe there are several portraits here somewhere." She moved toward the wall. "Oh, look, here they are!"

Charlotte pulled it away from the wall.

"Dr. Kennedy called him a fine, strapping lad," Claire said.

"Did he, now?"

Claire tipped her head to the side. "Mother Charlotte, why do you smile so much?"

"Come see your fine, strapping lad."

Claire stepped over to the portrait. There was a young girl with dark hair who looked like Charlotte. And the boy—

There was a lad of about eight or nine years old, clearly identifiable as Gray, standing proudly beside his sister.

But Claire couldn't withhold a laugh. "My word, look at his cheeks!"

"Yes," Charlotte said dryly. "He oft had his hand in the biscuit crock. His father called him robust. Jane used to tease him that he'd swallowed a pair of apples."

There were several other paintings stacked together. Claire moved to look through them. A quick glance at the next revealed a man and woman.

Beside her there was a sharp intake of breath. Charlotte spoke quickly. "That is Gray and—"

"Yes. Yes, I know. It's Lily."

Claire heard her own voice as if she were far, far distant.

Had the world turned on end, she wouldn't have been able to tear her eyes away from the portrait. There was Gray, standing with his hand on the shoulder of a beautiful, dark-haired woman. Gray and his wife Lily . . .

And the baby she held.

Chapter

Seventeen

*A*t breakfast the next morning, Gray rose from the table. "Forgive me, Mother, but I've some business to attend to today. Shall we say our good-byes now?"

Charlotte planned to leave for Bath that day. "Yes, indeed, my boy. I hope to see the two of you soon—no, wait—the three of you."

Claire remained where she was.

Gray had moved to kiss his mother's cheek. "Safe travels, Mama." He straightened up then and glanced at Claire. "Don't wait on me for dinner," he said. "I don't know when I'll be back."

Claire didn't look up. He was short. A little abrupt. She was stung. Stupid, foolish tears rose to the surface. She'd excused herself early from dinner last night but hadn't slept well. She kept seeing the portrait in the garret. Why had Gray never told her about his child? He should have.

Pride and embarrassment held her tongue. It was something that should have come from him.

She'd managed to keep the tears at bay last night. Now she couldn't. It was no doubt the baby; sometimes it seemed like she couldn't quite contain her emotions.

She tried to blink back the tears. No use! And now Charlotte had glimpsed her distress.

When Gray had left, Charlotte took both of her hands. "It's seeing that portrait, isn't it? I cannot make excuses for Gray, but I see in your eyes that you care . . . You do, don't you?"

Claire tried to hold it back, but a half sob emerged. "I don't want to. I don't. I shouldn't! He—he killed my brother. In a duel."

Charlotte sucked in a breath. "I didn't know. And yet you are here. His wife. And Gray . . ."

"I should hate him—I did. Oh, I do! And yet so much is changing . . . there's so much I don't know." Claire shook her head. "I sense it. I know it."

"Please, dear, listen to me," Charlotte said. "He cares about you—"

"He doesn't."

Charlotte smoothed her brow. "Claire . . . already I love you as a daughter. He cares . . . oh, you're wrong, dear. A mother knows such things. And I can only tell you this. He wasn't always so harsh. So cold. He is not an unfeeling man! I beg of you, take heart. Be patient. I see a change in him . . . I think you're exactly what he needs! You've spirit enough to match him."

By the time Charlotte was ready to depart, Claire's tears had dried. They hugged—and then it was Charlotte who leaked a tear.

Shortly after she left, Claire collected her cloak and sturdy boots. Her mind reeled every time she thought of the portrait.

There was a small graveyard out past the garden that she hadn't yet explored. Now, it was as if some unknown sense inside guided her steps. A part of her marveled at the age of some of the graves. Some dated from the fourteenth century.

And then, beneath the now barren limbs of a cherry tree, she saw the marker.

Gray's wife, Lily. The name meant chastity. Purity. Claire bent and brushed the leaves away from the headstone.

Lily Eugenie Sutherland.

She had died in 1811. Three years ago, as Paulette had told her.

And Lily wasn't buried alone.

The madonnalike figure held a babe in arms. Next to the graceful lily was an angel-cherub.

William Grayson Sutherland had also passed on the same year.

Buried together, mother and son.

And it made perfect sense . . . Gray's familiarity with the birth of Penelope's baby. He'd already gone through it with Lily.

She pulled her cloak more tightly about her. It was bitterly cold. Her head bowed, her gloved fingertips clasped together before her, was how Gray came upon her.

"Claire! For pity's sake, you'll catch your death out here."

She pressed her lips together. "I am in the best of health. Did Dr. Kennedy neglect to inform you?"

Gray didn't miss the censure in her tone. So. She'd realized Dr. Kennedy had come at his behest.

"It's time for tea," he said. "Come."

"No."

Gray's eyes narrowed. "I beg your pardon?"

There was an acid bite in his tone that hadn't been there before.

Claire matched it. He saw that her beautiful golden eyes were alight. Defiance burned into anger.

Gray held his silence. It was just as he'd told Clive. He'd thought to retire his bride to the country and think of her as little as possible. But no sparrow was she.

She gestured toward the grave. "You told me you had a wife, Gray. Shouldn't you have told me you had a child?"

His silence grated.

Claire was outraged. Finally he said, "I found no need to—"

"No need!" Her cheeks burned with hurt. "You married me, Gray. No matter the circumstances, didn't I have a right to know?"

"It happened long ago, Claire."

It might have been yesterday.

"It is a part of my life that has closed."

Fool! It will never close until you let it.

He gestured vaguely. "It changes nothing in our marriage. It doesn't change why we wed. It doesn't change why we must remain wed."

Claire choked back an angry sob. How could he be so cold? The man had a will of steel and a heart of stone.

"Go back to London, dear husband. Better yet, go to hell."

He slanted an acrid smile, turning her words around on her. "I'll return to London when I am ready, Claire. And, as you see, I am not."

Gray was stymied.

He should have gone back to London—he'd planned to once his mother left. He'd told himself he wouldn't stay. So why, two full weeks into January, was he still here? In the place he'd sworn he would never return to? Once the holidays had passed, why hadn't he taken care of what business there was and headed back to London?

Doubtless Claire thought he remained to torment her. But he was the one in torment!

She sat next to him at meals, her manner cool. But the child growing within Claire seemed to agree with her. She was thriving, her hair shining, her cheeks pink and glowing. And her body . . . He chided himself for taking such avid notice. Her breasts were plump and ripe and full, her skin like purest cream, offering titillating glimpses that overflowed her gown when she chanced to bend forward. He was disgusted with himself; he felt like a randy youth. She tantalized, she teased, she tempted. He suspected she didn't even know it. But he felt himself pulled ever deeper into that spell of awareness with every day that passed.

He couldn't forget what it felt like to lay naked with her. Each day brought renewed memories. If he were to reach out and touch, he knew her flesh would be warm. The scent of lilac—the scent of her—lingered in the air. It remained long after she'd left the room. He felt like a lovesick fool. He tried to freeze his heart against his beautiful bride. It rankled that she appeared oblivious to his state.

If he didn't know better, he'd have called himself smitten.

A foolish notion, he decided with a twist of his heart.

Gray spent his days seeing to estate business. They saw each other at mealtimes, each of them polite and reserved. Claire usually retired shortly afterward.

Gray went in search of her one morning when she wasn't present for luncheon. One of the maids told him she'd last seen the mistress upstairs near the master suite.

He found her in the room next to her own. He stepped inside—

And swore.

"Claire! What the devil are you doing standing on that chair?"

Claire stayed where she was, tugging at one of the draperies. "Dr. Kennedy said—"

"I'm sure the good doctor did not intend for you to be clambering up and down like a monkey. Come down here this instant."

His jaw tight, he reached up and plucked her from her perch, swinging her around so quickly she clutched at his shoulders.

His hands steadied her. "There, you see?" He frowned. "Must I secure a companion to watch over you?"

Her soft lips were compressed. "I thought I'd move the nursery to this room. It's close to mine, and the sunlight in the morning is wonderfully bright and cheery. What do you think?"

"Whatever you wish, Claire."

"There's also a cradle in the attic. I thought perhaps we could paint it white. May I have your permission to—"

"Claire, I thought it was understood. You may decorate as you please."

She tipped her chin up. "Pray don't treat me like a child playing with her dolls, Gray. This is—"

She broke off. An odd expression flitted across her face.

"What is it?"

She bit her lip. "I'm not sure." Her hand had strayed to the swell of her belly. Her eyes widened. She was half stunned, half frightened . . . and then filled with delight, the purest delight she'd ever known.

A sound that was half laugh, half cry escaped. "I think it's the baby. It's just as Dr. Kennedy said—like the wings of a butterfly." She laughed, her eyes shining. She didn't realize she'd caught at his hand, placing it on her belly. "There! That's it. Do you feel it?"

"I'm not certain." Gray withdrew his hand quickly, then cursed himself mightily. Claire looked like a wounded doe.

He couldn't explain what came over him. A voice warred within. *This was his child. The mother of this child.* But it was like a fist knotted in his breast.

It reminded him of Lily. Of William. And it was as if a sword cleaved him keenly in two, a pain so acute he wanted to scream aloud.

Claire faced him, her eyes flashing. "Sometimes I think you wish me and this child dead!"

For the space of a heartbeat Gray was very still. Then he snatched her up against him, utterly fierce. "Don't say that. Don't ever, ever say that."

Claire wrenched away. "Go back to London!" she cried. "I don't want you here. Do you hear me? Go back to London!"

His mouth twisted. "As you wish then. I bid you good-bye."

Claire was shattered, her joy bled dry. The first time her baby moved inside her, she thought bitterly . . . Despite all that had gone between them, she wanted to share it with someone—with Gray! Her husband. Her baby's father.

She cried herself to sleep that night. And when morning came, a deep-seated resolve came with it.

This was the last time she would shed a tear over him.

She continued to redecorate the nursery. But in the days that followed, her plight weighed heavy on her mind. What would happen when this child was born?

This was his responsibility as well as hers. It was Gray's duty to provide for her and their child, and by heaven, she would not allow him to shirk it. Certainly she couldn't imagine that they would live together as husband, wife, and child.

To that end, she took it upon herself to make the choice.

She wrote to Gray one afternoon. She was blunt and to the point.

Gray,

I have come to a decision I believe you should be aware of. I have decided it would be best if I returned to Wildewood. I'm sure you will agree, it's best if we live apart. If you wish, I will remain until the child is born. It is my belief, though, that there is little point to be gained in me remaining here at Brightwood. Of course I will inform you when the child is born. Should you wish to see him, or her, of course you may visit from time to time as you wish.

With regard to our marriage, I'm sure you are aware that since we will have a child, it cannot be annulled. Perhaps that is the penance we must pay for both of us. Dr. Kennedy tells me he anticipates no problems with my lying-in. I continue to be in excellent health.

I await word from you on this matter.

Claire

She had sorely underestimated her husband's response.

In London, Gray reared up behind his desk.

"Dawes!" he shouted. "My horse!"

Within minutes he was riding hard toward Brightwood.

Claire had just moved to a wing chair in the small sitting area in her room when Gray stormed inside. He pointed at the startled maid who had delivered the tray.

"Out!" he bellowed.

Claire raised a brow, casting him an arched look. "Is it possible," she said in as icy a tone as he'd ever heard, "for you to be civil to the servants? They needn't endure the beastly moods of their master."

Gray ignored the remark. He pulled the letter from his pocket and shook it in his fist.

"What the devil is behind this?"

Claire lifted her chin. "This? I assume you mean my recent letter to you."

"I bloody well do, and I cannot help but wonder at the reason why! Have you seen Lawrence?"

His eyes impaled her.

Her lips parted. "What?"

Gray swore, a blistering, vivid curse that made her ears burn. "You have, haven't you?" Anger fed the accusation. "Did you think I'd let you run off to him with my child?"

"Gray . . . I received a note from him once, several weeks ago . . . It was brief . . . He merely inquired as to my well-being"—her chin climbed aloft—"an inquiry I've not had from you, dear husband."

"You gave me no reason to believe you wanted it. But I tell you here and now that I won't let you run off with my child. I refuse to allow Lawrence to be father to my child. You will not live with him as husband and wife!"

"And I won't allow you to take my child from me!"

His jaw thrust out. There was no give in his voice. "Is that what you think I want?"

"I don't know what to think!" The one thing she did know was that she would not yield to this cold, hard man.

Three steps brought him before her. He snatched the cloth she'd been stitching and flung it to the floor. The air between them was charged with emotion.

At the sight of the tiny little gown at her feet— sewn in love for the impending birth—a dam broke inside her. Against all reason, against all expectation, Claire did the one thing she swore would never happen again.

She dissolved into tears. Helplessly. Uncontrollably. In sheer despair.

Stunned, shocked, shaken to the depth of his being, Gray could only stare. Her expression squeezed his chest. Finally he pulled her up. His arms closed slowly around her; he gave her no chance to deny him. Somehow he'd never thought of her as vulnerable.

He felt the shudder that racked her body. Tired and exhausted, she offered no resistance when he sat on the chaise, leaning back and pulling her against him.

He had brought her to this state.

His hand hovered above her hair. "Claire. Claire, please stop."

With his thumb, he guided her face to his. His gaze scoured hers. "This cannot be good for your health, Claire."

Her throat clogged tight. "Dr. Ken—"

"Yes, yes, I'm well aware of his opinion. I begin to wish I'd never let the man near you! It pains me to see you like this, Claire. It pains me to know that I have made you weep. You are right. I have a ghastly temper."

She swallowed. "I cannot bear to live like this, with such strain between us." Her fingers curled and released in the front of his shirt.

"I only stayed in London because I thought you wanted me to," he confided. "I am the man who killed Oliver. I am the man who brought you into these circumstances. You have every reason to hate me."

Claire didn't know what she wanted these days. But she did know she didn't hate him. Far from it.

His arms tightened. She was shaking, he realized. His gaze didn't waver.

His thumb beneath her chin, he guided her eyes to his. "Claire," he whispered. "Please stop."

He nuzzled the soft skin of her temple.

Her tears were wet between their cheeks. Gray didn't care. Unable to stop himself, his mouth closed over hers.

She didn't stop him. "God," he muttered when he drew back. "I've been wanting to do that for weeks."

"Gray—"

He heard the uncertainty in her voice. Her eyes were locked with his.

"This feeling between us," he said tautly. "Deny it, Claire, but it's there. I know you feel it, too."

He kissed her again, a kiss that caught fire. Locked in the moment, locked in her, his hand slipped inside her bodice. He could feel the difference from the time they had made love. He remembered everything. Her breasts were rounder. Fuller. He toyed with her nipple, his palm grazing back and forth, feeling it tighten against his palm.

He dragged his mouth away. Desire ruled. In his head, in his heart, in his body. The need for fulfillment pounded in his rod. It strained to be free. He ached with the need to release himself into her hand. He wanted to be against her, inside her. He was a breath away from loosening his breeches . . . lifting and settling her over his rod.

She raised her face to his. Her hands splayed over his chest. "I haven't seen Lawrence, Gray. I haven't. His letter—"

His knuckles skimmed her cheek. "Shhh. It's all right."

Her eyes clung to his. "Do you believe me?"

His embrace tightened. "Yes. Forgive me, Claire. I'm as beastly as you say."

Forgive me. The words tumbled through her mind. A frisson of guilt nagged at her. Not until then did Claire realize that her thoughts of Oliver had grown fewer. And now the mere sight of her husband made her heart leap as nothing before.

He spoke quietly, his gaze direct. "I believe we need a truce, Claire. Is that agreeable to you?"

She nodded, her eyes clinging to his.

"Excellent." Gray moved her gently away from him and rose.

"Are you going back to London?" The question slipped out before she could stop it.

He shook his head. "I shall stay."

Her heart was glad of it. Taking her hand, he pulled her to her feet.

"As long as I am here," he said, "I'd like to visit a neighbor. I'm thinking of purchasing several horses for my stable. It's not far. Will you ride with me this afternoon?"

Her eyes widened. "Ride?"

"On a cart." One corner of his mouth turned upward. "I think you're some months away from being able to ride again."

It struck Claire that this was the first time she'd ever truly seen him smile. An odd little tremor went through her. Impossible though it seemed, he was even more handsome than the last time she'd seen him.

"Meet me downstairs at half past the hour."

Chapter Eighteen

*D*ressed in her warmest cloak, scarf and galoshes, Claire met Gray promptly in the entrance hall.

He tucked a lap blanket around her knees. The weather had warmed throughout the week, though the nights remained cold. Snow had begun to melt during the day, making the track rutted and rather mushy. The cart jostled along. She was acutely conscious of the way his long stretch of muscular thigh nudged hers—and felt hers against his. Her shoulder bumped his as well. There was no avoiding his closeness.

Her emotions were scattered in all directions. The memory of his kiss was still fresh. Did he regret it? She couldn't control the bend of her mind.

His attention was occupied with controlling the cart. His hands were gloved, but her gaze kept straying to them. The kiss rushed back in vivid remembrance—she had to wrench her mind away from it.

And he was going to stay. She cringed inside. Why, she had practically begged him to! But how long would he be here? How long before he returned to London? Had he resumed his old life when he was there? How many women had lain with him? Heaven help her, was she jealous? All at once her mind seemed barraged with uncertainty.

As Gray had said, it wasn't far. Despite the cold, it was a beautiful day. The sky was brilliantly blue. They passed a stand of maple trees, branches bare and naked. The sun's warmth had begun to melt the snow and ice from the branches; it was as if the world glittered with silver pinwheels.

They neared a long, white-fenced pasture. Gray pointed out the roan he was interested in purchasing. "A beauty, isn't she?"

Claire echoed the sentiment. She was unaware of his scrutiny moving over her profile.

When they rolled up to the Bennett home, Edgar and his wife Rosetta came out to greet them. This was the first time Gray had introduced her as his wife. Claire felt her face heat. It seemed odd to think of herself as Claire Sutherland.

Edgar was a robust man with ruddy cheeks. Rosetta took her inside for tea, while the men conducted their business. Claire said good-bye with genuine reluctance. Though she and Penelope corresponded often, she hadn't seen her friend for months, and it made her realize how much she missed female companionship.

The shadows had begun to deepen before they departed for home. They were perhaps a mile away when Claire pointed through the trees toward snow glistening in the sun like crystal.

"Oh, how beautiful. Is it a pond? What a wonderful place to skate in the winter."

"It's a lake. And it's deep. Not a good place at all."

His abruptness caught her off guard. "Well, doubtless it's a good place for fishing. And you'll recall," she teased, "I caught a good many more fish than you. My father and Oliver—"

She broke off. An awkward silence descended. To cover it, Claire asked if she could see another arm of the lake that stretched to the east.

Gray jumped down to adjust the horse's bridle, so Claire walked down the path toward the lake. It would indeed be a lovely spot to pass a warm, lazy day, she decided. But her pleasure was bittersweet.

She didn't know where she would be come summer—here or home at Wildewood.

The day had warmed enough that the path was slushy with snow and mud. Wanting to see the shore, she moved down an embankment, picking her way carefully. Frowning, she peered over the edge. She didn't realize she stood in the shadow of a large boulder where the ground had yet to thaw. She turned—

Her legs went out beneath her and then she was plunging through the ice.

A frenzied scream tore from her throat. Darkness was everywhere. It was cold beyond comprehension. She could not see. She could not breathe. The water sucked at her, as if to bring her down . . . down.

Terror iced her veins. She opened her mouth to scream again. Water filled her mouth; it was as if her lungs turned to frost.

Then she knew no more.

Gray gave an affectionate slap to the horse's rump. He glanced in the direction of the lake, then up at the sky. Night's haze had begun to fall. They should be on their way.

In the midst of that thought came a shattering scream.

He bolted down the path.

Never in his life would he forget the sight of ice and water closing over Claire's head. There was a glimpse of slender arms raised high, as if in pleading.

Wild panic surged. A desperate fear that plunged him back . . . All he could think was that he had to save her.

He had to save her.

He scrambled across the icy surface, praying as

never before. Her cloak was dragging her down, he realized. A frantic dive and he grabbed hold of the hem.

He broke free of the surface, one arm around her chest. He heaved her from the water. Would the ice hold her? It did.

"Claire! *Claire!*" he shouted then, while pulling her to the bank. Her eyes were closed, her body limp and unmoving, her lips the color of wax.

Dread surged high in his chest. "Claire," he muttered hoarsely. She gave a heaving cough. A wheezing breath racked her body. Her lids fluttered open.

Gray was never as thankful as he was in that moment. Relief rushed through his veins. He wrapped his arms around her.

He had saved her.

He had saved her.

They were both soaked to the skin. Gray grabbed the lap blanket in the cart. He quickly wrapped it around Claire, then carried her to the cart.

Moments later, back at the house, he yelled for help. Rosalie came running.

Claire had thought she was going to die.

Minutes later, trembling violently, she stood while Rosalie and Gray pulled her clothes off. Gray settled another blanket over her while the bath was filled. Another servant came in to build a roaring fire.

Gray dismissed Rosalie once it was full. "I'll tend her from here," he said.

She still wore her underclothes. Gray reached for them and she batted at his hands. "Let me," she cried.

Gray was undaunted. He peremptorily pushed aside her hands. His brow furrowed in concentration, he tugged her chemise down one shoulder, then the other. Ignoring her protestations, he dragged the gown from her shoulders.

Claire quivered, not from cold, but shock. Mortified, she realized she stood naked. With a gasp, she clamped her hands over her breasts.

Gray had already begun to strip. Piece by sodden piece, his clothing slapped on the floor beside hers. Shirt. Breeches. She was still dumbfounded when he stood as naked as she.

A steely arm slid under her legs. He lifted her effortlessly from the floor and into the steaming water.

What happened next made her heart leap. "What—what are you doing?" she cried.

Gray didn't answer. He was intent on warming her. Water sloshed as he climbed into the wooden tub. To her dismay, it was big enough for two. An arm about her waist, he pulled her naked back against his chest, between the vise of his legs. Her bottom was nestled intimately against his loins.

But Lord above, her teeth wouldn't stop chattering. She sank lower, beneath the surface of the water, not quite sure what warmed her most, Gray's body or the bath. Nor did she know which was worse, his nakedness or hers!

"Come," he said finally. He rose behind her and brought her to her feet. Briskly, impersonally, he dried her, then pulled a robe around her. Claire had little memory of Gray donning his. She sucked in a breath—she didn't want him to see the round swell of her belly where her child dwelled. Oh, Lord, her child . . .

Fear consumed her. "My baby!" she cried. "My baby!"

Gray's reassurance was quiet and soothing. "I sent a message to Dr. Kennedy. He'll come have a look at you as soon as he is able."

Briefly, there were others in the room then, and someone pressed a hot drink into her hand. Seated on a stool in front of the fire, a robe around her form, Gray brushed the tangles from her hair while it dried. Claire's throat locked tight. She was reminded of the other times she'd felt his fingers in his hair . . . It now seemed more intimate than ever.

He put her into bed, then dragged his robe from his shoulders and dropped it in a chair. But not before she saw him.

His chest and belly were brazenly visible, matted with curling dark hair. She didn't want to look down, but something commanded her attention, something she couldn't stop. Her mouth went dry. Her breath caught. He was so— She cut the thought short. He was climbing into bed with her!

Pulling up the counterpane, Gray brought her back against his chest once more. Burned into Claire's mind was the memory of the night he'd taken her virginity. Her heart fluttered like a trapped bird's. Gray had seen her naked. Her stomach knotted. It was as if she could feel the heated strength of his fingers sliding over her skin again. Her breasts. Belly. The secret place between her thighs.

Time hung suspended. They lay toe-to-toe. Thigh-to-thigh. Sharing warmth. Sharing breath.

She could feel his sex, every inch of him—the spear of that part of him that had made her flesh sting and burn. Her thoughts were wild and disjointed. Every time she chanced to glance at his profile, she relived those unforgettable moments when his mouth trapped hers.

His every kiss.

His every touch.

Her feelings were all blurred inside her. She was both fascinated and wary. She began to tremble again, not from cold, for Gray's body was so very, very hot! She tried to speak, but no sound passed the lump in her throat.

It was almost as if he knew what was in her mind. "Lie here with me, Claire." He stroked the slope of her shoulder. The valley of her spine. "Lie with me. Don't be afraid."

Little by little her trembling ceased. She nestled against him, her breathing deep and slow and easy.

That wasn't the case a few nights later. Claire was tired and decided to retire early. Gray was working in his study.

In her chamber, she stirred the fire. Since that day at the lake, it seemed she hadn't been able to warm herself. She crawled into bed, piling covers over her shoulders. Sleep came quickly, but it was a restless sleep.

She dreamed she was in her nightgown running blindly toward the lake. Her heart pounded. A woman raced at her heels through the snowy woods. In her arms was a small bundle.

It was her baby.

And the woman was Lily.

There was nothing where her face should have been. She didn't know why, only that the woman spelled danger. Then all at once she was at the water's edge, ice beneath her bare feet. It cracked beneath her. She sank through the half-frozen surface, her lungs burning as the frigid waters closed over her head.

Strong hands curled around her shoulders. "Claire! Claire, wake up!" She was still screaming when she realized it was Gray.

"You're dreaming. It's just a dream, love, just a dream."

Her scream gave way to a fractured sob. A strong hand smoothed a long curl behind her ear. His thumb traced across her cheeks, wet with tears. It was as if she looked through him, not at him. His expression was grim.

"What were you dreaming?"

"I was running and I—I couldn't get away." Her voice was thready with tears. She didn't want to tell him it was Lily.

"From what?" He caressed her cheek with the back of his knuckles. "Tell me, Claire."

She shuddered. "My baby . . . My baby is in my arms. And I can still feel it, Gray. I can! And she wouldn't stop chasing me. She wouldn't!"

"Who?" There was an odd note in his voice.

Claire hesitated.

"Tell me, Claire."

"It was Lily."

Gray's skin had gone ashen.

Claire shook her head. "I don't understand, Gray. It was so vivid! Did Lily die at the lake? She did, didn't she?" Her cry was jagged. "And now my baby's dead. Now it's my turn!" A sob welled inside her. Once again she could feel the weight of that small, lifeless body cradled in her elbow.

"No, Claire. You aren't going to die. I won't let you."

Her eyes were half wild. "You couldn't stop Lily and your baby from dying, could you? And now I can feel my poor, dead baby in my arms again!"

He shook his head. Taking her hand, he pressed it across her belly. "No, Claire. Feel."

There was a reassuring—and unmistakable—kick beneath her palm. "You're right," she said haltingly. "Of course you're right. It's silly of me." Her gaze moved over his face.

"But I still don't understand. I—I saw the portrait in the garret, the portrait of the three of you. And I went to the graveyard—and found their graves. I thought they both died—Lily and William—when William was born." An eerie foreboding gripped her. "They didn't, did they?"

There was a heartbeat of silence. "No," he said at last. "They didn't die in childbirth."

Chapter
Nineteen

There was a painful heaviness in his chest. Gray didn't want to remember. It hurt—like a blade thrust into the heart.

He could never forget. Never. He had spent the last three years trying.

"Lily and I had been married a year before she conceived. She wanted a child more than anything." A remnant of a smile curved his lips. "She was like that, vivacious and excitable. She was so convinced she was barren—and ecstatic when she found out she was expecting a child."

Claire's heart constricted. Clearly he had loved her deeply.

"It wasn't a difficult pregnancy. Oh, she would take to bed at times, but all in all it wasn't a difficult pregnancy.

"There was a thunderstorm the night William

was born." A sad smile curved his lips. "Dr. Kennedy couldn't make it here through the rain."

"So you brought him into the world?" Claire was gently encouraging.

Gray nodded.

So that was how he'd known what to do with Penelope.

"Lily was so happy. She tended most of his needs herself. Why, she could scarcely stand to let him out of her arms—even to me."

Claire had the sensation Gray was purging himself. Perhaps he was.

"William was a good baby, a bit colicky at times. Nothing out of the ordinary, according to Dr. Kennedy."

A feeling of helplessness grabbed hold of her heart. Had the baby taken sick?

Gray went on. "I had business in Kent one week. I don't remember why . . . but I was eager to be back, so I rode hard. It was midnight when I arrived home."

A shadow seemed to slip over him.

"William was four months old. He'd begun to sleep through the night. But that night . . . Lily was still awake."

Her foreboding grew stronger. Gray stopped. She didn't press him. It seemed he was gathering himself before he continued.

"Lily was in the nursery with him. Rocking him. William was quiet—asleep, I thought. But

Lily continued to rock him. I remember thinking she rocked him almost frantically—"

Claire's eyes were riveted on Gray's face now. His voice was half choked. She hurt . . . as he was hurting. Never in her life would she forget his expression. His torment.

It was as if he was cutting his heart out.

"I tried to take William from her, to put him in his cradle."

The muscles in Claire's throat locked tight. No, she thought. Oh, no.

At some point she had taken his hand. He gripped it so hard his nails left marks on her palms.

"She fought me. She didn't want to let go. She just kept rocking William . . . rocking him, rocking him furiously. And when I took him from her—"

It hurt to watch him. It hurt unbearably. She felt the exact moment his control began to crumble.

"William was dead. I held my boy in my arms . . . and he was dead."

Nothing could have prepared Claire for what Gray said next.

"Lily said . . . he wouldn't stop crying. *He wouldn't stop crying*, she said over and over and over."

And so was Gray now. He made no secret of it.

"She shushed him, she said. She put her hand over his mouth to stop his crying."

His features reflected a helpless despair. It was as if she could see his heart breaking. He didn't bother to wipe away his tears.

"Lily didn't know . . . she didn't realize what she had done until later. She was horrified."

Claire couldn't hold back her anguish. She couldn't help but remember her dream.

"No," she cried. "Never say that she—"

"She killed herself. She walked into the lake—and never walked out.

"I remembered other episodes," he said. "Times when she was melancholy." His mouth twisted. "It was my fault. I should have known. I should have realized what might—"

"No, Gray. No. You can't blame yourself. How could you have known? No one could."

Claire was beginning to understand. It still haunted him . . . Was this why he was so wild? So reckless? His tarnished reputation . . . Was it his way of blotting out the past and all he'd endured? His wife's death? His son's?

His mother's voice tolled through her mind.

He wasn't always like this. So harsh. So cold.

Now she knew what Charlotte had meant. Gray had loved his family deeply.

His pain reached all the way into her heart. Claire bled for him, for she, too, was no stranger to heartache. And yet a violent tug-of-war raged within her. She, too, had endured tragedy. Oliver's death could never be erased; his death had come at this man's hands yet! Was his loss any greater than her own?

Everything inside her was tied into a knot. Never in her life had she been so confused.

Her mind clouded, she didn't trust herself to speak. Her hands acted of their own volition. She drew his head to her breast and lay back against the pillow, stroking the dark hair that grew low on his nape.

In time, they slept.

Life fell into a pattern. Gray attended to estate matters during the day. Claire tended to household affairs. They dined together. After dinner, sometimes they played chess, or had tea and port together. She was not wan or pale, and continued to be in good health. But more often than not, Claire excused herself early. There were two months left before their baby was born and she tired early these days.

Oh, yes, indeed, on the surface they might have been any country lord and lady. But like the waters of a stream, calm and serene on the surface, beneath lurked a swirl of unpredictable currents.

They did not sleep together.

They did not speak of that night.

They spoke but rarely of the impending birth of their child.

Nor did they speak of the future.

And when Claire's dreams returned—and

they did return—she cried alone, too proud to let Gray know.

A frigid February gave way to a rainy March. By mid-April bountiful flowers pushed through the earth. The countryside was vibrant with color. Wanting to enjoy the sunny day, she took her sewing basket out to the garden. She seated herself on a bench and lifted her face to the warmth of the sun. Remembrance touched her. Her mother had often taken her embroidery to the rose garden. If she were to stay here—

"There you are," said a voice. "I've been searching for you."

Gray stepped through a doorway on the verandah. He frowned.

"You should have a wrap on, Claire."

"Oh, I'm fine. After such a dreadful winter, it's wonderful to feel the sun shining down, isn't it?"

"Mmm." A tacit agreement.

He stepped close, so close that she had to look up to meet see him. Claire's stomach lurched. Tight breeches tucked into his boots emphasized every powerful muscle in his legs. His loose white shirt was open at the neck, baring a tangle of dark masculine hairs.

"What is that you're sewing?"

Claire flushed, remembering the day he'd taken the baby gown she was stitching and flung it to the floor. "It's nothing," she said, holding it tight in her lap.

"Of course it's not. May I see?"

Before she could stop him, he took it and held it between both hands.

"It's for the baby," she said defensively.

"It's—very tiny, isn't it?"

Claire had the sensation he didn't know what to say. "Dr. Kennedy says it appears as if the baby will be small."

"You must take every care, then."

Her cheeks grew hot. Concern? She wanted desperately to believe it. All at once sudden yearning took hold of her. She longed for all the distance and tension to disappear, to be able to know him as a husband and father—nothing else—no remnants of the past between them.

Quickly she tucked the cloth back in her basket. "You said you were looking for me."

"Yes." He pulled her to her feet. "I wanted to tell you I've been called away. I have a small estate in Lincolnshire. The caretaker there has taken sick. I must secure a replacement until he recovers."

He paused. "I would ask you to come with me, but I don't think it would be wise for you to travel now."

Claire nodded. She sensed a curious uncertainty in him.

She moistened her lips. "Are you coming back?" she blurted.

Gray looked at her sharply. "What?"

She wished she'd never spoken, but it couldn't be undone. "I . . . are you coming back?"

He captured her chin between thumb and forefinger. "Do you want me to?"

Conflicting urges had taken hold. A part of her longed to turn and run. She hadn't known she would say that until it was already out! And now—now she wanted to lay her fingers against Gray's lean cheek, feel the slight roughness of his beard against her fingertips.

"Of course," she heard herself say. "How long will you be gone?"

His pale blue gaze scoured her features. "A week. No more."

His eyes suddenly darkened. His voice went very low. "Will you miss me, Claire?"

Before she had a chance to answer, a mask seemed to shutter his features.

"No," he said almost harshly. "Don't answer that."

Powerful arms wrapped her close. His head came down. Their lips clung, an exchange both passionate and tender. Claire was breathless when Gray finally raised his head.

He ran a fingertip down her cheek. "Think of me," was all he said.

When he was gone, she put a hand to her lips. "Hurry back," she whispered. "Hurry back."

Chapter Twenty

*C*laire missed her husband dreadfully. The days were long, but she tried to fill them with her usual activities. It had become her habit to take a bit of exercise daily, so one afternoon she bundled snugly into a warm cloak and hat and went outside. The cold was crisp and bracing, and the sun was out. It felt good. She didn't venture far, but stopped at a spot that offered a view of the road—and the house.

It was beautiful, the house sitting amidst trees that had begun to bloom. Winter was definitely receding. She paused, a faint smile on her lips.

It was not quite spring yet, however, and after a while she decided it was time to return home before she took a chill.

On her way back she spied a carriage rattling down the road and assumed it was Gray. Her brows drew together. Why was he coming home in a carriage? He'd left on horseback.

Her heart lurched. Had he been hurt?

Claire set out for the house.

The carriage rolled to a halt in front of the double doors as she approached, hurrying as fast as she could. She stopped then, surprised when it wasn't Gray who stepped out.

It was Lawrence.

Disappointment flooded through her. She hid it behind a smile.

"Lawrence! How wonderful to see you!"

"It's good to see you again, Claire." He smiled back at her, his gentle eyes crinkling. "Your note said so little . . ."

"Here, come inside and warm yourself. It's getting chilly, isn't it?"

"Indeed."

A servant appeared, and Claire ordered tea brought into the drawing room.

"Please, sit down," she invited. She waved him to a chair in front of the fireplace. Lawrence held his hands toward the fire, warming them.

When the tea arrived, Claire poured for both of them.

Lawrence blew on the surface to cool it. "Is the viscount here?"

"Actually, no." She felt awkward. "He's gone for several days at one of his properties."

"Good. We can speak freely, then."

Her guard went up. She inhaled sharply. "Lawrence—"

"Claire, please don't be alarmed. I'm on my way to visit my sister in Essex. I won't stay long, I promise." He paused. "You are well?"

"Yes. Very well, in fact. Thank you for asking." She thought of her babe. Her condition was readily apparent now.

"I've thought of you often, Claire."

She didn't know what to say. She decided to be frank. "I'm not sure how to respond to that." She fell silent for a moment. "Lawrence," she said finally, "I don't mean to hurt you, but I don't believe marriage between us would have worked out."

"So you are truly happy with the viscount?"

"We are both looking forward to the arrival of our child." She laid a hand briefly on her belly.

Did he see through her? There were still so many uncertainties. Stupidly, she felt a rush of tears sting her throat.

"Ah," he said.

It appeared she wasn't a very good liar.

But what she said was true. She wouldn't have been happy with Lawrence. And he was a dear, dear man. He deserved a woman who loved him, who could offer more than companionship.

It was Claire who changed the subject. They finished their tea, chatting about several goings-on at Wildewood.

In the entrance hall, Lawrence donned his coat then took both of her hands. "I want you to make me a promise, Claire. Should you ever need me—for anything—will you let me know?"

Her eyes softened. "I promise." She leaned up and kissed his cheek.

"Farewell, my friend."

Gray rode hard to get home. He'd missed Claire. He'd missed being home. But did she truly think he wouldn't return? Thoughts of his wife had been with him nearly every moment he was gone. He was eager to see her. In some deep-seated part of his soul, he knew something was happening inside him. Something he couldn't control.

He leaped down from his horse and tossed the reins to a groom. He bounded up the stone stairs to the wide, double doors.

At that moment the front doors opened wide.

Never in this world did he expect the sight that met his eyes.

Lawrence stood there, his hat tucked beneath his arm, gazing down at Claire, a smile on his lips.

At that precise instant, Claire leaned up.

And kissed him, damn her hide!

Gray saw red—and Claire saw him. He felt like an intruder—in his own home!

"Gray," she said breathlessly. "Lawrence was just leaving."

"Yes. I trust you are well, my lord?" Lawrence offered his hand. Gray ignored it.

Aware of Gray's eyes burning into her back, Claire descended the stairs in front of the house with Lawrence and bid him good-bye.

Inside, Gray followed her into the drawing room. Seething, he removed his hat and tossed his gloves on a table.

Claire set her jaw. "What the devil is wrong with you? You look as if you'd like to challenge Lawrence to a duel."

"Perhaps I damn well should. The last thing I expected was to come home and see my wife kissing another man."

"A kiss between friends," she said coolly.

"Friends?" His laugh was brittle. "You planned to marry the man."

Claire wet her lips. "He was on his way to visit his sister in Essex. Is it so wrong for him to stop and inquire as to my welfare?"

"How long was he here, Claire?"

"I beg your pardon?"

"How long was he here?" The harsh line of Gray's mouth matched his voice.

"Not long. I asked him to tea." She raised her chin. "I offered him the hospitality due a guest."

"What else did you offer him?"

Claire's look hardened. She couldn't believe what he was suggesting.

He gazed at her with an intensity that was

almost frightening. "Did he lay with you in your bed?"

"I will not dignify that with an answer."

"Did he lay with you in my bed?"

He presumed. She would not capitulate. He demanded. She refused.

He considered himself blunt. She considered him rude.

Most of all she despised his imperious air.

"Is he the father of your child, Claire?"

"I will pretend you did not say that," she said between her teeth. "Now please leave my room."

His jaw came together with a snap. "I will not. Need I remind you the lies came easily to your lips when we first met, didn't they?"

Her eyes flashed. "You foolish man. You accuse blindly, and for what?"

"I am a man of passion," he said tautly, "and you are my passion."

"You have no passion!" The words were snatched from deep inside her. "You have no heart!"

Desperation filled her. Moored in her breast was a cold reality. Almost from the start she had sensed his pain, his wounded soul—

There was a painful catch in her heart. Heaven above, was she falling in love with him? No. She could not. To love this man would be to betray her brother.

"Do you truly believe that Lawrence would seek to share my bed?"

Gray's lips were drawn into a thin line.

"You do." Claire was incredulous. "For pity's sake! Do you imagine any man would desire me with the way I look?" Her hand came to rest on the burgeoning swell of her belly.

Gray's gaze stabbed into hers. "You are a fool if you think he would partake of no pleasure. You are a fool if you think I would partake of no pleasure."

"You are mad!"

"Lawrence is not unaware of your beauty, Claire. No man could be unaware of your beauty. *I* am not unaware of your beauty."

He moved to where she stood near the bed. His mood was black. He was pricked with jealousy, jealousy spurred into reckless anger.

She flung out her hands. Certain she was not desirable, she did not feel desirable. In but an instant her hands were imprisoned in his. He pulled her close, so close her slippers lodged between his boots. So quickly her breath was jarred from her lungs.

His arms closed around her. His features were searingly intense. She couldn't look away. She'd accused him of having no passion. But the need reflected there stunned her.

"Come to me," he whispered. "Come to me, Claire."

She lifted her face to his. Her heart tripped. Desire grappled with reason. *He was not unaware of her beauty*, he had said. Was it true? Conscious of the babe she carried, she was shy about letting him see her.

His mouth covered hers. It was a kiss that carried with it the flame of desire escaped, a soul-shattering kiss between lovers.

She could do naught but yield her mouth. He stole her breath from her. And if she let him, he would make her yield her very soul.

It didn't matter. Claire tried to slow her pounding heart—a fruitless effort. It felt too good.

And Gray betrayed no hesitation. He divested her of her gown, pushed her chemise from her shoulders. He bared her breasts, splayed his fingers wide across full, ripe flesh as her body prepared for the impending birth. Shivers of delight danced across her skin when he touched her nipples. Drawing, sucking, pulling, it was as if she'd died and gone to heaven.

Would she regret this? She didn't care. In the heat of the moment, nothing else mattered.

Bold male fingers trespassed beneath the hem of her chemise, dragging it up to her waist. Unable to help herself, she let her legs fall apart. Her fingers tangled in the hair on his nape.

Gray had already shed his own clothing. He trembled inside. It was a heady sensation, knowing he was the only man who had touched her thus. For he did know, deep down inside.

A finger dragged up her furrowed channel.

Protecting her modesty, Claire tried to push it aside. He persisted, tracing with the wet heat of his finger, first one side and then the other.

Again.

And again. A rhythm that drove her half mad. The air around them was scorching.

"I want you, Claire. Tell me you want me, too."

It was tauntingly erotic, that touch. Her nipples were drenched with the wash of his tongue, dancing from first one and then the other.

His eyes were riveted to hers. Between her thighs, she felt herself grow damp and hot beneath his fingers. One slid within her cave, finding the spot and rhythm that would give her the most sensation. Her flesh closed around his finger, hungry and tight.

A jolt went through her. She sucked in a breath. "Gray—"

With unfailing intent, he took her hand and covered it with his own. The back of her knuckles skimmed the rough, curling hairs around his shaft. His fingers around hers, he brought her hand down between his thighs—

To close around his burning shaft. His fingers covered hers, showing her the tempo, faster and faster, pulsing in time with the throb of his flesh.

Her breath left her in a scalding rush. She was shocked—and pleased beyond all measure.

Sometime, he thought, he would feel her

mouth—her tongue—circle and close hot and damp around his velvety head.

He brought her to pleasure—how could he not? He heard her cry against his mouth, felt her throbbing around his finger, every pulse and shiver.

The trickle of her breath began to slow. He knew Claire was confused. So was he.

For this was fulfillment replete in a way he'd never known. But Gray knew he had made love to her—no matter that he hadn't yet received his own completion.

And now he would. Her thighs parted beneath the pressure of his knees. He spread her wide. His belly nudged hers—

Something stirred, there where her belly pressed his. It was unmistakable. As if he knew he was the subject under discussion, the babe moved within her, an unmistakable quickening.

Gray froze.

Gut-wrenching pain ripped through him, the most powerful wave of emotion he'd ever felt. Each breath was like fire in his lungs. This was his child. A part of him. A part of Claire. Nothing could ever change that. Nothing.

But he was torn, caught squarely between heaven and hell. Touching him—or her—feeling the life inside her . . . it was like tearing his heart out! He'd been dragged to the limit already . . .

Claire would never understand. Gray wasn't sure *he* did.

And his hand didn't leave her. Not yet. Pain ripped through him anew.

In time, Claire grew quiet, her eyelids heavy.

Gray's knuckles caressed her cheek. He brushed a stray hair from her temple. His touch immeasurably gentle, he kissed the curve of her cheek, the sweetness of her lips.

There was no sleep for him. He lay awake long into the night, his heart in torment.

S pring settled in and the days grew warmer. That night was foremost in Claire's mind whenever she saw Gray. She could not rid herself of the vision painted high in her mind's eye— the lean strength of Gray's naked body, poised against her own. Had he stopped out of concern for her? Concern for the baby? She longed to ask—

She didn't, for fear of disappointment. Fear of being hurt. He had already rejected her. She couldn't blame him, she supposed, with her ungainly presence.

There was so much between them. Words, both spoken and unspoken. Deeds, which could never be erased.

Would she ever be truly his wife? Would his heart be forever buried with Lily?

She both longed for and dreaded each night

Gray walked with her to her room. Both were polite. But distance yawned between them. She longed to cry out her yearning. Though she despaired of her weakness, she couldn't find the courage to step beyond it. She didn't want to shatter the fragile state of affairs between them.

Nor was that the only thing between them. Awareness sizzled. Whenever Gray was near, her mouth grew dry. Her heart stopped when she discovered those ice-blue eyes following her every move. Sometimes she would turn—and he was gazing at her in that disconcerting, impenetrable way he had. He was adept at shielding his feelings.

Claire was not.

In the night there was nothing between them. No resentment. No pain. She had been sleeping heavily at night. She did nothing and yet she was exhausted at day's end. Refuge? she wondered. Or curse?

But there was something Claire did not know.

Her husband lay beside her hour upon hour. And he knew if she discovered it, she might well kick him out!

He crawled from her bed at dawn.

He crawled from her bed with bittersweet candor.

The one thing that bound them together . . . could also tear them asunder.

* * *

Temperatures had warmed to hint of the approach of summer days. After being closeted inside for most of the winter, it became Claire's habit to take the buggy out each morning. Sometimes she rode the entire circuit. Sometimes she stopped and walked, simply enjoying the sunshine and fresh air. Once she stopped at the lake, but didn't venture down to the shore.

On one such day, she stopped the buggy beneath the sheltering branches of a huge oak tree. She walked away, making a sound of pleasure when she spied half a dozen strawberry plants. Sinking down, she plucked one fat strawberry and popped it into her mouth. Another followed, and two more. They were sweet and ripe, oozing with juice. She put her finger in her mouth and licked it clean.

Pushing herself to her feet, she heard a noise that came from the direction of the cart. Frowning, she looked down the incline.

It was Gray.

She watched as he dismounted and tied the reins to the buggy. A hand upon his brow, he squinted toward the little hill, then began to climb.

Claire ducked behind the massive trunk and scooted down. Something came over her then. Her eyes danced. Her lips curved into a mischievous smile. She picked up three plump berries. Half rising, she flung one toward his back.

It landed with a satisfactory *splat!* squarely in the center of his back. Red juice stained the white of his shirt. He turned abruptly.

The next glanced off his shoulder.

Two more sailed through the air, in rapid succession.

These last two landed on the front of his shirt. With a rather black curse, he strode forward. Claire ducked to the other side of the tree.

She couldn't help it; she bent down and began to laugh. Gray's boots stepped into her line of vision. Claire was laughing too hard to straighten upright. When she was finally able to rise, she discovered Gray looking anything but pleased.

A dark brow climbed high. "I have a question for you, my lady. Is turnabout fair play?"

Claire laughed harder. "I can hardly run away and escape, now, can I?"

"No, you cannot. You're mine now." His hands closed over her shoulders. "Tell me, Claire. I'll wager you were quite the imp when you were young."

"Only because I was forever trailing after Oliver."

She spoke before she thought better of it. Gray's smile faded. An awkward silence ensued. Claire decided a change of subject was in order.

"Where are you off to?" she asked.

"To find you." He took her hand and tucked it into his elbow. "Claire, I'm not so sure you should be off on your jaunts alone. What if your time comes?"

His concern made her feel warm inside.

"But now I have you, don't I?" he said.

"So you do, sir."

"Perhaps you should head back. I believe Mrs. Henderson is waiting luncheon for you."

Claire chuckled. "Yes, we're starving, both of us." Her hand rested on her belly.

Gray said nothing. He walked her down the hill, lifted her into the cart and handed the reins to her.

"Thank you, kind sir. Onward home it is, then." She nickered at the horse.

"Oh, and Claire?"

Eyebrows raised, she glanced back. "Yes?"

His grin was decidedly roguish. "You might want to wipe the juice from your cheeks, my love."

She wrinkled her nose at him. His chuckle was low and deep. Deep inside, she realized this was the first time she'd seen him smile with genuine mirth. Her breath caught and her heart turned over.

As it happened, they didn't have luncheon together. The estate manager waylaid Gray. Claire was on the verandah finishing tea when Gray strode up.

"Will you stay and have tea?" she asked.

He shook his head. "I'm hardly fit to be seen. Come, we can talk upstairs."

He took her hand and walked beside her up the wide staircase—

Into his room.

Joseph, one of the house boys, was pouring one last pail of steaming water into the large tub in front of the fireplace.

Gray's boots hit the floor. His shirt followed. Now his hands were at his breeches.

Blast her foolish naiveté! She hadn't realized quite what Gray had meant.

It appeared he intended to bathe before her.

Wrenching her eyes away, she inspected the window and every diamond-shaped pane within it. From the corner of her eyes there was a flash of impossibly long—impossibly naked—limbs as he climbed in. When the splash stopped, she cleared her throat.

"It's quite safe now." His low tone reflected his amusement. "I believe all pertinent parts are safely out of view—at least all that should satisfy my prim little wife."

A hot tide of color surged into her cheeks. Summoning the courage that was proving to be so elusive, she looked at him.

His arms were stretched out on the top of the bath, literally covered with a dark netting of hair. The plane of his chest was covered with that same thick, dark forest of hairs. It spun through her mind to wonder what their child might look like.

A boy would be a handsome child indeed, if he resembled his father. And a daughter? She would be an exquisite beauty, with Gray's ice-blue eyes and shining black hair.

Gray's eyes were alight with laughter, a laughter reflected in his tone. "Will you hand me that sponge, please?" It was around at the far end of the tub, where an assortment of brushes and sponges had been laid out.

Claire found it and gave it a toss. An odd sensation flitted in her belly. She sought desperately to still the pounding of her pulse.

Drat! It fell far short, several feet from his right knee.

Gray cocked a brow. "Hmmm. My dear, the way I see it, you have but two options. You can fetch it again, or I can stand and—"

It had already landed with a *plop* near his chest. He laughed. "There! Now come have a seat on the stool beside me and tell me what is on your mind."

"I doubt you would wish to trouble yourself with my musings," she said breathlessly.

"Let me be the judge of that."

She could tell by the way his brow arched that he would be insistent.

"Very well, then. I was merely speculating as to this child's appearance." Claire's hand rested unknowingly on the center of her belly. "If the babe is a boy, what will he look like? Me? You? I confess, a boy with your hair and eyes would be quite handsome. And a girl—"

"I daresay a beauty like her mother."

Claire caught her breath. Did he truly find her beautiful? All at once it seemed almost impossible to breathe.

Uncertainty clutched at her insides. She suddenly didn't know where to look. Droplets of water glittered like tiny diamonds in the curly mat on his chest. His nakedness made him more handsome than ever. And his eyes were suddenly smoldering, as if in a fever. She couldn't breathe, she couldn't even move as she watched his gaze slide down her neck.

All at once she needed to break this strange spell that had cropped up between them.

"Perhaps you should finish your bath, my lord."

"I would much rather finish with you to share it."

She swallowed. Surely he wasn't serious.

The gravity of his long, slow perusal lent the truth to his statement.

"Gray," she said, the pitch of her voice very low, "please do not jest with me. When you say such things, I don't know what to do. I . . . You know that I have no—" All at once she sucked in a breath.

On his back, near his left shoulder blade, his skin was pitted and white with scars.

She was aghast. "What is that?"

His lips pressed together.

"Gray! My word, gunshot?"

He neither confirmed nor denied it. His withdrawal was almost palpable.

"Were you in the war?"

"No." His tone was curt.

She ran her fingers over the uneven edges. "What, then?"

He did not shirk. Their eyes tangled.

"Let it be, Claire."

"No."

"You don't want to know."

"I do."

"No"—he cut her off—"you do not."

A sickening dread washed over her.

"Oliver?" Even as she spoke, she knew it was true. "I don't understand." Her fingers touched his back. "This—this is where the bullet came through, isn't it?"

Again that oppressive silence.

Claire was still reeling. "We were told there was only one shot—yours. Tell me what happened, Gray."

No words.

"Tell me!" she almost screamed. "We were never told that Oliver fired."

"I wanted it that way, Claire."

"Why? What did it matter?"

His mouth twisted. "Surely you know how a duel plays out, Claire. We chose seven paces.

There was an exchange of fire. He turned, I fired. Oliver had no choice but to shoot in return."

"Did you intend to kill him?" It hurt to say the words.

His mouth twisted. "Isn't that the purpose of a duel?"

He reached for a length of toweling and threw it about his naked form.

"Who shot first, Gray?"

"I did."

Liar! screamed a voice in her mind. Yet if she believed Gray, it was a betrayal of her own brother! If only she could be sure.

A rending ache sheared her soul. Never had she been so conflicted!

Gray set his lips together. "If I could take back everything"—his tone was gritty—"if I could give back anything, I would—"

"You can't, Gray. You can't."

All the closeness of this afternoon was bled dry. Claire felt as if her very soul lay naked and exposed.

"How much better if I had left well enough alone. My need for revenge . . . it brings no satisfaction." She touched her swollen belly. "This babe . . . should never have happened. This marriage was for naught. Now both can never be undone. I should have left well enough alone, Gray. I should have left well enough alone!"

Gray had donned his robe. "Claire, for heaven's sake, don't look like that."

Her skin had turned pale. He read the bleakness inside her. She turned, as if the weight of the world was hers to bear.

His jaw clenched. "Dammit, Claire, stop! Listen to me. It's too late to change what happened. But we must do what we can to make it right."

Sudden tears welled in her eyes. "Nothing can ever make this right, Gray. Too much has happened," she said tonelessly. "So leave me be. I just want to be alone."

Gray's hand fell to his side. There would be no talking or reasoning with her just now. His expression grim, he watched Claire enter the hallway. He let her go.

The door between their rooms closed. Claire stopped just inside the threshold. There was something wet between her thighs. Frowning, she lifted her hem and gazed toward the floor.

A tiny puddle of bright red stained the periwinkle carpet.

"I'm bleeding," she said, puzzled. Realization dawned. "Gray," she whispered, then it was a scream . . . *"Gray!"*

Chapter
Twenty-two

Never in his life would Gray forget Claire's stricken cry. Ice ran through his veins. Terror filled him, a frantic terror that he would never forget in all his days.

Claire was white as mist. She was bent protectively over her middle.

"What is it? What's wrong?"

"I'm bleeding," she cried. "I'm bleeding!"

Gray had already noticed the growing pool on the carpet. Her knees gave way. Swearing violently, he caught her and swung her shaking form high in his arms. "Hold tight to me, love, hold tight."

He called for the servants, who soon scurried to and fro. One dashed for clean sheets, another with a message for the stables. Rosalie spread a blanket over her bed and helped Gray to disrobe her. A messenger tore out the front gates to summon Dr. Kennedy.

"It's too soon," Claire sobbed. "It's too soon. He should not come for over a month."

"Ah, and what if this wee one is a girl?" Gray tried to tease as he helped Tina pull a nightgown into place. They wadded clean cloths and packed them between her legs to staunch the bleeding.

"It's a boy. The firstborn is always a boy."

Now was not the time to debate the point, Gray decided.

She flung out her hands. "Gray?"

"I'm here, sweet one."

"Please. Don't leave me."

"I'm here, Claire. Feel me." With one hand he stroked her cheek to quiet her, the line of her jaw. He squeezed her hand, cupped possessively in his.

When Dr. Kennedy arrived, he banished everyone from the room to examine Claire.

"All of you, out. Let me have a look at my patient."

Gray didn't budge.

The doctor peered at him over his spectacles. "My lord? It's been my observation that husbands do not cope well in situations such as this."

Gray set his teeth. "I'm the one paying your fee, Doctor, and I am not leaving."

"Very well, then." He frowned his disapproval.

"You may stay, but sit across the room there and don't interfere with my examination."

Gray nearly lost his temper with the man but finally relented.

Dr. Kennedy nodded and stroked his mustache from time to time as he examined Claire. At the conclusion of his assessment, he patted her shoulder.

"The bleeding has nearly abated, my lady. A good sign. Now tell me . . ." He took off his spectacles and polished them with his handkerchief. ". . . what were you about when this bleeding began?"

"Nothing—that is to say, I had just arisen"— Claire glanced at Gray—"and when I did, there was a peculiar . . . I do not know how to say it . . . heaviness . . ."

"A sensation of pressure?"

"Yes, yes. A feeling of pressure from within. Doctor, surely that was not the pains of labor?"

"No, child. I don't believe so. If this child can come to within two weeks of when he is due, with the best of care I believe all will be well. However," he propped his glasses on his nose, "there are certain things you must do, and others you must curtail."

Gray reached for Claire's hand where it lay on the counterpane. Her fingers curled tightly around his. He wondered if she was even aware of it.

"You must rest as much as possible. A nap in the morning. At least two in the afternoon. You must curtail your walking. And no stairs, by any means."

"No, of course not," Claire hastened to assure him.

"There are other things you must refrain from as well." He glanced pointedly at Gray.

"What? What things?" Claire tried not to panic.

"My good woman, how shall I say this with regard for your tender ears—you must refrain from . . . conjugal relations."

Claire's mind was slow to respond. "Conjugal relations?" she echoed blankly.

Gray rescued the good doctor—and had a laugh at the doctor's expense. "My love," he stated smoothly, "I believe Dr. Kennedy means that we must refrain from the same marital relations that resulted in your condition."

She shook her head. "My con—" she started to say. Her eyes went suddenly huge. Her face flamed.

There were a few more instructions, then the good doctor left.

Gray gripped both her hands within his own.

Very quietly he spoke. "You frightened me, love."

"Gray, Dr. Kennedy is gone. There is no need for pretense, for silly endearments."

"Of course, sweetheart." An unexpected grin played at his lips. "But what makes you think they are silly?" He suddenly realized how naturally they had come to him.

Claire stared down at their joined hands. "Do not jest with me," she said, her voice very low. She paused, then lifted her eyes to his. "You know what this is, don't you?"

Gray frowned. "What?"

"I know why this is happening. This is our fault, Gray. Our penance. For all the lies. He punishes me for my desire to avenge Oliver's death. He punishes both of us for Oliver's death. For my sins. For yours."

"Claire, stop this at once."

"You didn't want this baby. Neither of us did. We have to pay for all the lies. We weren't married when we lay together. Both of us are sinners."

"You are distraught, Claire."

"No! Don't you see? This is what He intends. For my babe to die. Because I don't have anyone but him. I don't have anyone but my baby and that's why He will take him."

Her fingers twined in the front of his shirt. There was fear laden in her voice. Her mouth was tremulous. His heart twisted. She was wrong, he thought. She had him.

"I don't want my baby to die, Gray. I don't."

Her agitation was growing.

The doctor had left a draught containing laudanum in case she needed it. Gray reached it on the bedside table.

"Drink this." Coaxingly, he tipped the glass to her lips.

She sipped, and had finished nearly all of it. But suddenly her hand came out and she knocked it from his hands.

"No! It's poison, isn't it? You want my baby dead! You want me dead. Then you will be rid of both of us."

Her accusation pierced him to the quick. "You are overwrought, Claire."

"No!" she screamed. "You never wanted him in the first place. You never wanted either of us!"

"This is not good for you or the child. Calm yourself, sweet."

She fought him. Tears slid unheeded down her cheeks but she fought him with all the strength she possessed, until he had no choice but to wrap his arms around her and hold her until her struggles began to subside.

But all at once she twisted again. "I'm strong," she burst out. "I'm not weak like Lily. I won't kill my baby like Lily. I won't!"

Gray froze.

I won't kill my baby like Lily.

Pain ripped through him. He felt as if someone reached inside and squeezed his heart. Claire quieted in his arms while the laudanum took hold. He stroked her back, the shallow groove of her spine, the movement of his fingers monotonous. He held her, his mind beset by haunting images of the past.

Lily's face spun through his mind. Shame pricked him deeply; he hadn't thought of her for oh-so-long now. And William. His boy. His son. To this day he wondered what had gone wrong. How he could have changed the outcome. Somehow, he had failed her. Failed them both.

His child kicked. Kicked strongly against his father's hand.

Claire was right. No woman could have challenged him as she had. She was strong and brave and he'd never known a woman so courageous.

She fell into a light sleep, her hair tickling his chin. But there was no such release for him. There was no peace. He knew only that he couldn't lose her, too.

Because then he would be forever damned. Forever lost.

Forever alone.

Claire was not a good invalid. She disliked being treated like an invalid. To pass the interminable time, she read. She played cards. She played chess with Gray when he was able. She sewed for the baby, who surely had enough little blankets and gowns until he was ready for small clothes—she was still convinced she carried a boy.

By the end of two weeks she was at wit's end.

Perhaps Gray and the household were as well.

He walked in one afternoon to find her sitting on the window seat, gazing outside.

His brows shot immediately up, his mouth down. "Did you summon Rosalie?"

"Whatever for?"

"Claire, do not test me. Did you summon Rosalie or Paulette?"

"I did not."

"Did you summon anyone?"

"No, good sir."

He glanced pointedly from the bed to the window seat. "Then how, pray tell, did you get there?"

"How do you imagine I got here?" she asked with amusement.

Gray scowled.

"Very well, then. The usual way," she replied, wrinkling her nose. "No, wait. I have it. I ran as quickly as I could."

He leveled on her a shrewd consideration. "Were you cheeky as a child, my love?"

"I daresay I was. Were you, sir?"

Her pulse had picked up its rhythm. She was rather enjoying the banter.

"I daresay I was, as well. Now, then, I thought you might like to go downstairs for dinner tonight."

Gray had been taking a dinner tray along with

Claire every evening thus far. Her eyes glowed. Her little trill of delight warmed him to his soul.

"A little persuasion might be in order," he said.

"Persuasion?" Her tone turned breathless.

"Mmmm." He was studying her mouth.

Claire's heart began to pound. She wet her lips. "Please? May we have dinner tonight in the dining room . . . please?"

"That was not the kind of persuasion I referred to."

"It was not?" Her cheeks were flushed a most becoming shade of rose, Gray decided. "What sort of persuasion did you mean?"

A slow smile crept across his lips. "Perhaps I should show you."

"Yes," she agreed. "Perhaps you should."

Bending low, strong fingers curled around her nape. His thumb beneath her chin, he brought her mouth to his. There was a low sound deep in his throat. He lifted her upright, enough so he could lean back, angling her against him, pulling her atop him.

Snug between the vee of his legs.

It was a kiss that began with melting sweetness. Only moments after their lips touched, it turned hungrily fierce. Claire's lips parted—yielded—to the demand in his.

She shivered. Every fiber of her body clamored. She loved the scent of his cologne; relished the wide plane of his chest against her breasts.

It spun through her mind that she didn't want to go downstairs. She didn't want to ever leave his arms.

All at once he shifted. Her heart nearly stopped. His mouth demanding, almost wild now, he guided her against his rod, the rock-hard measure of desire.

It was Gray who broke away. His laugh was shaky. "I am hungry, Claire, so hungry that I think we'd best go down for dinner."

Thus began their to-and-fro wordplay.

Gray encountered Claire one afternoon, halfway down the stairs.

She bit her lip. "I only meant to dash down to the library. Five minutes, no more."

"You won't be dashing anywhere," he said sternly. "Most certainly not up and down these stairs. You should have rang." An arm beneath her knees, he swung her up and into his arms.

Claire pouted.

One of his brows climbed high. "Is this a display of temper?"

Claire locked her fingers around his neck. He had stopped at the landing, halfway up the stairs.

She glanced pointedly to the top of the stairs. "Is this a display of strength, milord?"

"I am prepared, dear lady, to hold you this way forever."

Her heart constricted. She wasn't certain how to take that.

"And what if I said that I am prepared to let you?" she asked daringly.

The truth was, she loved being near him like this. She loved the feel of his chest, the power of his arms as he held her high, seemingly with no effort.

"I would tell you it's not a test of strength, but a test of the strength of my desire."

She was stunned at the fervor burning in his low declaration.

But far more thrilling was the hunger in his expression.

L ittle by little Claire resumed a limited number of duties. Either Mrs. Henderson's or some of what had been her usual activities; planning the meals and so forth. Though she still chafed at having to remain in her room, Gray soberly reminded her that a fall could kill both her and the baby.

She loved Gray's evening visits. They ate dinner at the small table before the fireplace. There was no need to have it lit, for the weather was warm.

She sat at the dressing table one night, brushing her hair. The day had been hot, and she'd already changed into her nightgown. Gray usually watched from a chair while enjoying his nightly brandy. Several times his intense regard made her heart trip.

Claire was daydreaming, lost in thought. She tugged her hair over her shoulder and began to absently pull her brush the length of her tresses. She tilted her head, unaware that it revealed the long arched sweep of her neck. A warm kiss on her nape gave her a start.

"Expecting someone else?"

Claire wrinkled her nose at him. Sensation still rippled across her skin. Almost nervously she separated her hair into three long ropes and began to braid it.

"Leave it," he said quietly.

A tremor of reaction went through her. In the mirror on the dressing table, their reflection gazed back at her. Wide golden eyes met hazy blue.

He gave a half smile. "Your hair is beautiful, Claire. Too beautiful to hide."

Beautiful. She felt the most absurd desire to cry. Indeed, the heat in his eyes made her feel beautiful.

"How are you today?" he asked.

"Very well, thank you." The reply was automatic.

"Mrs. Henderson said you did not feel well this afternoon."

Claire made a face. "Mrs. Henderson exaggerates. I chanced to mention that there was a wee bit of an ache in my back."

"Where?" Long brown fingers slid down her spine. "There?"

"No—"

Gray changed his position a little. "There?"

"Not quite. No, wait! Almost . . ."

"Let me help." To her shock, he pulled her back onto the adjacent bed so they both lay stretched out on their sides, Gray's chest to her back. It was almost as if the length of her lay tucked into him.

Her throat grew dry. He touched a spot at the small of her back and rubbed.

She sighed. "Yes, Gray, there . . . Yes, the very spot."

He gently massaged until she released a long breath.

"Better?" he whispered.

"Yes. Much. Thank you."

His hand was still anchored on her hip. "You need only call me, Claire, and I am yours to command."

He was teasing, surely . . . The thought was cut short as he brushed her hair aside, revealing her nape again. His mouth replaced his fingers, his tongue touching that very sensitive spot he'd kissed a few seconds earlier, a lazy rhythm that made fiery shivers ripple across her skin.

One hand came around to guide her bottom quite cozily into the notch between his thighs and lower belly.

Claire sucked in a breath. She could feel not only his thighs, but a rather telling ridge that seemed to grow with every breath.

She made a low, choked sound.

"Do I frighten you? I don't mean to, Claire. Tell me if I do."

"I . . . no."

"Then why are you trembling?"

With desire, she thought. With uncertainty. Not fear. Never fear.

"Gray, what Dr. Kennedy said about refraining from . . . conjugation . . ." Suddenly everything seemed to spill forth. She couldn't stop it. "Do you mean to say that men and women . . . and with a child on the way . . . Do you mean to say they want to?"

Gray chuckled. He couldn't help it. "I presume you mean—oh, what was it I said?—marital relations."

"Yes . . . yes!" Claire was aghast at herself.

"Yes, they can—and they do—make love."

Make love. How could the two of them make love when there was no love between them? Passion, yes. God, yes. But love? Her heart twisted. Was love this yearning—burning—to the depth of her soul and beyond? The thought sprang forth and she couldn't stop it.

She wasn't aware that he'd removed his shirt until she felt the hair-roughed plane of his chest against her back. Her heart stood still. A little shock went through her when he pulled her back against him once again. His hand laid claim to the curve of her belly. His breath was heated against the side of her neck.

"I want you, Claire. Can you feel it? I cannot hide all that fills me—all that calls to me. You make me burn inside."

His whispers were hot and torrid. He spoke of desire. Need. Passion.

But he did not speak of love. Never love, and God help her, her heart cried out.

And then he kissed her, turning her onto her back. Fingers along her jaw, he trapped her mouth beneath his. Claire had no choice. She relinquished all control, submitting to the demands of his mouth and hands. He kissed her with aching tenderness, with slow, languid thoroughness, a kiss that suddenly turned fierce. Afire with longing, she returned his kiss with a yearning that matched his.

The neckline of her nightgown was wide and deep. Gray pulled it down to expose one ripe breast. With his thumb he circled the swollen peak, in taunting play. Claire moaned. Her head arched back. Her hands came up to tangle in the dark hair on his nape. Her eyes riveted to his, she watched his tongue circle her nipple, pulling it into his mouth and sucking hard, leaving her shining and wet. A bolt of sheer delight shot through her.

He wasn't finished.

Once again his mouth covered hers in blazing conquest. His tongue traced the outline of her lips. Lean fingers slid beneath her hem, trailing up the insides of her thighs. Claire's heart lurched. Her lips parted. Her hands came up to clutch his shoulders.

"Gray—"

His whisper was smothered against her cheek. "I won't hurt you, Claire. Trust me. Just . . . trust me."

His mouth captured hers once more. He kissed her endlessly, until he felt her thighs give way beneath his touch, until she was breathless and dizzy. His fingertips traced along her furrowed cleft in taunting play.

Her heart pounded and she nearly cried out. She needed his touch, there at the base of her thighs. Her hips came up, a wanton, seeking movement. Then she felt it, the tips of his fingers drawing rhythm, up and down her cleft, teasing damp, plump flesh. Everything inside her seemed to cry out. She was desperately waiting, desperately wanting to feel his pulsing shaft drive home inside her. In some far distant part of her, she acknowledged that they did not dare.

But Gray knew another way. He was aware of just what she needed. His fingertips traced soft, weeping flesh, a taunting foray that drove her half wild. His thumb brushed there, at the pearl hidden deep within her cleft. With sheer abandon he plied her, exposing her core, swirling around and around in sweet sensation until at last everything exploded inside her.

He rolled to his side, taking her with him. His hand at his breeches, he allowed his member to escape. Strong fingers captured hers. With unerring intent, he curled his hand around hers, slowly shaping her fingers, one by one, against his rod. She could feel every throb, every pulse-beat of desire, against her hand. Her palm was filled with the burning thickness of his shaft. His hand now moved apace with the pounding of his heart, almost wild now. His breath scraped faster and faster, in tandem with his heart. The cords in his neck stood out while he sought the tempo to end his torment.

When it came, the cords in his neck stood taut. He buried his head in the hollow of her shoulder.

Spent, it took a moment to recover. Gray's laugh wasn't entirely steady. "There, sweet Claire. You see? There are indeed other ways to make love. Everyone safe, everyone satisfied."

Claire's face was still burning, aware of what he meant—aware of who he meant. Him. Her. Their child. A boast? Reassurance?

She spoke then, the words that would haunt them both, shearing him, branding him, scalding him inside and out.

Her voice was barely but a breath. "Did you do such things with Lily?"

Too late, she realized her blunder. Too late, she realized his pain. She fought to hold back tears. She stared at him with eyes that stung painfully—yet he beheld her with a blistering regard, his expression icy as the northern seas.

"Gray!" His name came out half choked. "I am sorry! I—I don't know why I asked such a thing. Please! Forgive me!"

She hadn't wanted to bring Lily into this moment. She didn't want to bring Lily between them, and call forth the very thundering emotions that stood between them now.

"You're right," he said through lips that barely moved. "You shouldn't have."

Claire had never heard him so cold. And now, through her own folly, she feared that Lily would be forever between them.

"I want no harm to come to you or this child, Claire. Yet it seems we are ever at odds. Therefore, I will remove myself from your presence."

He gave a stiff bow and grabbed up his shirt.

Shock flitted across her features. Claire was stunned. She pushed herself to a sitting position. "Gray! What are you doing?"

He thrust his arms through the sleeves of his shirt. "I would have no harm come to you or this child. I thought we could make this marriage work, Claire. But all we do is hurt each other."

It was like a stake, his speech, driving deeper with every word. All the tension was thrown up between them once more.

"There are things that must be settled between

us, but now is not the time. There have been too many angry words."

Claire stared at him. It was like one of her nightmares. An icy shroud surrounded her. The tumult inside her was almost unbearable.

Gray shook his head. "All this"—he waved a hand—"is not good for you and the child. You need peace and quiet. Rest. I can grant you that, Claire. I *will* grant you that. The child must come first. I'm sure we are in agreement on that score."

Claire stared at him in shock. The tentative peace they had built was crumbling all around her. The urge to cry was overwhelming. Her lungs burned with the effort it took not to break down.

"Gray," she whispered, "what are you saying?"

"I think we are better apart, Claire. At least for the moment." His lips twisted bitterly. "Can you deny it?"

"I can and do!" she cried.

"Can you?" He picked up a tear glistening on the end of a fingertip, which he now gently rubbed, and held it high. It sparkled in the light. "I think not," he said. In her mind he was almost being deliberately cruel. "It seems all I do is hurt you."

Tears scalded her throat. But Claire had her pride, too, and she would guard it as closely as he. "Go then! Run away, Gray. Turn your back and run away the way you have done these past few years. Go and leave me be!"

Something flitted across his features. A spasm of pain? "I will be in London should you need anything. Stay well." He dropped a hand on her hair, a kiss on her cheek.

Once he was gone, sitting amidst the covers, heartbroken, Claire began to sob. It was all a lie. His tenderness. His concern. Foolishly—so very foolishly!—she had blinded herself. She had feared her heart was in peril.

Heaven help her, it was.

A fortnight later Gray was on his way to his town house during a light spring rain. The night was half over when he'd made his excuses and left the Dudley ball. He had stood idly on the sidelines, there in presence if not in spirit. And while Clive went home with a lovely French widow, Bram and Lucian with their own lovelies, he went home with only his thoughts for company.

In his study, he lit a candle. Another drink and perhaps his head would be buzzing enough to sleep.

A figure rose from the chair across the room. "I grow tired of making excuses for you," came a voice from the shadows.

"Mother! What are you doing here? I thought you were in Bath."

Charlotte Sutherland arched a brow. "I received a letter from your wife. She told me you were in London. She assured me all was well, but I sensed something was wrong. I might add, my son, that your presence here embarrasses me."

Gray dropped his hat atop his desk, then sat. "You needn't make excuses for me, Mother. If one needs to be made, I will do it."

Charlotte's regal chin came up. "It's not for you that I make them. It's for your wife. It appears to be up to me to salvage the family name."

Gray sighed. "You exaggerate, Mother."

"Perhaps. Perhaps not."

"Mother, I assure you it's better this way—"

"Better . . . better! How can it be better for anyone with you in London and your wife at Brightwood alone, waiting to birth your child? How long since you've seen her, Gray?"

Gray stiffened. "This is not your affair, Mother. However, to reassure you, I make certain I have word from Dr. Kennedy every day. And I just received a letter from Claire yesterday. She tells me she is well."

Charlotte's blue eyes flashed. "You are a fool, Gray. Don't you know your own wife? What Claire said was one thing. I daresay her well-being is another."

Gray went pale. "She assures me she is in good health, Mother. If Claire were in any danger, Dr. Kennedy would have—"

"Kennedy! I never did like the man. You

should know, Gray, the man is quite terrified of you. I imagine he's loath to report her true state. But I wonder, Gray, does that allow you to live with your conscience?"

Indeed, guilt arrowed through him. But he resented his mother's presence here. If it were anyone but her, he would have tossed her out on her ear.

"Are you trying to shame me into returning to Brightwood?"

"No woman should go through this alone. Lily did not. Is Claire any less your wife than Lily?"

"Do not tell me how to live my life, Mother."

"Well, perhaps someone should! You don't seem to be doing a very good job of it! Now, I'm going to Brightwood to see to your wife's well-being. She should have a shoulder to lean upon, and it appears mine is the only one willing to do so!"

Chapter Twenty-four

*W*ith every sunset, Claire sent a prayer of thanks heavenward. The bleeding was gone—it had been since before Gray left. Thank heaven her child remained safely sheltered in her womb.

But time seemed never-ending.

More than ever, she feared what the future would bring. Her spirit dragged. Conflict raged in her breast. Confusion warred in her heart. Charlotte came to visit, went off to London for a few days, then returned. Indeed, if not for her presence, Claire was not sure what she would have done.

She was careful to hide her melancholy—or so she thought. During the day she was ever ready to summon a smile. But the nights . . . oh, the nights! She was afraid of the storm of feelings she felt for her husband—

The nights were never-ending.

Everything inside her was bruised. He had hurt her immeasurably, and that pain was still ripe within her breast. Yet her heart was in peril—filled with feelings she could not banish. He had run when Lily and William died, afraid—unable—to confront his pain. It haunted him still. Claire was certain of it. And now he chose to run once more, to turn his back—

If only he would run back to her!

When Charlotte returned to Brightwood again, Claire didn't delude herself. Charlotte had doubtlessly seen her son. Claire asked her point-blank if she had.

Charlotte didn't lie. "I did," she said quietly. "I will not make excuses for Gray. He is a fool, and so I told him." She touched Claire's shoulder. "I'm sorry, Claire. I realize now I was wrong to see him."

"I think he still loves Lily." Claire's voice was half choked.

"She was his wife, Claire. William was his son. Is that wrong?" Charlotte chided her gently.

"You don't understand. There's no room for me and my baby."

"I think you're wrong, dear."

"He can't forget her. He will never forget her. His bitterness holds him hostage."

Claire wondered fleetingly if Charlotte knew

the truth, that Lily had killed little William. But no. Somehow she knew Charlotte didn't know. Gray had shared that with her . . .

And no one else.

If only he could share his heart! She was desperately afraid he could never forget his heartache.

"I was wrong to come here," Charlotte said. "If you wish me to leave, I will."

"No! Please stay and see your grandchild!"

They tearfully embraced.

Indeed, the very next day after Charlotte's return, the master walked through the door.

Claire was at the top of the stairs. Gray looked up at her.

"Hello, Claire," he said.

Her knees went weak. Her pulse gave an odd little leap. The very sight of him did that to her. A part of her ached for him to touch her. To kiss her into oblivion until nothing else mattered. But the very next instant, raw pain splintered through her breast.

"Why are you here?" she asked.

"This is my home." There was an edge to his tone.

All at once Claire was reminded of what he'd said . . . *I thought we could make this work. But all we do is hurt each other.*

Almost wildly she wondered . . . Was it shame

that had brought him back? The thought made her ache bitterly. Was it shame that would bind them, then? She wanted none of it.

She wanted his heart.

But her own had been wounded. He had hurt her, hurt her immeasurably. It would take time to heal—

Time and love.

And she was tired. Tired of hiding her feelings. She didn't know if she could find it in her to forgive him.

He began walking up the stairs. His gaze never strayed from hers.

"No!" she cried. "I haven't changed my mind, Gray. I told you I don't want you here. Go away! Go back to London!"

Gray paid no heed, but continued past the landing. At the top, he extended a hand.

Claire knocked it away.

"If I could travel," she told him, "I wouldn't be here. I'd be home at Wildewood. As soon as we are able, the baby and I will be gone."

"Do you think I wouldn't find you?" He took her by the shoulders. "Claire," he said softly. "Look at me."

What little control of her senses shredded. All at once she was trembling. Two fat tears rolled down her face. "You leave me no pride. You leave me nothing!"

He drew her shaking body into his arms.

She wrenched away. "Don't touch me," she said. "I'm a fool, Claire. I should never have left."

"But you did, Gray, you did. Do you truly think you can come home and pretend that nothing happened?" It was the naked truth.

"I'll make it up to you, I swear." Gray could see her vulnerability. He could *feel* it.

Claire's exhaustion gave way to despair. It seized her heart like a clamp. "Why did you have to come back?" she sobbed. "Why?"

He brought her shaking body close.

Her fists were poised upon his chest, as if to push him away. "Release me, Gray."

"Claire, please listen."

"No!" she screamed. "You didn't want me. You didn't want us!" She pushed back from his chest.

Then she felt it—a gush from inside her. She stared down, puzzled by her wetness, the puddle on the floor.

Above her, Gray sucked in a breath. "It's the baby. The birth waters . . . The baby is coming. The baby is coming!"

She was in Gray's bed, she realized. His face swam above her. How strange, to be here in his bed, not hers. He stood near the foot of the bed. But his expression was most odd; he appeared almost frantic. But there was pain in her belly— her back—pain that squeezed, then receded.

It was the baby, she realized. Everything came

flooding back. It was too early. Too early, and she couldn't erase the choking fear inside.

Pain seized hold of her once more. Tightening her muscles, she held her breath, as if she could hold it back.

"Claire! Let it come, child. You will lose your strength."

It was Charlotte. Her image danced before Claire's eyes. Gray said something to her. Charlotte hovered near while Gray sat next to her. A hard arm supported her, pulling her clothes from her shaking body. He was ever so careful as he pulled a clean nightgown over her head and thighs, letting it settle over her knees. Her womb tightened once more.

He took her hands. "Don't fight it, Claire. Trust me."

"Why are you here?" she asked. Her voice was half stifled. His name trembled on her lips. "Why are you here?"

Gray's eyes darkened. Her cry tore at his soul. It struck him then . . . "You didn't think I'd be back, did you?" Guilt enveloped him. Had she thought she must endure this alone?

He cursed himself. With a cloth he wiped the beads of sweat from her forehead. "Claire," he whispered. "Trust in me. Believe in me."

"No! I want my baby!" She pushed his hand aside and gave a half-strangled cry. "I will fight you, Gray. I won't let you take my son."

She would have said more, but another spasm knotted her belly.

Gray laid aside the cloth and gripped her hands. They were ice cold.

Through a fog, Claire stared at her husband. Through a haze she heard him.

"Breathe, sweet. That's the way. There now. Rest while you can."

A painful wave of emotion broke inside her. Not a pain in the body this time, but an ache of the soul. His tenderness wrenched at her.

There was another contraction, more intense this time. She heard Charlotte urging her, Gray coaxing her through the next spasm and the next.

"You're close, love, so very close."

From the foot of the bed came Charlotte's voice. "Yes, Claire, yes!" She was half crying. "Oh, darling, just one more contraction!"

Claire gave a half moan. Her hips came off the bed. Her head came off the pillow. A tremendous pressure built between her thighs—

A wavering little cry filled the air.

Tears glazed her eyes. Charlotte held a tiny little body. She cried while Charlotte cleaned the baby, then she held out her hands.

"Let me see him! Let me see!"

Charlotte wrapped the little one in clean clothing while Gray helped his wife sit up. Claire was shaking with weakness. Charlotte placed the bundle into her waiting hands with a laugh. "Prepare yourself, darling. Your son is a daughter!"

Charlotte departed to leave the new family to themselves.

Claire undid the swaddling to unveil the tiny little form, needing to see that all was well. She uncovered ten fingers and ten wee toes and kissed every one of them.

She stared raptly at the babe. "Isn't she the most beautiful baby ever?"

"Of course she is." His tone was husky.

A tremor of gladness went through her. Gray's smoky blue eyes made her heart turn over. She fought exhaustion as long as she could, savoring the feel of that warm little body in the crook of her elbow. She tucked the baby at her side and slept.

Gray swallowed. The babe was tiny, with a sweetly impudent little mouth—like her mother. Her head was perfect, covered with golden brown fuzz.

Memory gripped him. The first time he'd ever seen William came rushing back. He'd been so proud, so very proud of his son—

Darkness spilled through him. He felt locked in time. He couldn't banish the remembrance of that horrible night when he held his son's lifeless form in his arms. So limp . . .

And he could not bear it. A tearing pain ripped through his heart. He acknowledged a bittersweet truth—a painful truth that must be faced.

He was grateful the child was well. He loved her—how could he not? She was a part of him.

But he felt trapped, his soul blistered with guilt. He should hold the babe, he knew. Yet he couldn't bring himself to. It hurt too much. So much he wanted to scream his pain aloud.

He stretched out a finger toward her face . . .

It dropped to his side.

His heart squeezed. He and Claire were forever joined together in blood now. The proof lay nestled at her side. But the birth of this child did not assure him of happiness, none of them. If only it could be so easy!

The torment in his breast was beyond his control. It seared his very soul.

And in that mind-shearing instant, he bitterly acknowledged that Claire must never know. It would tear her apart.

No, he and Claire could not remain at odds. They had clashed too many times. They must find a way to live together.

He would never walk away from her.

And he would never allow Claire to walk away either.

Somehow he was going to have to find a way to make her forgive him.

A way to make her love him.

Somehow.

Chapter
Twenty-five

*L*azy spears of sunshine tumbled through the draperies into the room, lighting a path of gold. Claire slept heavily. She couldn't remember ever being so exhausted. She recalled being wakened twice to have the babe put to her breast. Stretching slowly, she realized she was still in Gray's bed.

She bit her lip as she moved her legs. She was distinctly sore between her thighs. The babe lay sleeping in the corner, in the cradle she had found in the attic.

Rosalie fluffed up her pillows. The maid had no sooner finished than there was stirring from the cradle. Claire's gaze homed in on it. The baby gave a forlorn little wail.

Rosalie picked up the baby, looking a little uncertain.

"Many ladies do not nurse their own," she said

as she changed the baby's swaddling. "My lady, his lordship has engaged a wet nurse."

"What!" Claire was already shaking her head, a vehement no. "I will see to her nourishment, Rosalie." She was adamant.

Rosalie settled the baby into the crook of Claire's arm. Joy lit within her. She experienced her first thrill of motherhood. With the baby nestled against her breast, her heart turned over. She cradled the baby's tiny head as love poured through her, pure and sweet. Pressing her lips against the fine golden fuzz, she decided that nothing had ever felt so right.

A little awkwardly, she lowered the bodice of her nightgown. With the exception of observing Penelope's little one, she had no other experience with childbirth.

This would be an adventure for them both, she thought.

Her daughter fussed, rooted around and found what she wanted. That tiny little mouth tugged at her mother's nipple and quieted.

Another thrill of motherhood.

There was a knock and the door opened. Claire looked up eagerly, thinking it was Gray.

Charlotte peered inside. Claire motioned her forward.

Charlotte moved to the bedside and kissed her on the forehead. When she drew back, there were tears in the older woman's beautiful blue eyes.

"Oh, don't cry," Claire laughed, her own eyes misty. "You'll have me blubbering as well."

The babe slumbered at Claire's breast. Charlotte let that tiny hand grasp her finger.

"You look beautiful," she said. Her smile widened. "Both of you."

Claire smiled up at her. She tried for an even tone. "Has Gray seen her yet?"

"My child, Gray was here throughout. Don't you remember?"

"Of course. Now I remember. It appears he has taken on the role of midwife." Claire explained how Gray had helped assist Penelope. Charlotte paused, then softly told her that Gray had been present at little William's birth as well.

"Now," Charlotte said crisply, "I beg of you, dear daughter-in-law, may I hold my grandchild?"

Claire relinquished her. Charlotte stayed a few minutes longer, and when her mother-in-law announced that she was returning to London, Claire was genuinely sad. She had come to love Charlotte like a mother.

"This is a time for new family, for mother, father, and child." Charlotte was resolute. "But of course I'll be back for the christening—should this precious little girl have a name by then." Charlotte arched a brow.

Claire smiled. "I'll let you know the instant we've decided both." Another order of business would be the choosing of godparents.

She and Charlotte made their good-byes, a warm leave-taking.

Rosalie bustled in with a tray for her mistress. Claire wasn't particularly hungry but knew she needed the strength. While she ate, Rosalie had her bath prepared. Still no sign of Gray. Claire was suddenly fearful. Where was he? Was Charlotte wrong? Perhaps he had merely put on a face for his mother. Was he displeased with a daughter?

Such was the bane of her thoughts.

Slipping into a hot bath, she winced as her torn flesh hit the water. With the next breath she sighed and let the waters soothe her aching muscles. Leaning her head back, she soaked until the water grew cold.

Rosalie brought a clean nightgown. Claire sat in a chair in front of the fire and combed her hair dry. She instinctively began to plait it, then suddenly stilled.

Gray liked it long and loose.

The thought had no more than crossed her mind that she heard a sound at the door. All at once he was there, standing on the threshold wearing breeches, boots, and loose white shirt. He looked so tall and starkly masculine, her knees felt weak.

She reached for a nearby table to push herself upright. She'd been a little unsteady when Rosalie helped her into the bath.

"Hold!" he ordered. "Those pretty little feet are not to touch the floor for at least a week."

Striding across the carpet, he swept her up into his arms effortlessly. When he didn't move, Claire raised her brows expectantly.

His regard was very solemn. It roved her features as if to take some silent measure of her.

His gaze settled on her mouth. Claire sucked in a breath, a little uncertain. She had thought, for one mind-spinning instant, that he was going to kiss her. She wanted it so much she ached inside.

And his eyes were still fixed unwaveringly on her mouth.

Claire lifted her chin. Her lashes drifted closed. She made it clear what she wanted.

But the kiss was not to be. Instead, there was a whisper of breath as he brushed his mouth fleetingly across her cheek.

Had he kissed Lily this way after the birth of William?

Claire despised the renegade thought that spun through her mind, hating herself for it. No. He would have kissed Lily long and lingeringly, a kiss that spoke of pride and love.

She ducked her chin. Her throat was hot. She didn't want Gray to know what was in her mind. She had her own pride, too.

He lowered her to the bed, pulling the counterpane up and over her lap.

He sat then, reaching for her hand. His fingers began to toy with hers. Claire's heart caught. His smile, that sudden smile—so rare and so precious—shot straight into her soul. Tears sprang to her eyes.

Gray caught her chin. Her tears speared him to the core. "Claire! What's wrong? Why are you crying?"

She could not say precisely where they came from. A sudden vulnerability flooded over her. Perhaps it was the irony of it all.

If not for Oliver's death, if not for Lily's and William's, this beautiful child of theirs would not be.

Such was the burden of truth.

But she could never say that to Gray. "I'm fine. Truly."

He stared at her intently. "Are you certain? I remember Lily sometimes—" He broke off. A strange expression flitted across his features. No doubt his memory had been stirred.

Claire sensed his difficulty. This wasn't easy for her either. She didn't want Lily to forever stand between them.

"It's all right, Gray. We should be able to let Lily's name pass between us with no awkwardness. Now tell me, please, what about Lily?" This was their first day as parents and she didn't want a battle.

Gray acknowledged that she was right. "Lily was prone to crying spells from time to time after William was born." His tone grew quiet. "They were there, then all at once gone. Perhaps I should have told Dr. Kennedy." There was a pause. "Speaking of which, do you remember Dr. Kennedy's visit?"

"What," she muttered, "you mean he deigned to come?"

Gray chuckled. "Yes, for a time. He had another delivery to attend to."

"I am immensely grateful that you were here, then." Claire was still pale, but her eyes were pure topaz, a-shine with love for her daughter. Gray caught his breath, bringing her knuckles to his mouth.

"And I, too." He meant it. "He pronounced both of you in good health."

"We should name her, Gray."

"Indeed."

"What if I decide her first name, and you choose her second?"

"A fair bargain."

"Then I choose . . . Alexa." Claire paused. "Alexa was my mother's name," she explained. "And perhaps we might call her Lexie."

Gray tipped his head to the side. "Then perhaps we should have Charlotte as her second name. My mother will be greatly pleased."

Claire tried it out on her tongue. "Alexa Charlotte Sutherland." She smiled. "What do you think?"

Just then Alexa Charlotte Sutherland gave a little cry from the cradle in the corner. The covers started to shift.

Claire laughed. "Let us take that as approval."

When Lexie fussed at noonday, Rosalie was quick to change her. Claire readied herself, easing to a sitting position in the bed, her arms uplifted and ready to receive her daughter. When her maid carried the baby toward the door, Claire protested.

"Rosalie! What are you doing?"

"I am taking the wee one to her wet nurse." The maid was nervous.

"We discussed this," Claire said sharply. "I will nurse my daughter."

"Yes, my lady, but . . . his lordship told me again that my instructions are to take her to her wet nurse." Rosalie was clearly uncomfortable with her position. "Perhaps you should know, too, mum, he has ordered the little one be moved to the nursery."

Claire didn't know if she was more incensed or incredulous.

"Give me my child, Rosalie."

The girl delivered the child into Claire's waiting arms.

"His lordship will not be pleased, mum."

Claire muttered a not particularly flattering remark aimed at "his lordship."

Her hands were shaking as she tried to turn little Lexie toward her breast. But Lexie was impatient, frantic; she had been kept waiting long enough. Claire touched her cheek to direct that oh-so-tiny mouth toward her nipple. But as soon as the baby latched on, she lost it and cried the harder.

The more Claire tried to direct her to the breast, the more the baby fretted and wailed in earnest.

"What is going on?"

It was Gray. He stood on the threshold.

Lexie was still in her mother's arms. His gaze swung to the maid. "I thought it was understood that Alexa should go to her nurse to feed."

"No." Claire clutched her baby. "I am her mother and I will feed her!"

"Claire, listen to her cry! A wet nurse knows how to deal with a hungry infant."

"And I will learn. She is my baby, Gray!" No doubt sensing her mother's discord, the little one's cries had reached a fevered pitch.

"Be reasonable, Claire."

"Reasonable! I know what you want, Gray. You want to take her from me. You would take her!"

"I'll do no such thing."

Claire fought to keep hold of her senses. "You already are!"

"Claire, of course I am not. Well-born ladies do not nurse their own."

"To hell with well-born ladies!"

Lexie had at last caught hold of Claire's nipple and began to suck. Claire adjusted her gown, trying to cover her flesh, unwittingly baring more of her smooth, milk-white flesh. She didn't realize how Gray's eyes fastened hungrily on the sight.

"If you think you can take her from me, you— you will not! I will take her where you cannot find her."

He showed no sign of allowing her privacy. "Is that a threat, Claire?"

"It is a promise. Now allow me to feed my babe!"

He fell silent. His gaze had fastened on the fullness of pale, pink flesh, open to his gaze. He made no attempt to hide it, to give her privacy.

When the babe finished with a gentle hiccup, with trembling hands she pulled her nightgown up over her bare breast and covered herself. The babe was already asleep.

"Claire," he said quietly, "you will not take this child. You forget, I know where to find you."

The insolent bastard! "Not where I will go!"

"Do not threaten me or you will regret it, Claire."

She ignored him. "Let me be!" Her baby cradled in her arms, she made as if to rise.

She was still trying to climb from the bed. She almost made it to her feet when Gray caught her beneath the arms. "Sweet, you cannot stand. You're too weak. Let me help you."

"No!" Her voice was choked. She was wild,

almost hysterical, trying to pound his chest. "Don't you see what you're doing? She's mine. Don't take my baby from me. I won't let you. I'm not mad like Lily, Gray. I'm not!"

She sobbed wildly, her mind blunted by fear. Gray held her shaking body close and smoothed her tumbled hair.

"Of course she is yours, Claire. I merely thought to see to your health. You're still weak. Let me help you."

You forget, I know where to find you.

Little by little her sobs eased. Drawing back, she peered at him. "You won't take her from me?" Her voice was thready with tears. Faith, she was so confused! His sudden tenderness made her come all undone.

He wiped away her tears with the pad of his thumb. "No. Trust me, Claire. Believe in me."

Chapter Twenty-six

*C*laire was young and healthy, and quick to recover. Several weeks after Alexa's birth, she brought up the subject of godparents at breakfast one morning.

"I would like to have Lexie christened soon, Gray."

He took a sip of coffee. "Have you anyone in mind as godparents?"

"I thought perhaps Penelope and Theo."

He was silent for a moment. "You and Penelope are like sisters, are you not?"

"Indeed." She wiped her fingers on her napkin and smiled, thinking of Penelope and Theo and little Merry. How lovely it would be if Merry and Lexie grew to share such closeness.

She looked at Gray. "Do you object?"

"No. I, too, think Penelope a good choice for godmother. But as godfather, I would prefer to ask Clive."

"The duke?" Her voice was clipped.

"Just as Penelope is your greatest friend," he said quietly, "so is Clive to me."

Claire didn't want to argue. "Pray do not be difficult, Gray."

"Difficult? I'm being difficult because I prefer Clive?" He confronted her with a cool stare. "One might say you were being difficult by refusing my choice."

"I do not refuse. I merely prefer to have Theo."

"Claire"—his tone was implicitly polite—"it is only fair that you should choose Alexa's godmother. Therefore, I think it equally fair that I should choose her godfather."

"Gray, I do not want to argue—"

"Then do not." His jaw was tight. He looked at her. "Why do you object to Clive?"

She glared at him. "Since you ask, I'll tell you. I do not like the man. He is arrogant. He is a rake and a womanizer."

"The very kind of man that I was called. How very revealing. I expect it's good for one to know what one's wife thinks of one." She heard the bite beneath the words.

"He is not the kind of man I want to godfather my child."

"Yet Penelope chose me as godfather to her child." His tone was less than pleasant. He dropped his napkin on the table. "I might point out, Claire, it's quite a privilege for an infant to have a duke stand as godfather."

She couldn't quibble with that. And it appeared that Gray was set.

"Very well, then. May I have your permission to set the date the Sunday after next, provided it is agreeable to Penelope and the duke?"

His tone was short. "Certainly."

It was not a good way to begin the day. Claire rose to her feet. "If you will forgive me, I am going to look in on Lexie."

"Perhaps I should mention, Claire, I think she should be moved to the nursery."

"What! Why?"

"I don't believe that a child should occupy the parents' bedchamber beyond the first few weeks. I think it's best for the child." He sat back.

"Then I will have her in my room. In any case, I think it's time I go back to my suite."

"I think not."

"I beg your pardon?" Claire couldn't believe her ears.

Gray had risen to his feet now as well. He towered above her. She hated that it made her feel distinctly at a disadvantage.

"I've been meaning to discuss our sleeping

arrangements, Claire. You've slept these many nights without me in my bed. It's time that changed."

"We didn't sleep together before Lexie was born! Why should we now?" The words were fairly flung at him. There was no time to think, to reason.

"I don't want the guests to know that we sleep apart."

"The christening won't be for several weeks, provided everyone is able!"

His jaw clenched. "Nonetheless, those are my wishes."

"You are ordering me to sleep with you?" Claire began to tremble.

"I am not ordering you. I am asking."

"Asking! You are not!"

His eyes narrowed. They shone like fierce blue fire, but his expression was glacial. "I don't believe you found it as unpleasant as you pretend, my lady. If that were the case, we would not be wed. We would certainly never have conceived a child together."

"Don't do this, Gray." Her eyes were huge, her voice half choked. "I beg of you, please do not. After Lexie is christened, let me go back to Wildewood. Surely you agree it would be best—"

"I do not," he stated flatly.

Desperation filled her. "You do this only to spite me!"

"You are mistaken, Claire. There is no spite in my heart."

"You have no heart!"

She turned away then. The last thing she wanted was for him to glimpse her tears.

The gulf between them yawned wider than ever.

Claire knew no peace. The first night that Gray walked into the bedroom, Claire was pulling on her dressing gown. She was sorely tempted to take a blanket and pillow and sleep on the chaise lounge. His closed expression nixed the idea.

An arm's length was between them. They slept together . . . yet slept apart, and the distance between them was never greater.

Rosalie woke her when Lexie was hungry at night. Claire slipped out to the nursery to feed her. If Gray noted her absence, he said nothing.

They shared meals. Small talk was the only discourse between them.

Several days before the christening, Penelope, Theo, and little Merriweather arrived. The moment the carriage rolled to a halt, Penelope was out the door and running up the wide stone steps. Claire was already standing at the top.

"Claire!"

"Pen!" Claire was half laughing, half crying. "Oh, Pen, I've missed you dreadfully!"

"And I you."

By now both Gray and Theo were observing the reunion between their wives. They shook hands. Theo laughed.

"They've been this way since they were a mere twelve years old."

"Ten." Penelope wrinkled her nose at her husband.

"I second that!" Claire raised a hand. "Now, let me see Merry."

"And Lexie."

"Lexie just woke from her nap."

A nurse stood nearby holding Merry. Claire squealed and eased Merry into her arms. "I cannot believe how she's grown!" Claire marveled. "Come, let's be off to the nursery."

The two men were left looking at each other.

"Time to adore the little ones," Theo said dryly. "I doubt we'll be seeing them for some time."

"Indeed," said Gray. "You've come a long way. You must be thirsty."

"Parched, actually."

"I have an excellent bottle of Bordeaux I've been saving. What do you say?"

"Sounds just the thing."

As it happened, roughly an hour later Clive arrived—and Charlotte as well.

The next day, the men went out shooting while the women spent much of the day walking, talking, and playing with the little ones. Merry was a bubbly child who was learning to walk, and she put on quite the show. Claire decided she couldn't wait until the day Lexie began to walk. She ignored the niggling little voice in her mind that asked where she would be on that day—here at Brightwood or at Wildewood?

Several other guests arrived the next day. Lexie's christening was set for nine o'clock on the following morning.

Claire thought Lexie looked beautiful in her silk and lace christening gown and bonnet. She was a perfect angel until the minister blessed her with holy water. It seemed Lexie wasn't fond of the little shower.

After the ceremony, Clive picked up Lexie. "I hope you don't mind if I hold her," he told Claire. "I think my goddaughter and I should get acquainted."

"But of course." Claire wanted to snatch her child back. She was cordial, hiding her distaste. It didn't set well when Clive put her over his shoulder, quite content.

Oh, yes, Clive proved quite the charmer. Even her daughter seemed enamored of the lout!

Several mornings later, when Charlotte and Pen and her family gathered to leave, Claire genuinely hated to see them go. Charlotte kissed her with tears in her eyes.

"Invite me back soon, my child."

"You do not need an invitation to see your granddaughter—or me." Claire laughed, then they embraced. "Hurry back," she urged. "Your granddaughter will be eager to see you."

Theo and Penelope were next. Claire kissed Merry, hugged Theo, and turned to Pen, whose eyes were overflowing.

"Pen! Don't! You'll have me blubbering as well."

The previous day, the two of them had talked long into the night. Though Claire was guarded about her marriage to Gray, she was aware that Penelope knew her too well not to sense it. Penelope did not push her, and for that she was grateful. It was silly, but somehow it hurt to see Theo and Pen so happy and content.

"You know me too well, Pen."

"Lovely as your home is, you won't bury her here in the country forever, will you?" Penelope teased Gray. "You'll bring her up to Town?"

Gray slid an arm around Claire. "You may count on it," he said smoothly.

He kept his arm around her until the dust from the last carriage faded from view. Then his arm fell away.

An empty hollow filled her breast. All at once she realized she'd never felt so alone.

* * *

Clive's departure was planned for shortly after luncheon. He had business at a nearby estate. Claire saw him leave the dining room, headed toward the stairs.

"Your Grace!" she called.

He turned. "Clive to you, my lady."

"Very well, then . . . Clive, I would like the opportunity to speak with you for a moment." Claire reached him and touched his sleeve. "May we? There's no one in the music room." She opened the door.

Clive followed, a bit wary. He was aware that new godfather to her daughter or not, Claire tolerated his presence. She had no liking for him.

Claire closed the door after them. She indicated a nearby chair. "Please sit."

"I prefer to stand. This won't take long, will it?"

"I expect not. No doubt you are curious." She gathered her hands before her; she was nervous.

"I—would like to talk to you about the day my brother—Oliver—died. Were you Gray's second?"

Clive was even more wary. "I was. What of it?"

"I want what happened to be clear in my mind. There are . . . several things I must know—"

"Perhaps you should ask your husband."

"I have," Claire said quietly. "We—my father and I—were never told that Oliver shot Gray. But I've seen the scars. When I asked him about it, he said only that shots were exchanged, first Gray, then Oliver . . . and, oh, I cannot explain it! But I think there is something more." Wide eyes met his. "Will you tell me, Clive? Will you tell me what happened?"

Clive hesitated. Apparently Gray did not want his wife to know the truth of what happened. Yet he couldn't lie either.

"Very well, then."

"Gray said they chose seven paces," Claire said. "Upon completing them, they each turned. There was an exchange of fire. Gray said that— he fired. That Oliver had no choice but to fire in return." Her eyes never wavered. "Is that what happened?"

Clive hesitated. "In a manner of sorts," he said slowly.

"So it happened exactly as Gray told me?"

Clive held silent.

Claire was beginning to tremble. "No, then," she whispered. She clasped her hands imploringly. "Clive, please! Please tell me the truth."

"You won't want to know."

"That's what Gray said! But you're wrong, both of you. I have to know what happened that day! I need the truth of it."

"Very well, then," he said slowly. "Gray chose seven paces, but Oliver turned early. He fired. Gray was hit. The shot took him down. It all—"

He gestured vaguely. "—it happened so fast. I ran to Gray when he went down. He hadn't even raised his weapon. He was talking about the code . . ."

"The code?"

"On the field of honor, there is a code. If one party fires, so must the second, or the first party will lose all respect from his peers. He will be shunned.

"That's why Gray shot, Claire. I was on the ground with him when he reached for his pistol. He could hardly hold it! There was mist all around, and then rain began to fall. It was almost impossible to see—the second shot went off."

"Killing Oliver?" Claire was still trembling.

"Yes," the duke confirmed. His gaze met hers. "Oliver fired before the count was finished, Claire, at six paces."

Claire shook her head. "Gray told me that he shot first. But it was Oliver—"

"Yes. Oliver got off the first shot, striking Gray. And somehow—Gray thought he shot high—it somehow managed to hit Oliver."

Gray had wanted to spare her, she realized. That was why he'd told her he was the first to shoot.

"Thank you, Clive, for telling me. May I trust this will remain between us?"

Clive bowed his head. "Of course."

Hesitating, she reached up and kissed his cheek.

Her eyes were swimming so that she could scarcely see. Clive had affirmed what she had begun to suspect.

Swiftly, she moved down the hall, dashing away a tear.

She didn't understand the man she had married. She didn't understand him at all.

But she loved him. She would love him till her last breath.

Chapter
Twenty-seven

*W*hile Claire willed for peace between them, it remained elusive. Gray hated the awkward silence that cropped up—hated it but knew not how to breach it.

So continued the divide.

Each night, Gray escorted her to their room. He often returned downstairs to his study. A maelstrom of longing swept through him.

Almost desperately he wished he could make her love him. Motherhood became her. She was lovelier than ever. There was an air of maturity about her. Sometimes he came close when she was nursing the babe, his gaze hungry. Her skin was creamy white and smooth, except where it was traced with veins. The naked expanse of her breast laid bare made desire burn inside him. The blood rushed to fill his loins. The need for fulfillment scorched his veins. He couldn't tear his gaze away.

He knew Claire was embarrassed, yet he couldn't tear his eyes away. At other times he came up behind her while she worked at her sewing. He stared longingly down at the fragile skin of her nape, so fair and feminine. He wanted to kiss the velvety spot that flowed into her shoulders.

Awareness pounded through him. He had only made love to her three times, but once to completion. He chafed inside. At night sometimes he pulled her softness into his arms, her bottom sweetly cradled in the valley between his thighs. How he managed to restrain himself, he didn't know. Did she know? He already knew that if he turned her, she would fit him perfectly.

He also knew that Claire had never expected that a baby would be conceived during their night together. Nor had he. A part of him used to wonder if she would hate their baby because he was the father. Not so now. She was entirely devoted to her daughter.

He thought of Lily. His soul burned inside whenever he did. And then it was as if his mind had been tainted. Guilt pricked him deeply. He'd loved her so much.

Loved her . . . while hating her for killing his son.

And what about Claire?

He wanted Claire past bearing. He yearned for her beyond measure. He wanted to plunge deep inside, to her very soul. He wanted her more than ever.

Did he love her?

The days that followed were far from easy. Each night, he gave Claire a chaste kiss on the cheek, hating that he'd insisted they sleep together. And so each night their bodies were warm and close. Each night he slept with her—

His heart in limbo.

What a fool he was.

Gray didn't know how desperately Claire wanted to heal the breach with her husband. With each day that passed, she wanted it more. She wanted Gray to love her. To love their child and to carry another. She wanted a true marriage.

But she was afraid to love him. Afraid he might never give his heart again after his tortured past.

A part of her despaired.

Another part of her was determined.

At six weeks, Lexie began to take long naps in the late afternoon. Claire came down from the nursery after nursing her and rocking her to sleep.

One day, humming, she went outside to the rose garden to cut her favorite peach-colored roses for a bouquet. Their scent was particularly strong and sweet, and she wanted them for the bureau in her room.

In Gray's room.

It struck her then that she had begun to think of the chamber as theirs . . . not simply Gray's. Not simply hers, but theirs.

The thought made her pulse quicken.

What did it mean?

Her mind thus wondering when she returned, she crossed the room and placed the vase on the polished wood top, rearranging a few of them before she stepped back.

"There!" she said in satisfaction.

"Very pretty," said a voice behind her.

Claire turned. Her husband surveyed her. He sat in the large wooden tub, his forearms extended along the sides, his shoulders wide, sleek and taut with muscle. Tiny droplets of water winked like jewels in the dark forest on his chest. The sight of him at any time was enough to shorten her breath.

The sight of him now, naked was enough to stop it in her breast.

Granted, he wasn't totally nude. Well, he was, but not all of him was visible, thank heaven.

"What are you doing here?" Her tone was breathless.

Gray arched a brow.

Her cheeks grew hot. "I mean, what are you doing here in the bath—in the middle of the afternoon," she rushed to clarify.

"I was in the barn with the horses. I don't think you'd want me at the dinner table smelling the way I do."

"No." She wet her lips, unaware how his gaze followed the tip of her moist, pink tongue. "I suppose not."

She met his gaze, then averted her eyes.

"Oh, come, Claire, it's no worse than the last bath we shared." His eyes pinned hers. He leaned forward. "Will you wash my back? The sponge is on the table there."

Her senses clamored an alert. Melting heat spread low in her middle. He was a presence that made her quiver inside.

Claire picked up the sponge but remained rooted to the spot. Her heart was clamoring wildly. Her fingers still clutched the sponge.

Gray caught her wrist. "Every moment you stay," he said quietly, "is a moment that costs you—another moment I want you. And you know where play such as this will lead."

She stood frozen in place.

"I see," he said softly. "If you run, Claire, I'll catch you, though I daresay the servants might be aghast at seeing the master chasing after his wife."

Claire swallowed but remained where she was.

"Lock the door, sweet, and come here."

She did as he asked.

"Your gown, Claire. Remove it, if you please."

She lifted her fingers to the ribbons at her bosom. Her hands were shaking so that she fumbled with the ribbon, unable to untie it.

"Kneel down and I'll help you."

She did as he bade her. Lean male fingers parted the material and swept it from her shoulders. It seemed that, all at once, she was naked. But she was afraid she would fall while climbing into the bath. She felt shaky inside and out.

"Gray, I don't know if I can—"

Water rushed down his body. A hand gripped hers, the other her waist. The instant she was in the tub, she sank down. She'd had one fleeting glimpse of his naked body before he lowered himself across from her.

There was no hiding his nakedness. There was no hiding the power of his form. There was no hiding his rod, rigid and thick and thrusting from the dark hairs at his pelvis.

She knelt between his thighs. Gray handed her the soap, marveling at his control. Quickly she began to soap his chest, loving the slight abrasive feel of the hair against her palm.

His chest rose and fell more quickly. He gritted his teeth. The feel of her small hands running over his skin, stroking, kneading, was almost heart-stoppingly arousing. Unwittingly she touched the clefted head of his rod. It leaped beneath her touch.

Into it.

The soap slipped from Claire's fingers.

Now it was Gray's turn.

His palms slick with soap, they slid over the mounds of her breasts, taking particular attention to her nipples. She made a soft, sweet ragged sound of need.

In one fluid move Gray stood. Water rushed down his body. He caught Claire's waist and brought her upright, his hands splayed wide against her buttocks.

His chest expanded . . . and so did the proof of his desire. Against the part of him that swelled more with every breath, with every heartbeat.

They still stood in the bath, the water swirling around their calves. He pressed her against his length, twining his fingers in her hair and turning her face up to his. He caught her leg and dragged it around his hip. There was something raw and possessive in the way he kissed her, the way he held her. Her arms crept around his neck, sending his heart soaring. Gray couldn't remember a time when he'd wanted a woman as much as he wanted Claire.

At last he lifted her from the tub. She clutched

at him. He made a halfhearted effort to dry them with a length of toweling. They tumbled to the bed. If there was doubt, he swept it away with the heat of his passion. She sensed the fierceness in him and thrilled to it.

"Claire," he whispered. Their mouths were but a breath apart, touching as he spoke. They lay face-to-face. Her hands imprisoned within his, Gray brought them down. "Touch me, Claire. Touch me now."

His voice was strangely thick. She felt the muscles of his belly clench—he was so hot! Her body hummed, matching and meeting his fervor.

Over and over he kissed her mouth. With languorous exploration. With bone-deep sweetness, with bone-deep tenderness that melted her heart . . . and melted her against him.

His lips caught the tips of her breasts. Claire felt them swell into his mouth. With his tongue, he traced lazy circles from one breast to the other, down the valley of her chest, down her belly, clear to the fleece at the apex of her legs.

He did not stop, but kissed the inside of her thighs.

"Gray!" She lay open to him. Bare and open and . . . almost breathless with expectation.

"Let me, Claire. Let me in."

With only his thumbs, he parted her cleft, with its pink, womanly flesh. A tremor went through her. She wasn't quite sure of his intent but every sense inside clamored a warning.

She couldn't look away as he parted her with his thumbs.

She couldn't look away as he parted her with his lips.

She jerked at the first wash of his tongue, down furrowed flesh already damp, slick and hot with liquid heat. Quivering inside, she stared down at his dark head poised between her legs. He raised his head and gazed at her, his eyes burning.

"Let me, Claire. Let me."

His voice was taut and ragged. Her shyness receded. A strange dark thrill ran through her. She felt wanton. Wicked. And she couldn't look away as his tongue pressed the pearl of sensation hidden within . . . pressed and kissed her in an incredibly erotic caress.

She gasped. Pleasure exploded.

It didn't end there.

Gray's breath was hot and raspy. He raised himself over her. Her legs fell wide apart.

He thrust inside her.

He couldn't hold back. There was no hope for it. He could feel her hunger and it aroused his passion to a fever pitch. He plunged, fierce and almost wild.

"Claire . . . I don't want to hurt you . . ."

She caught his head in her hands. "You won't. You don't."

Something gave way in her as Gray lunged, again and again. Her flesh clung to his, tightening—contracting—again and again. Release came in a blinding rush of sparks.

His fingers combed gently through her hair. "Claire," he said. "Claire." His mouth exquisitely tender, he kissed her.

Chapter Twenty-eight

There was a subtle change in Gray's behavior after that. He no longer seemed so foreboding, so remote. They made love at night . . . and in the afternoon. In bed. On the floor. At first the passion he aroused in her was almost frightening. His lovemaking was fierce and explosive. It thrilled Claire as much as it frightened her. At other times he was exquisitely tender and protective.

When they were wrapped in each other's arms, it was a time of discovery, a haven from all the chaos between them.

Claire wanted him more with every day.

She loved him more with every day.

Yet even as passion flamed, no words of love passed between them. She would not yield surrender when it was not returned. Her pride would not warrant it. Was it wrong for her husband to want her in equal measure? Oh, the feelings were there! The lights in his blue eyes turned a soft silver when they were together. But she wouldn't give up hope. Not yet.

She could point the way. But she could not lead him to it. She *would* not lead him to it.

Claire awoke one morning to find her husband propped on his elbow. "What are you doing?"

"Watching you sleep."

Her lips quirked. "How exciting."

A slow grin edged across his mouth. "Indeed it will be. I am going to kidnap you, you see."

They lay facing each other, now palm-to-palm. Fingertip-to-fingertip.

"That sounds . . . intriguing."

"Didn't I tell you?"

Claire felt giddy inside. "You sinful, sinful man."

He pulled her up to her feet. "Shall we bathe together again?"

Just then someone knocked on the door.

It was Rosalie with breakfast.

After feeding Lexie, she joined Gray downstairs a short while later. She raised her brows when one of the maids handed him a wicker basket.

"What is that?" she asked him.

"You've a short memory, m'lady. If you recall, I did once promise to kidnap you."

Claire laughed. "You did kidnap me," she pointed out. "At Clive's house party."

"Well, then, fair warning. I'm about to kidnap you again."

His smile made her heart turn over.

Outside, Gray tucked the basket and a blanket into the space behind the seat of the gig. With a snap of the reins, they rolled forward.

A peaceful contentment settled over them as the gig rolled forward. But all at once there was a pang in her heart. She wanted more nights like the last. More days like this one.

A lifetime like this.

They stopped at the top of a rolling hill. It looked down across the valley where a stream gleamed in the sunlight. Gray threw out a blanket for them to sit. He unpacked wine and cheese, bread and fruit. Claire discovered she was famished.

Afterward, they packed the basket away and Gray returned to the blanket. He stretched out, pillowing his head in her lap. Claire stroked the hair from his forehead and drew a long breath, poised squarely between heaven and hell.

She wanted more days like this. She wanted a lifetime like this. What would it take for him to see her? What would it take for him to love her?

Gray frowned. "What's wrong?"

"Nothing." She ducked her head, then gathered herself and summoned a smile. Reckless abandon came back in searing remembrance as she thought of the shockingly erotic way he sometimes made love to her.

She had wondered what it would be like to touch him in that way.

To taste him as he had tasted her.

When he would have swung up to face her, Claire stopped him with a slender hand upon his chest.

There was a faint puzzlement on his brow. "Claire . . . what are you doing?"

She gave a shake of her head. "You'll see."

Small hands wrested the buttons of his shirt. With her hands she parted it wide.

His breeches were next.

His belly clenched. He jerked as her hands slid beneath the waistband. Cloth parted at the urging of her fingers.

She knelt between his thighs.

Gray went very still. All but his rod—

Swollen stiff and erect.

Brazenly, she brushed the very tip of him, circling it with a fingertip.

Again. Yet again.

Slowly she leaned down.

There was a jagged intake of his breath. His heart surely stopped.

"Claire," he said thickly.

Small fingertips closed around the root of him, a gentle but insistent guidance.

Gray couldn't look away. She swirled her tongue on the inside skin of his thighs, as he had done with her.

He gritted his teeth, holding back a groan. How long would she taunt him? How long would she tease him?

Her hair slipped from its knot atop her head, trailing down over him, over them.

"Now," he grated out. "Do it now."

And she did. She laid her tongue against the most acutely sensitive part of him.

Warm, sweet breath swirled around his helm, that boldly arching tip of him, clear to the very root of him. She waited . . . waited endlessly, it seemed—

Air rushed from his lungs.

He pushed himself up on his elbows and stared down at her. He watched the circle of her tongue, watched her fill her mouth, watched her tongue scale his length, gliding hot and slick over the cleft of his member. Licking. Tugging. Sucking.

He'd never dreamed she might indulge such blatant eroticism. But he couldn't bear it if she stopped.

He liked it, indeed he whispered it over and over.

Powerful arms dragged her up and above him. "I want you in the dark. I want you in the day. I want you now." He spoke the words that made her come all undone, a dark heated whisper.

"Wrap your legs around me," he directed.

His gaze roved the delicate features upturned to his.

He kissed her with naked possessiveness. Her lips parted as she began to pant. The ivory column of her neck. Loving the tight feel of her passage as he lifted her, then plunged into her, again and again. Fierce. Explosive. The wet heat of her passage clamping hold of his flesh.

The world seemed to give way. Again and again he thrust into the sleek prison of her channel. Her breasts bobbed with every fiery plunge of his hips.

His features were strained, taut with need. His hands locked on her hips, lifting her ever higher, lunging ever deeper, ever frenzied and torrid.

She buried her face against his neck and cried out her release, a second after his. Her name trembled on his lips. "Claire," he said hoarsely. "Do you know what you do to me?"

Claire was beyond speech.

One slim leg entwined between his. He caught her chin between his fingers. With lazy amusement, he echoed the sentiment that she had proclaimed earlier. "You sinful, sinful woman."

Later they would both wonder how such a perfect day could possibly turn so brutal.

It was early evening, time for Lexie's bedtime feeding. Claire usually fed her first, then went down for supper. Gray stood in the hall just outside the nursery door, looking in. Lexie was fussing in her cradle.

Gray didn't move.

Claire shook her head. "What, sir! Are you afraid to pick up your own daught—"

She broke off. Her laughter died.

The strangest sensation crept through her. Everything inside her seemed to freeze.

Her tone turned very quiet. "Your daughter is crying, Gray. Will you not pick her up? Will you not hold her?"

Something surfaced in his eyes, something she couldn't decipher. Something almost beyond comprehension.

No, she thought. No. She glimpsed half pain, half plea.

"You should feed her," he said.

"Yes." Claire walked toward the chair in the corner. There was a violent tug-of-war going on inside her. It was as if she were being pulled apart inside. "Will you bring her to me?"

He didn't move.

"She's crying, Gray. She wants to be held."

He remained immobile.

A halo of pain began to encircle her chest. It was as if the strength of that emotion was strangling her.

Reeling, Claire searched her mind. "I just realized . . . I've never seen you hold her, Gray. Not once. I've never seen you touch her. Not once. You call her 'the child.' But she has a name. Your daughter has a name. Why don't you use it?"

Perhaps Lexie sensed the discord between her parents. In her cradle, she cried harder. Claire snatched her up and sat in the chair in the corner. She began to rock forward and back.

"You'll hurt her," Gray said sharply.

Claire clutched her even closer.

Rocked her faster.

"You'll smother her!"

"I told you once before I'm not like Lily!" she cried. "And I'm not! I would never harm my baby. Never!"

All that would quiet Lexie was her breast. With trembling fingers she loosened her bodice. Lexie latched frantically onto her nipple and began to suck.

The sudden silence was overwhelming. She was aware of Gray moving, standing over her.

How could she salvage her pride without risking her heart? Nothing in the world could ever hurt like this.

"I don't mean to be cruel, truly I don't! But William died at Lily's hands. Not yours. You aren't to blame for either of them. Don't you know that?"

Lexie had fallen back to sleep, now oblivious of the battle between her parents. Claire deposited her in her cradle and turned back to Gray.

"Haven't you blamed yourself long enough? Haven't you punished yourself enough? You have to forgive yourself. You have to forgive Lily! I can't make you. I—I can't give you anything because you will take nothing. You want nothing! You turn me away, Gray. You push me away!"

His countenance was like a thundercloud. "You don't know what you're saying, Claire. Aren't you forgetting Oliver? Aren't you forgetting I took your brother's life?"

"You've given me another life in return, Gray— our daughter. Don't you see that?"

The silence seemed never-ending.

Wrenching pain tore through her. "We cannot live like this. I won't. I don't want Lexie cheated of a father's love. I—I think it's better if we go away now."

"Don't leave me, Claire."

"Don't make me!" she cried.

Her throat was thick with tears. Bitterness stole through her. All her angry hurt flooded out.

"You loved Lily and William. Why can't you love me? Why can't you love Lexie? Why can't you love us?"

They were shattering, those words—

Just like her heart.

And agony for both of them.

"Gray! Don't you see, you're tearing me apart! I can't live with ghosts between us."

She meant Oliver. She meant Lily. She meant William.

An icy shroud of despair descended. There was so much tumult inside her, she could scarcely bear it. She understood his pain, in an anguished kind of way. But it didn't eclipse her own, and the rawness of her heart etched a bitter scar upon her soul.

"I will not live with only a part of you. I want all of you . . . or none at all."

Gray's mouth twisted. "What do you see when you look at me? At the man who killed your brother?"

Claire did not speak.

"Answer me!"

"I no longer see the man who killed my brother. Once—once I did. Once that was all I could see. But not any longer. I've let go of Oliver. But so must you. Let go of Lily and William, or they'll haunt you forever."

His voice was gritty. "You didn't answer, Claire. Tell me. What do you see when you look at me?"

"I see the man I married. The father of my daughter." *The man I love. Oh, don't you know you have another child,* she longed to cry! *You have Lexie! You have me.*

A burning ache stung her throat.

"I want more nights with you, Gray. I want more days like today."

The cords in his neck stood taut. He spoke not a word.

"How can you do this?" she almost screamed. "You don't love me. You don't even love Lexie!"

"That's not true. Of course I love her."

"I want to go home," she sobbed.

"You are home. This is your home. My home. Our daughter's home."

"It's a prison—and you're trapped here with Lily and William!" The truth was like a stab in the heart.

"I want to go home," she said again. "Home to Wildewood. I cannot live like this. I won't! Let me go, Gray. Let me go!"

Chapter Twenty-nine

When Claire left for Wildewood the following morning, Gray had already departed for London. It was in his mind that when he was able, he would close up the house for good. There were too many broken dreams left behind. Too many hurtful memories.

In London, he shut himself away in his study.

The trays left in the hall by the butler were left untouched.

When he came out, it was to have Dawes fetch another bottle of brandy.

Such was the state of affairs when Dawes admitted the Duke of Braddock.

Clive did not ask admittance into the study. He simply strolled in boldly. "Gray, I saw your carriage—"

Gray reared up from the shadows. He'd been sleeping on a small settee. "What the bloody hell—"

"Yes," drawled the duke. "My sentiments exactly." He went to the windows and tugged the drapes wide. Sunshine flooded the room.

Gray scowled. He sat back, shoving his fingers through his hair. His shirt was half in, half out. "What the devil are you doing?" He regarded his friend through bleary, bloodshot eyes. "Get the hell out, Clive."

"I think not," said the duke.

He took a step toward his friend, only to stop cold.

"Good Lord! Is this stench what I smell like when I'm sotted?" He sniffed in distaste.

"A good deal worse," snarled Gray.

Clive picked up the cravat that lay unwound on a chair, the jacket thrown to the floor.

Gray glared at him. "For pity's sake, you are not my maid! If you want to do something for me, get me another bottle!"

A black brow hiked upward as Clive considered his friend. "I think I shall join you, after all." Clive claimed a glass from the tray and poured while Gray moved to sit behind the desk. Then Clive took the chair across from him.

"Gray," he said quietly, "what the devil are you doing? What the blazes is going on?"

Silence spun out. For the longest time Gray said nothing. Then: "She's left me."

"Claire?"

"Of course it's Claire! She's gone back to Wildewood."

"Whatever for?"

His mouth twisted. "I am doing as my wife wants. She wants me to leave her alone, and so I have."

"Is that what she said?"

"She didn't need to."

"You fool." Clive didn't bandy words. "You blind, bloody fool."

Gray's eyes narrowed. "I am your friend and so I will forget you said that."

He lifted his glass to his lips, but did not drink. Slowly he lowered it.

"It hurts to love her," he whispered.

"Then treat her like it. Don't turn your back on her!"

"I did not turn my back. Is that what you think?"

"It doesn't matter what I think." Clive was frustrated. "For God's sake, man, she's your wife. You should be with her!"

"She accused me of running away. But I'm not! I just—couldn't stay there. It's too . . . empty."

"And so you will wallow in self-pity, the way you have since Lily died."

"Watch your tongue, Clive!"

"Oh, come. You know it's true."

Gray's lips thinned. "Clair is better off without me."

"Yes, I suppose you're right. She's better off without you." The duke gave a nod.

Gray's eyes glinted but he said nothing.

The duke set aside his glass. "Listen to me. I'm the last man to offer advice when it comes to love—"

"Yes," Gray bit out. "You are the last man who should offer advice. So don't."

"You stupid fool, would you throw away what you have?"

"Clive, didn't you hear me? She doesn't want me."

"And you will not fight for her? For the both of you? For all of you? Will you just give in?"

Gray reached for the bottle. "Another?" he drawled.

The duke's eyes narrowed. Bluntly, he spoke. "You will lose her, Gray."

"What do you know of it? You have no experience with marriage. You have no experience with love!"

"Listen to me. I've seen the way you look at her, Gray. I know you love her."

"Yes, well, that's all well and good, but it doesn't seem to matter to my wife."

"Have you told her you love her?"

Gray's eyes slid away.

Clive sighed. "I thought not."

As it happened, Clive hadn't been gone more than a few minutes when the knocker sounded again.

The butler admitted Charlotte Sutherland. "Good day, Dawes," she greeted him. "Where may I find my son and daughter-in-law?"

Dawes looked almost guilty. "You'll find my lord in his study."

Charlotte smelled the odor of stale smoke and liquor even before she entered. "Gray! My word, what are you about? Where are Claire and Alexa?"

"They're at Wildewood, Mother."

"Gray!"

"Have you come to counsel me, too? You needn't bother. I've already received a lecture from Clive."

"Clive!"

Her son smiled grimly. "Yes. That's what I thought, too."

"Gray, what is going on?"

"As I told Clive, my wife has left me."

Charlotte was shocked.

"She's better off without me, Mother. I deserve this."

"Rubbish!"

"She thinks I don't love Lexie."

"Poppycock!"

Gray was sprawled on the settee. Charlotte sat and took his hands in hers. "Gray . . . it was hardly an ideal situation when the two of you first wed. But Claire loves you. I've seen it. You must trust her, my son. You must trust yourself."

Gray shook his head. He stared straight ahead until his eyes grew dry and began to water.

"You don't understand." His voice grew hoarse. "I—haven't been a very good husband. I haven't been a very good father."

"Dearest, we all make mistakes. Don't let the past get in your way. Don't let it stand in the way of your feelings for Claire. She will heal you, if only you will let her."

As it happened, at that moment, Penelope sat in the drawing room at Wildewood. She had come immediately upon receiving a letter from Claire.

Penelope held her old friend's hands, her eyes swimming. "Claire," she whispered, "Gray loves you. I know it! You're not a coward. Give him a chance. Give your marriage a chance."

"I'm afraid," Claire whispered. "I want . . . what I'm afraid he can't give."

Penelope laid a hand on hers. "I don't believe that, Claire. Give him a chance. Give your marriage another chance."

* * *

"Go home to your wife," said Clive.

"Go home to your husband," said Penelope.

"Go home to your family," said Charlotte.

In London, Gray pondered.

At Wildewood, Claire pondered.

She wasn't yet ready to give up.

Neither was Gray. But first—first there was something he knew he must do.

Upon arriving at Brightwood from Wildewood, after Penelope had come to speak to her, Claire was disappointed to find that Gray had gone to London. Lexie was sleeping, sweet little mite, so she put her to bed in the nursery. A nap was in order for her as well. After dinner and a good night's rest, she decided, she and Lexie would travel to London.

She would go to the ends of the earth for her husband, if that's what it took.

London seemed a small enough distance to travel after the long, long journey they had endured. She was more determined than ever. They belonged together, she and Gray. She wanted more children. Gray's children. As many as God willed. She wanted them to share the present, future hopes and dreams.

She didn't hear when Gray arrived home. Mrs. Henderson told him Claire was napping, so he headed for the stairs.

He started to pass the nursery, but a rustle

caught his attention. He glanced inside just as his daughter began to cry.

Her nurse didn't appear. He stood uncertainly.

Finally, he stepped in, slowly crossing to the cradle.

The baby was squalling in earnest now. Her cries gained pitch and volume.

Gray stood as if paralyzed, staring down at her.

Dammit, where was her nurse? Gray stood helpless above her.

"Hush, little one. Hush."

She cried harder.

Unable to bear it any longer, he reached out and slid his hands beneath her body.

She stopped screaming the instant he touched her.

Time stood still.

Slowly, as if it hurt—as indeed it did!—he brought the babe toward his chest.

There was a blanket covering half her face. Perhaps that was why she cried. He pushed it aside, away from her nose and mouth.

Everything inside him seemed to freeze.

He remembered holding William—on his chest—rubbing his back during those times he fussed at night . . . holding him while Lily slept.

Not once had he done that with this babe.

She drew his gaze helplessly. Gray allowed himself to look at his daughter—really look at her.

Soft, golden hair covered her scalp, a shade

lighter than Claire's. Her cheeks were rosy and plump.

His chest grew tight. Raw emotion seared his soul. He touched her cheek. Clasping her tight against his chest, he looked into eyes as pure as the skies above. *His* eyes—

A dry, jagged sound broke from his throat.

"Lexie. Oh, God, *Lexie.*"

Chapter Thirty

C laire watched from the doorway, the back of her hand dammed against her mouth to keep from crying out. Her heart constricted; her eyes were misty and wet. She couldn't hold back a sob, and Gray looked up.

Wordlessly, he held out a hand.

On shaky legs she crossed to him.

He laid his hand alongside her neck and tipped her face up to his. "I pray that you can forgive me, Claire. I've done so many things—"

His voice wasn't entirely steady. The catch in it cleaved her in two. Her fingers stole up and pressed against his lips. She gave a shake of her head. "I don't want to think of that. It's been a long journey, but what matters is now. What matters is the future."

His gaze roved hers. "I love you, Claire. I love

you more with every breath. I need you more with every breath."

Joy surged through her. She buried her face against his neck, her throat hot. "Oh, Gray, I love you, too," she cried. "I love you so."

His thumb slid down her throat. He lowered his head to hers.

A sudden cry reminded them they weren't alone. Lexie was nuzzling against his chest, her face turned toward him, crinkling as she gave a demanding cry.

Gray's laugh was rusty. "My pet, I can't help you. I think you need your mother."

He passed her to Claire.

Later, when Lexie had been fed and lay sleeping in her cradle, Gray caught her hand and brought it to his lips.

He took a deep breath, his gaze searching hers. "There's something I need to do," he said quietly.

Claire lifted her chin. "I know," she whispered. The muscles in her throat locked tight. She read what was in his mind. In his soul.

A few minutes later she watched from their bedroom window as Gray's legs carried him toward the hill near the church.

He was going to say his good-byes to Lily and William.

Her eyes grew damp all over again.

He returned a short while later. As he entered their bedchamber, he raised his head.

Her eyes clung to his. Clung . . . and held.

She sensed a peacefulness within him, a peacefulness that had never been there before.

Wordlessly he held out his hand.

This time when Claire raised her face to his, her smile was dazzling.

"Welcome home, my love," she whispered.

In the nursery, Lexie had just begun to sit upright by herself.

"I can't believe how quickly she's growing," her mother marveled.

"Soon she'll be walking to us," said Gray.

Claire laughed. "I can't wait!"

Gray's eyes turned a smoky blue. He captured her in his arms and nuzzled the side of her neck. "What do you say we give her a brother? Or a sister?"

Claire tried to hold back a smile and couldn't.

Gray's lips quirked. "I know that look, my love. What is it you're hiding?"

She splayed her fingers wide on his chest, loving the muscles beneath her fingertips. "So you think we should give our daughter a brother or sister?"

"I do."

"And what would you say if I told you we already have?"

His lips quirked. "Well," he chuckled, "I can't say I'm surprised . . ."

If you love Samantha James
and her delectably wicked heroes,
pick up the latest from
award-winning author Anna Campbell.
Turn the page for
a peek at Anna Campbell's

Midnight's Wild Passion . . .

AVAILABLE NOW

The Marquess of Ranelaw will never forgive Godfrey Demarest for ruining his sister—now the time has come to repay the villain in the same coin. But one intriguing impediment stands in the way of Nicholas's vengeance: Miss Antonia Smith, companion to his foe's daughter. Having herself been deceived and disgraced by a rogue, Antonia vows to protect her charge from the same cruel fate. She recognizes Ranelaw for the shameless blackguard he is, and will devote every ounce of her resolve to thwarting him. But Antonia has always had a fatal weakness for rakes . . .

London
April 1827

*B*eneath hooded eyelids, Nicholas Challoner, Marquess of Ranelaw, surveyed the whirling snowstorm of white dresses. A debutantes' ball was the last place the *ton* expected to encounter a rake of his appalling reputation. A rake of his appalling reputation should know better than to appear at any such respectable gathering.

With his arrival, the chatter faltered away to silence. Ranelaw was accustomed to causing a flutter. Neither curiosity nor disapproval distracted him. As the orchestra scratched a trite écossaise, he scanned the room for his prey.

Ah, yes . . .

His jaded gaze settled upon his mark.

The chit wore white. Of course. The color symbolized purity. It convinced buyers in this particular market that no human hand had sullied the merchandise.

For Miss Cassandra Demarest, he'd ensure that promise was a lie. Nothing much excited him these days, but as he contemplated his victim, satisfaction stirred in his gut.

After the brief, shocked silence, the room exploded into hubbub. Clearly Ranelaw wasn't the only person convinced he belonged elsewhere.

A fiery, subterranean elsewhere.

The guests were right to be perturbed. He carried mayhem in his soul.

A smile of wicked anticipation teased at his lips as he studied the girl. Until a caricature in black stepped between him and his object of interest, spoiling the view. He frowned, then turned when Viscount Thorpe spoke beside him.

"Sure you're ready for this, old man? The tabbies are giving you the cold eye and you haven't asked Miss Demarest to dance yet."

"A man reaches the age to set up his nursery, Thorpe." He glanced up again, seeking his quarry. The black barrier hindering his inspection resolved itself into a tall woman with a nondescript face. At least what he saw was nondescript, under tinted spectacles and a lace cap with ugly, dangling lappets.

Thorpe scoffed. "Miss Demarest won't give you the time of day, my good fellow."

Ranelaw's smile turned cynical. "I'm one of the richest men in England and my name goes back to the Conquest."

Thorpe released an unimpressed snort. "The name you've done your best to disgrace. Your courtship won't be the doddle you imagine, my fine friend. Miss Demarest has the kingdom's most fearsome chaperone. You might gull the filly, but the redoubtable Miss Smith will send you packing before you get your paws on the girl's fortune. Before you get so much as a whiff of it, I'll wager."

"I'm not interested in Miss Demarest's fortune," Ranelaw said with perfect honesty. "And surely you don't rely on some sparrow of a spinster to circumvent me. I eat chaperones for breakfast."

He ate courtesans and widows and other men's wives for lunch and dinner, with much more pleasurable result. He trusted very little in his life, but since his first heady experience of sex, he'd trusted the fleeting delight he found in a woman's body. He asked nothing more of his lovers, frequently to their chagrin.

Thorpe's eyes brightened with greed. "A hundred guineas say Miss Smith dismisses you with a flea in your ear when you make your bow."

"A hundred? A paltry risk for a sure thing. Make it five."

"Done."

Lady Wreston wove through the throng to greet the arrivals. Thorpe had made sure his aunt sent Ranelaw a card for the ball. Nonetheless she looked less than overjoyed to see him.

A pity. She'd looked overjoyed to see him yesterday afternoon in her summerhouse. She'd looked even more overjoyed half an hour later with her drawers around her ankles and a hectic flush heightening her famous complexion.

Devil take their delicious hides, but women were a capricious sex.

Ranelaw glanced past his comely hostess to where Cassandra Demarest shifted back into sight. He'd had the girl followed since her arrival in London a week ago and he'd observed her himself from a distance. She was a fetching little piece. Blond. A graceful figure. Ranelaw had never been close enough to read her expression with accuracy. Doubtless it would reveal the same vacuous sweetness that shone from the face of every maiden here.

If one excepted the chaperones.

His attention returned to the woman leaning over Miss Demarest like a sheltering tree over a ewe lamb. As if divining his thoughts, the chaperone stiffened. Her head jerked up and she focused on him.

Even across the room, even through her spectacles, her gaze burned. Severe, assessing, unwavering. Absolutely nothing fetching there, but he found himself unable to look away. Uncannily the surrounding cacophony faded to an expectant hush.

As blatant as a tossed glove, she flung down a challenge.

Then she turned to answer something her charge said, Lady Wreston bustled up in all her plump glory, and the instant of hostile awareness splintered.

Unaccountably disconcerted by that wordless exchange of fire, Ranelaw bowed over his hostess's hand and asked to meet the Demarest heiress. Millicent, Lady Wreston, couldn't hide her flash of pique, but she knew what their world demanded. Girls were born to be wedded then bedded. Single men did the honors. Even single men who had sown a continent of wild oats required a legitimate heir.

The polite fiction of his interest in the marriage mart was convenient, although he rarely used respectability to cloak darker intentions. Hypocrisy counted among the rare sins he didn't commit on a regular basis. Nor did he indulge in willful self-deception. He knew that he'd roast in hell for what he plotted. Cassandra Demarest was an innocent who didn't deserve the fate he intended. But what he wrought was too important for him to ignore how perfectly the girl fitted his purposes. He couldn't allow scruples to discourage him.

Scruples and he had long been polite strangers.

He lingered to soothe his hostess's vanity, all the while watching Miss Demarest's every move. She'd accepted a dance, and her partner now returned her to the fearsome chaperone. The fearsome chaperone was a long Meg under that loose, rusty black gown at least five seasons out of date.

Then the Demarest chit spoke and the uninteresting Miss Smith smiled.

And became no longer quite so uninteresting.

Ranelaw felt winded, like someone had just punched him in the belly.

Ridiculous, really, to be intrigued. So the crone possessed a lush mouth. Except now that he sauntered closer, he recognized Miss Smith wasn't a crone after all. Her skin was clear and unlined, with a soft flush of color like the pink of dawn. He found himself wondering about the eyes behind those unbecoming spectacles.

Good God, what was wrong with him?

The haggish chaperone demonstrated signs of desirability. Who the hell cared? He had other fish to fry. Young, unsuspecting fish trapped in a net of vengeance.

Lady Wreston performed introductions. "Lord Ranelaw, may I present Miss Cassandra Demarest, the daughter of Mr. Godfrey Demarest, of Bascombe Hailey in Somerset? This lady is her companion, Miss Smith."

Out of the corner of his eye, Ranelaw watched

the chaperone straighten as if scenting danger. She was more awake than her charge, who blushed and dipped into a charming curtsy.

"Delighted, Miss Demarest," he murmured, bending over her gloved hand with a deference he knew the girl—and her dour companion—would note.

"My lord." Cassandra Demarest had long, childish eyelashes tipped with a gold darker than the luxuriant curls framing her piquant face. She inspected Ranelaw from under their shadow.

A natural coquette.

He wasn't surprised. Nor was he surprised to discover a beauty. She was as bright as a daffodil.

His skin prickled under the chaperone's glare. Curse the crowlike Miss Smith. He needed to concentrate on his goal, not some disapproving and insignificant old maid. Although with every second, he revised his estimate of the chaperone's age downward.

"May I have the pleasure of this dance?" A waltz struck up.

"I'd love—"

Miss Smith interrupted. "I'm sorry, Lord Ranelaw, but Miss Demarest's father strictly forbids the waltz. She has a country dance free after supper."

The dragon didn't sound sorry. Her husky voice was surprisingly resolute, considering she rebuked a man so far above her in rank.

"Toni, surely Papa wouldn't mind under these circumstances," Miss Demarest said in a winning tone.

Toni—an intriguingly pretty name for such a starched board—arched a blond eyebrow. "You know your father's rules."

Miss Demarest was clearly used to wheedling her own way. Ranelaw prepared for a childish outburst, but the girl took denial in good spirit. Apparently he was mistaken in both women. Miss Demarest wasn't altogether a brainless flibbertigibbet. The black beetle showed unexpected promise.

How interesting . . .

More white-clad butterflies joined the group. Introductions were performed. The chaperone hovered protectively.

Wise chaperone.

Lady Wreston wandered away while Thorpe questioned Miss Demarest about mutual acquaintances in Somerset. Thorpe was related to half the nation and anyone he wasn't related to was apparently his dear acquaintance. The quizzing could continue into tomorrow. Taking advantage of the diverted attention, Ranelaw shifted nearer to the companion. She was even taller than he'd thought. In bed, she'd fit him perfectly.

What particular Gehenna spawned that thought?

"The chit won't take if you terrify all the eligible gentlemen, Miss Smith." Music and conversation restricted his taunting remark to her ears.

She started but didn't retreat. He found himself respecting her courage if not her sense of self-preservation. She kept her gaze fixed on Miss Demarest, who giggled at one of Thorpe's quips in a way Ranelaw found remarkably irritating. Would she giggle when he fucked her? He feared it likely.

"My lord, I hope you will permit me to be frank," Miss Smith said sternly.

He could imagine what the dragon wanted to say. She'd displayed only dismay when Lady Wreston introduced him to Miss Demarest. His reputation had preceded him. He counted on it as a weapon in his arsenal of seduction. Young girls found his wildness deplorably romantic.

Silly poppets.

"And if I said no?" he asked lazily.

"I'd still find myself compelled to speak."

"So I imagined," he said with a boredom that was completely feigned. Most people disapproved of him. Few had the backbone to tell him so to his face.

"Pray suffer no insult when I tell you I consider you neither eligible nor a gentleman, my lord. Miss Demarest can do considerably better than the Marquess of Ranelaw, even if your intentions are honorable, which I take leave to doubt."

He burst into laughter. His first unguarded response since entering this stuffy ballroom.

The woman had nerve. Damn him if she didn't. His interest, reluctantly aroused, became intent. He'd have the girl. No question. And before he was done, he'd have the chaperone as well.

He'd strip away that ugly gown. He'd unpin that wrenched-back hair—whatever color it was under that horrible cap—until it tumbled around her shoulders. He'd kiss those untouched breasts. He'd teach her to relish a man's caresses.

He reminded himself that the duenna was a side benefit of the main game. But his instincts didn't accept that. Right now, his instincts were pitched to hunting sharpness because of a desiccated maiden of uncertain age.

"You don't mince words, Miss Smith."

"No, I don't," she said calmly. Still, blast her, without moving away. Didn't she know he was dangerous?

He waved off a footman bearing a tray of orgeat. He despised that sickly sweet swill. Bugger it, he wanted a real drink. And he wanted to get his head screwed on right. For God's sake, he was accounted a connoisseur of the frail sex. He refused to let a prune-faced virgin divert him from his quest.

A prune-faced virgin who stood so close, he caught teasing hints of her scent. Something wholesome and clean. Something indicating innocence.

Of course it did.

"I make a difficult enemy," he said in a low voice.

She shrugged, still without looking at him. "Set your sights on another heiress, Lord Ranelaw."

"And that's a commandment from my lady disdain?"

At last she stared directly at him. The tinted glasses obscured her eyes, but he couldn't mistake her jaw's stubborn line. "You can't possibly consider this a challenge. A country miss and a harridan of a chaperone?"

He felt an unaccustomed urge to laugh again. He had the oddest conviction that she knew him better than anyone else here. "Why not?"

The primming of her mouth only drew his attention to its pink fullness. A spinster companion had no right to such kissable lips.

Now he'd actually met her, the prospect of bedding Cassandra Demarest flooded him with ennui. Whereas the idea of shutting Miss Smith's delectable but scolding mouth with passionate kisses, then thrusting hard between her spindly thighs made him vibrate with anticipation. Vinegar became his beverage of choice. He must have a maggot in his brain. He rarely found troublesome women appealing. Miss Smith had *troublesome* written all over her scrawny form.

Years of practice helped him conceal these unsettling reactions. Instead he tilted a knowing eyebrow and spoke in an indolent drawl that would irritate her to her undoubtedly thick and scratchy undergarments. "You know, for a woman little above a servant, you have a damned impudent manner."

Again she didn't back down. Her drawl almost matched his for self-confidence. Who *was* this woman? "Only impudent? How disappointing. When I strove for insolent, my lord."

This time a huff of laughter did escape. No female crossed swords with him, no matter how high born.

Miss Smith provided a refreshing change.

Perhaps that was why he found her so compelling. He couldn't possibly have developed a taste for hatchet-faced maypoles with sharp tongues and no dress sense.

"Miss Smith," he murmured in a silky voice, "if you seek to discourage, you're failing miserably. The prospect of besting you becomes irresistible."

Still she didn't take warning. Her chin tipped at a defiant angle. "Prove yourself a better man than the world believes and resist temptation, Lord Ranelaw."

A smile curled his lips. She was delicious. Tart like lemon curd. A sharp, fresh taste that wouldn't pall. Oh, he'd have her in his bed. She'd be his reward for ruining the poppet.

"Temptation is impossible to resist. That's what makes it temptation."

"You would know."

"Miss Smith, you'd be amazed at what I know," he said with as much salacious emphasis as he could manage. And a man with his experience could manage a great deal.

Through her spectacles, he felt her withering glance. Brava, Miss Smith. Seducing this woman would be like training a leopard to eat from his hand. She hissed and snarled now, but under a master's tutelage, she'd learn to purr.

"Lord Ranelaw . . ." she began, an edge to her voice.

The promise of a tongue-lashing was devilishly exciting. What a pity he couldn't whisk her away and teach her to use that tongue for other purposes altogether.

The wench would have an apoplexy if she could read his mind.

Although something told him little disconcerted the stalwart Miss Smith. No wonder she was accounted the dragon of chaperones. Ranelaw rather liked casting himself as St. George. And this St. George would steal away both maiden and monster. Lucky fellow.

"Toni?"

Cassandra Demarest's uncertain question exploded into the tension bristling between him and the chaperone like a grenade tossed into an enemy line. With a reluctance he resented, Ranelaw wrenched his gaze from the outwardly uninteresting woman who so inexplicably aroused the strongest interest he'd felt in a donkey's age. He found himself and Miss Smith the cynosure of all eyes, and most of those eyes glinted with speculation and curiosity.

Hell, this was the last thing he wanted. His sudden decision to pursue the chaperone was purely a private matter, whereas he wanted his interest in the Demarest girl to become the talk of the *ton*.

Miss Smith's fine, pale skin reddened with humiliation. Her gloved hands strangled her plain black reticule. Ranelaw's lips twitched—he knew whom she really wanted to strangle.

A companion's employment relied on pristine reputation. An extended conversation with the notorious Marquess of Ranelaw would do Miss Smith no good. No wonder she looked furious enough to release a blast of dragon fire upon her tormenter.

Not that she glanced at him.

"Cassie, did you require something?" Ranelaw heard how hard she worked to steady her low voice.

Cassandra, to her credit, looked troubled rather than annoyed at her chaperone's lapse. "I was wondering if we received cards for the Bradhams' musicale."

Miss Smith's color heightened. In that moment as a blush warmed her creamy skin, Ranelaw's suspicion cemented into certainty. This was no aging spinster. The woman behind those tinted spectacles was young. Young and ripe for a man's picking.

His picking.